A DREAM COME TRUE . . .

"My—my lord," she managed, her breathing caught in her throat.

"Are you all right? I heard you calling—you must have had a bad dream." He shifted his position, and she saw he knelt above her on one knee. Through the open collar of his bed gown, she saw the hair that curled in black clusters on his chest.

"Yes," she said. "I'm fine. It was only a bad dream."

He said nothing, and in the dim moonlight, she saw his eyes run down the length of her body, hidden as it was beneath the shift and the quilt. "Come," he said, at last. "You're cold."

Without waiting for a response, he picked her up as easily as if she were a child . . . He eased the door open, and carried her to his—their—bed. . . .

A Once and Future Love

Anne Kelleher

JOVE BOOKS, NEW YORK

TIME PASSAGES is a registered trademark of Berkley Publishing Group.

A ONCE AND FUTURE LOVE

A Jove Book / published by arrangement with
the author

PRINTING HISTORY
Jove edition / December 1998

The Penguin Putnam Inc. World Wide Web site address is
http://www.penguinputnam.com

ISBN: 0-515-12409-5

A JOVE BOOK®
Jove Books are published by The Berkley Publishing Group,
a member of Penguin Putnam Inc.,
375 Hudson Street, New York, New York 10014.
JOVE and the "J" design are trademarks belonging to
Jove Publications, Inc.

PRINTED IN THE UNITED STATES OF AMERICA

10 9 8 7 6 5 4 3 2 1

Prologue

ENGLAND, 1214

THE ICY RAIN sluiced the blood from the gray faces of the dying and the dead, and pooled in the little valleys of staring eye sockets and gaping mouths. Lord Richard de Lambert, most recently appointed of all the wardens of the Welsh Marcher country by His Grace, King John, wiped the bits of flesh that still clung to the blade of his broadsword on his thick cloak of Frisian wool, and nodded as he surveyed the carnage. "This should teach them."

He looked over his shoulder at his ward, who sat hushed and grim faced on his horse amongst the men-at-arms. "What's the matter, Hugh? Never spitted a Welsh rabbit?" With the point of his sword, he nudged the crumpled body of a dark-haired child. She had been no more than five or

six. De Lambert grinned in the face of Hugh's obvious discomfort, showing even white teeth in a lean, tanned face that
might have been handsome had the expression not been so
savage.

Hugh shuddered. He was fifteen years old, and, but for a
few words never spoken by his parents before a priest, there
would have been no need for de Lambert's presence in his
life, or that of his half sister's. If he had been the legitimate
heir, rather than Eleanor, he would have proven to the king,
by force of arms, if necessary, that he had no need for a
guardian, especially not one so rapacious as this. He looked
down at his hands, already thick with calluses and rough
with scars, and said nothing.

Geoffrey de Courville, captain of the men-at-arms, and
himself the bastard of a Norman knight, glanced first at the
boy beside him, and then at the lowering sky. He cleared his
throat. "Shall we go, my lord?" He tightened his hand on the
reins of de Lambert's mount and pulled his own cloak closer
to his throat. The stallion stamped and pawed, as though impatient to return to a warm stall and dry oats.

"All right, Geoffrey. We'll go." De Lambert sheathed the
broadsword, and slung his sodden cloak over his shoulder.
"I've got a wicked appetite." He swung into the saddle, his
movements graceful and sure for such a big man. At the look
on his ward's face, he burst out laughing. "Have to toughen
you up, boy. A man without land must earn his bread—right,
Geoffrey? Unless, of course, you'd like to be a priest."

Hugh shifted, biting back a retort to the sneer in de Lambert's voice. He caught Geoffrey's eye and glanced away. He
would give nothing to these animals, nothing at all. "No, my
lord," he answered quietly. "I have no calling to the Church."
Rain found its way beneath his cloak, and trickled down his

neck, but he refused to allow his discomfort to show.

De Lambert cast one more look around the remains of the village. The empty huts stood in a forlorn circle, and the bodies littered the clearing, twisted in their final agony. "We'll come back and burn the lot when this cursed weather breaks."

He flapped the reins, and the horse broke into an easy trot. The other men wheeled around and followed after, hooves crashing through the undergrowth.

Hugh brought up the rear. Beneath the thick canopy of leaves, the downpour was reduced to a steady drip. It had been a cold spring, and a wet summer, and now it looked as though the autumn would be both. Out of sight of the rest, he allowed himself to shiver, and pulled his cloak higher. His nose was red. Water dripped from beneath his chain-mail hood. Before de Lambert and his minions came to Barland Keep, Eleanor would have met him at the door, laughing and scolding, with dry clothes and a bowl of steaming wine. But now, Eleanor would be hidden in her solar, and the hall would be a dark, dank cavern. The servants would be hiding in the kitchens, only to emerge when de Lambert bellowed for his dinner.

Lost in his thoughts, Hugh was startled when Geoffrey's horse reared and screamed, and one of the men in front of him fell to the ground with an arrow protruding between his shoulder blades. De Lambert wheeled his mount immediately, drawing his broadsword with one hand. "On guar—" His voice ended in a gurgle, cut off as an arrow sliced past his throat. Another arrow thudded into his chest. For a moment, he went rigid, as though astonished, and then slumped sideways in the saddle.

Amid the confusion, Geoffrey reached for his lord's slack

reins. As a volley of arrows fell on the hapless company, Hugh crouched low, spurring his horse on. He pushed past the milling soldiers, riding hard for the keep. Behind him, he heard Geoffrey calling for some semblance of order, and hoped God would forgive him for wishing them all dead.

Chapter 1

THE ROAD WOUND down through the thatched roofs of the village, past tidy garden rows of radishes and cabbages edged with marigolds, clotheslines heavy with sheets and underwear, and low stone fences where bicycles leaned like contorted grandfathers resting in the late afternoon glow. Richard Lambert slowed the borrowed little Morris to a near stop and ducked his head out the window, peering left and right at the crossroads.

On his right, an ancient church hugged the slight rise, as though it had been planted, not built, and the crooked tombstones in the churchyard sprouted like weathered mushrooms. Behind the church, reaching to the horizon, the mountains of Wales were a dark blue backdrop against the pale blue sky.

As he watched, four women in faded housedresses emerged from the church, carrying mops and buckets hung with damp rags. They paused on the porch and eyed him, suspiciously he thought.

He looked to the left. At the bottom of the row of shops, beyond the greengrocer and the butcher, the bakery and the post office, was a two-story half-timbered pub. Over the door was the word Courage. A swaying sign proclaimed that the name of the pub was The Lamb and Bears.

"Well, El." He spoke aloud, out of habit. That nickname had been a joke, based on Lucy's listing in the telephone book, at the time they met. "I made it." She had not been gone long enough for him not to notice her absence. Six months after her death, his first impulse was still to wait a few minutes whenever he got into a car, to call her at the end of a day, to check with her first before he made plans.

He eased his foot off the clutch and slowly guided the little Morris down the narrow street. What passed as a sidewalk would barely accommodate more than one pedestrian at a time, and when a car happened to be driving down the street, surely passersby were required to flatten themselves against the gray stone walls of the buildings.

It was like a miniature, he reflected, as he parked the car inexpertly in the tiny lot beside the pub. England was full of little cars, little streets, little houses full of little rooms with low ceilings and winding staircases. But England had been the land Lucy loved.

She had spent her girlhood here, somewhere in the West Country, returning to the United States when she was eighteen and her father's company had transferred the family. And she had never returned, not through college, nor any of the years of their marriage. They had been struggling students when they met, he in law school, she working on her doctorate in medieval history. Their courtship had been brief—from the day he'd met her, he'd never looked at another woman. But the children came so quickly after they married, and somehow, in all the years they had together, there was never the time to plan a trip across the ocean. Nor the money, between school loans and car payments, dentist bills and piano lessons. But Lucy had never forgotten her first love, and she had filled their home with English music, and English prints, and English books about English history. He remembered how she used to read medieval poetry in bed, her voice still husky from their lovemaking. Red-faced at the memory, he ducked his tall frame through the low door, and straightened slowly to his full height.

He was used to these random thoughts by now, odd recollections like scraps of paper that popped into his head for no apparent reason, and at any time. At first he had thought he might be just a little crazy, but a psychologist had assured him that grief was a complicated process. So he acknowledged the thought, and deliberately tucked it away.

A huge fireplace of blackened brick dominated the wall to his left, with a long bar on his right. The hearth was empty, and there were no other patrons. He checked his watch. Three o'clock.

A middle-aged woman with graying hair, wearing a blue smock, entered from the door in the middle of the opposite wall, wiping her hands on a towel. "May I help you, sir?" She spoke with the musical lilt of Wales.

"I, uh, I was just looking around. Would I be able to get something to eat?"

"The kitchen's closed. You're a bit late for lunch, and we

don't serve food again till tea time, but I could get you a ploughman's lunch, if that's all right."

"And something to drink?"

Her face folded into a smile. "That's available. Have a seat." She nodded at the round tables in front of the fireplace. "I'll be right back."

Obediently he sat and looked around. A coat of arms hung on the wall behind the bar, presumably the source of the pub's name, for it depicted a lamb between two bears standing upright. Lucy would have known the proper heraldic description.

He nodded at it when the landlady returned. As she set bread and cheese and tomato before him, he asked, "That coat of arms—is it yours?"

"Heavens, no. That's supposed to have belonged to the family that was here once—the Lamberts. They were the local squires until about the sixteenth—no, seventeenth century."

"What happened to them?"

"Well." She put her hands on her hips and seemed to settle more comfortably on her feet. "I'm no historian, but I believe they sided with the king against Cromwell. They all died in the Civil War, and if there were any survivors, they never came home."

"But you still keep the arms over the bar?"

"Three hundred years isn't so very long ago. You're American, aren't you?" When he nodded, she shrugged. "Time counts differently here than in America, I expect. Your country's still brand-new compared to this one. You're on holiday?"

"Sort of." He picked at the cheese. "My name's Lambert. My wife—she was a medieval historian. She thought that my family might have come from this part of England. We were supposed to make this trip together. But we never had the time."

"I'm sorry, sir."

He looked up quickly, into the woman's soft sympathetic eyes, but the catch in his throat made speech impossible.

"You'll want to see the ruins of Barland Castle."

He sliced the bread in half. "Ruins?"

"Of Barland. It's not far. But it does go back nearly a thousand years, all the way to 1066. The manor house was burned by Cromwell's men, and there's nothing left of that. And there's some graves in the churchyard you might care to see—though don't go there after dark."

"Why not?" He laughed. "Is it haunted?"

"They say that the first of the Lamberts was one of King John's men. He terrorized the country, to keep the peasants in their place, I suppose. But in later life, he settled down and built the church for the repose of the poor souls he slaughtered. But the murdered don't rest well, they say, even though the murderers sleep in peace."

Richard smiled. England was full of ghosts, Lucy always said, and she had delighted in collecting stories. What self-respecting village wouldn't have a few gray ladies or headless knights galloping down the streets at midnight? The landlady set a pint of dark ale before him.

"The ruins aren't far. Just down the road past the church, over the first two hills. At the bottom of the second, you'll see a lane on your left. Turn there. That's Harry Powell's road, but he won't mind. Go past his pasture, and the road will turn to gravel. Follow it right up the hill. You can't miss it."

Amused, Richard nodded his thanks. He finished his

lunch, paid for it, and left debating whether to go first to the
church or the ruins. There was still plenty of daylight. He
could see the ruins, then come back and stop at the church.
Lucy's friends in Hereford weren't expecting him until eight
o'clock.

He followed the winding lane between the tall hedgerows
misted with Queen Anne's lace. He turned on to Mr. Powell's road, hoped that Harry was as accommodating as the
landlady claimed. "In England," Lucy always said, "the very
air smells good."

He took a deep breath. The very air smelled strongly of
cow. The lane curved sharply up a steep incline. He shifted
the car down to second. As the Morris putted slowly up the
hill, Richard prayed that one of Mr. Powell's cows wouldn't
suddenly choose to cross the track. Finally the ground lev-
eled out, and a clearing emerged. He parked the car. He sat
for a few moments, wondering if he would feel some sense
of déjà vu, some genetic memory of the place, but all he was
aware of was an acute sense of loss.

This was Lucy's trip. She should have been here—listening to the coo of the wood pigeons, watching the sun-dap-
pled leaves stir in the late afternoon breeze. He took another
deep breath, and this time, the air was sweet, a blend of
moist earth, and green growing things. He breathed again, to
reassure himself that it was not his imagination, and this
time he caught the spicy fragrance of something like carna-
tions—gillyflowers, Lucy called them. "Oh, Lucy," he whispered. "Oh, El."

He wiped at the moisture in his eyes, and got out of the
car. Immediately he was struck by the size of the ruins.
There was certainly nothing miniature about the gray gran-
ite walls, the size of the huge stone blocks lying like dis-

carded giant toys amid the weeds. The shell of the central keep towered three stories above him. A deep depression marked where the moat must have been, as he walked slowly toward the great structure. Even after eight hundred years, it was imposing. He skirted the walls, arrow slits still visible high on the ramparts, and entered the keep. The roof had long since collapsed, the upper floors long rotted, but the stone staircase still spiraled up the interior wall.

Moss grew in a hearth high enough for a man to stand upright in it, deep enough to burn young trees. The back wall was black with the soot of centuries. Wondering, he touched the darkened stone. This was real, he thought, not like the sterile spaciousness of the Tower of London or Westminster Abbey, where the past was neatly catalogued and kept behind velvet ropes and clear glass. Here, one could believe that once knights had ridden out, broadswords in their belts, lances in their hands, ready to do battle for the honor of their king. England had not always been a country of miniatures. An owl hooted, and he turned, startled, to see a black shape flit across the sun.

Something red fluttered near his foot, and he bent to pick it up. A crumpled candy wrapper lay in the long grass, and then he saw that the ground was littered with wrappers, and bottles and cans, and that graffiti marred the rugged surface of the walls.

He started up the steps, walking carefully to avoid the cracks in the stones. The ragged walls looked like broken teeth against the sky, the gaping windows like empty eye sockets. At the top, he looked out over the countryside.

England stretched before him, a patchwork of shaded greens, bounded by hedges and fences and winding roads, dotted with cottages and barns, and far off, to the west, the

Welsh mountains loomed like sentries, as though they guarded their strongholds still.

"We're here, El." He gripped the edge, lonely as the ruined castle beneath the empty sky. It would have been different if she were here. She would have laughed, and scrambled from one thing to another, like a child on Christmas morning. She would have explained battlements and crenelations and buttresses, and would have dragged him up and over the stones a dozen times. "Here," she would have said, "this was the kitchen, and here were the stables, and here was where the lord and his lady would have slept. . . ." He would have listened, entranced, not by the information, but by the look on her face, the happiness in her voice. In the sunlight, her hair—mouse brown, she called it, ash brown, he called it—would have been edged in silver gilt, and her high cheekbones would have been blushed a delicate pink. And he would have found those gillyflowers and picked them all for her.

His throat thickened, and his eyes blurred. Blindly he turned to start down the steps. It was too late when he heard the crack. The stone beneath his feet crumbled into a shower of powder, and he felt himself falling, tumbling head over heels, helpless as a rag doll. He struck his head against the wall, and heard, as though from a distance, a sharp, distinct snap. He had just enough time to pray "Let me be with Lucy," before the world went dark.

Chapter 2

BARLAND KEEP, HEREFORDSHIRE
SEPTEMBER 1214

LADY ELEANOR DE Lambert pushed away from her loom. Her head ached, her neck was stiff, and her hands were sore from trying to manipulate the rough woolen threads with cold fingers. The rain beat a monotonous tattoo upon the shutters, and the ineffective fire snapped and hissed more viciously than the heat it generated warranted.

She got up, and stretched her cramped shoulders and knotted back. She was four months past her twenty-first birthday, but she felt like an old woman three times her age. Across the room, Ursula, who was nearly that old, spun industriously as though her salvation depended on it. Eleanor watched for a few moments as the older woman worked, oblivious to the scrutiny. Her thin lips were pursed as she hummed a tuneless little song, and her wrinkled, bloodless cheeks were flushed in the glow of the rushlights, the room's only other illumination.

No doubt, thought Eleanor, as she turned away with a sigh, Ursula was lost in the memory of happier times than these. She poked at the fire, glad to have an excuse to bend low over its heat. Ursula had been her mother's nurse, and then her maid, and now finally served Eleanor.

But to Eleanor, she was much more than a servant. Ursula had become a bulwark, a refuge, a comfort, in the months since the death of her father, the elder Hugh St. Clair, and Eleanor's subsequent marriage to Richard de Lambert at the king's decree.

Eleanor had not been surprised that the king had promptly sold her wardship to the highest bidder. John Lackland, John Softsword, as her father called him with a sneer, was notoriously low of funds. But she had been surprised at the sight of the man who came riding through the gates of Barland Keep to claim her lands and her person.

Richard could have had her heart, she thought bitterly, as she listlessly sorted through the rolls of new fabric. He was tall and dark, his body lean but muscular under his surcoat and armor. His hair curled in little waves at the nape of his neck and around his ears, and his eyes were a bright and piercing blue. But Richard made it clear he cared nothing for her, nor the rest of the people of her father's lands. Serf and daughter alike, he regarded as nothing but chattel for which he had paid dearly. And he intended to get the most for his money.

He worked the land and the villeins harder than they'd ever been worked before—demanded higher rents and more days on the manor lands so that the peasants had less time to till their own small plots.

He was cruel to her brother, Hugh, who had made no secret from the beginning that he resented de Lambert's presence on the manor. Richard had responded by making the boy the butt of his jokes, ridiculing him in front of the men-at-arms, ceaselessly goading him into a display of temper, then smacking him down as carelessly as he might a puppy.

He was ruthless to the Welsh, leading raid after raid over the border, even when the local chieftain had appeared on Lammas Eve and offered a treaty. When the chief, or the prince, as the Welsh styled their petty warlords, refused to leave his son and daughter as hostages, Richard had laughed, and torn the parchment to shreds before the Welshman's eyes. He had waylaid them as the party had crossed the border back into Wales, had slain the son, attacked the daughter, and brought the father back to rot in the dungeon until a substantial ransom had been paid.

Among the other marcher barons, he was known as a bully and a braggart, but his bravery in battle, and the reputation of his prowess with a lance and sword, were unquestioned, and had won him the grudging respect of the most courageous men in England. It was said of him that even old William the Marshal, the greatest soldier in England or on the Continent, had complimented his fighting.

And of Eleanor he demanded obedience, unquestioning, unassuming. Twice he'd struck her with the same offhand brutality he showed the servants when she had dared to question his judgments at the manor court. He also expected a son—and was furious that so far there was no sign at all that she carried his child. Privately Eleanor hoped she would conceive, for surely it would mean that de Lambert would leave her alone at night. But each month brought disappointment, and those few nights that he did not drink himself to sleep with his cronies in the hall found him rutting in her bed.

Last night had been one of those nights. Eleanor knew that dark smudges marred the delicate skin beneath her eyes, and dulled her pale complexion to a pasty white. She wished she could bathe, to remove the salty stench of her husband's body from her skin, but Richard sneered at her convent-bred sensibilities, and had forbidden the servants to carry hot water to fill the heavy wooden tub. "I want my woman to smell like a woman," he'd said with a nasty grin.

A shudder went down her spine, as she remembered how he'd caressed her in the glow of the firelight. He was a warlock, she'd thought then, as she had so many times before, because once in bed beside him, her body responded of its own accord. Will herself as she might to remember his petty cruelties, his jeering grins, she felt all her resolve melt like spring snow the moment he ran his hands down the length of her body. Richard was a skillful lover, there was no doubt of that, and he took great pleasure in whispering his shameful exploits in her ear, even while his flesh took possession of hers. Eleanor ran one hand over her eyes, and sighed softly.

"Tired, my dear?" Ursula laid down her distaff, as though hearing the echo of Eleanor's thoughts.

Eleanor shrugged. She couldn't talk to Ursula. How to explain that the very man who mistreated them all made her body shiver with unimaginable pleasure? If she said anything at all, Ursula was likely to say that that part of marriage, at least, was every woman's lot. Instead she managed a tired smile. "Just a bit. It's so dark, you'd think it was evening."

"And he's too cheap to allow a few candles." Ursula sniffed.

Eleanor said nothing, although she knew Ursula was right. Even the convent where she had spent her childhood was less parsimonious than Richard. The reverend mother abbess might have been strict, but she was never cruel, and although convent life had not been luxurious, it had never been harsh. And even when the harvest was lean and the sisters had had as little to eat as the villeins in the fields, there had always been light enough to read and write and sew and spin. And certainly she had never felt like the prisoner she knew herself to be here.

Eleanor sighed, momentarily homesick for the place she had spent most of her girlhood. The abbey near Rouen was more home than this stark stone keep overlooking the mountains of Wales.

After her mother had died in childbirth, her father, Hugh St. Clair, had sent Eleanor, his only child, then five, to his sister on the Continent. Eleanor had not wanted to leave the whitewashed walls, and quiet gardens, the long, high-ceilinged library and the clean refectory that always smelled pleasantly of herbs. But the reverend mother had insisted that she must spend time in the world before she ever contemplated returning to the abbey to take the veil, and Eleanor suspected that the old nun was shrewd enough to realize that her father would have laid siege to the convent before he allowed his daughter's inheritance to fall into the hands of the Church.

A log sent up a shower of sparks, jarring Eleanor out of her reverie. The past was gone. There was no sense mourning for it. "It must be nearly time for dinner anyway. Why don't you put that aside, and I'll go check—" Shouts from the courtyard interrupted her. Eleanor paused, wondering what possibly could have happened that the stout wooden shutters did not muffle the noise.

Footsteps pounded up the narrow stairs. Eleanor heard voices calling for her. She threw open the door. "Yes?"

"My lady, my lady, come quickly—" Ralph, the fat, red-faced steward puffed up the steps, his face puckered in distress. With a worried frown at Ursula, Eleanor gathered up her shabby skirts and followed the little man down the steps.

"What's happened? What's wrong?"

The little man could not answer. He only shook his head and gasped for breath. At the bottom of the steps, Hugh stood, stripping off his cloak, his garments streaming water.

"Hugh!" cried Eleanor, as she took in the scurrying servants, the wide-open doors where the men-at-arms shouted in the courtyard. "What's happened?"

"The bastard—" Hugh spoke through clenched teeth. "He finally got what he deserved."

"What do you mean—?" Eleanor broke off at the sight of men being carried into the hall. Geoffrey de Courville and two men-at-arms were struggling to bring in a heavy form that lay unnaturally still.

She reached for Hugh. "What happened? Tell me."

"My lady." Geoffrey stood before her, helm in hand, blood and mud streaking his hawk-nosed face. His broad shoulders sagged beneath his chain mail, and his cloak flapped like wet laundry about his legs. His dark, wide-set eyes were shadowed with an expression she could not read. "Will you come?"

She glanced once more at her half brother, who shrugged and turned away. "Will you please tell me what has happened here, Sir Geoffrey?"

He gestured toward the figures lying on furs and rushes by the hearth. The fire had been hurriedly stirred into roaring life, and the flames flickered over the still forms, the servants hurrying from man to man, with wine and bandages and blankets. She allowed him to guide her. "The Welsh, my lady." His voice was hoarse, his shoulders sagged beneath his cloak. "They were hidden in the woods—they shot at us—"

"Tell her why," Hugh seized the older man's upper arm and stepped in front of them. "Tell her the truth. Tell her why."

"Stand aside, little cock. That is none of her concern. Her husband is."

As Geoffrey and Hugh stared each other in the eye, Eleanor broke away from the men. She hurried over to the hearth, picking her way through the wounded men. Some moaned, some gasped for breath, some lay quiet. All were bloodied. She bent, searching for de Lambert. He lay beside the fire, the shaft of an arrow protruding from his upper chest, a bloody wound at his throat, another arrow in his side surrounded by a spreading stain. His face was ashen in the ruddy light. She touched his chest, and felt no movement beneath her fingers.

"My lady?" It was Ralph, holding a bowl of water, and clean linen over his arm.

She hesitated, held her fingers over de Lambert's mouth. The lips were bluish. His stubbled beard was a dark shadow on his chin, and she noticed, incongruously, how chiseled those lips were, and the cleft in his chin. There was no sign of breathing, and tentatively, grimacing as her fingers touched the sticky blood from his throat wound, she felt his neck for a pulse. There was nothing.

"I brought water for Lord Richard," Ralph held out the bowl.

"He's beyond that, Ralph." She rocked back on her heels, and wiped her blood-stained hand on de Lambert's sodden cloak. "Send for the priest. Lord Richard's dead."

She waited in the hall, watching with curious detachment the women tending the wounded, the men carrying out the dead. When one of the women tripped in the uncertain light, the cry of the wounded man roused her. "Bring candles," she said to Ralph.

"But, my lady, Lord Richard—"

"Lord Richard's dead." It was the fourth or fifth time she'd spoken those words, as though they were a charm, an incantation. Or a prayer, she thought. Hugh sat at the long table on the dais at the far end of the hall, watching with satisfaction, drinking hot wine spiced with the precious stores Richard guarded so jealously. Had guarded, she told herself.

She looked around for de Courville, but he had left to ensure that the manor defenses were sound in case the Welsh were planning an attack.

Ursula was among the women tending the wounded. Every now and then, she raised her eyes to her mistress, and Eleanor met her gaze calmly.

Ralph had seen that Richard's body was placed on a low pallet away from the wounded, and he lay, much the same as he had been brought in. There was no sense in laying out the body until it had been shriven. The body. It. *There,* she told herself. *That's all he—it—is. Not your guardian, nor your husband. He's dead, and you're free.*

Free as she had never been before. She was twenty-one now, a woman in her own right, and a widow. Not even the

king could force her to marry against her will. Oh, he could
pressure her perhaps. But she was no longer some helpless
minor in need of a guardian to be sold like a milch cow to
the highest bidder.

She glanced at Hugh where he sat watching, his gangly
legs stretched out before him. His face was hidden in the
shadows, but she knew he had not taken his eyes off
Richard's still body since she had announced his death.

The great doors banged open, and with a rush of water,
and swirl of wind, the priest, Father Alphonse, stood shaking the rain off his black cloak. "Lady Eleanor?"

Slowly she advanced, and gestured to the body. The priest
handed his cloak to a servant who had materialized out of
the gloom, and drew a vial of holy water from a pouch at his
waist. Over his long black tunic he wore a purple stole
around his neck. The ends hung almost to his knees. With
his long Norman nose, and thin shoulders hunched against
the chill, he reminded Eleanor of a raven dressed for church.

She curtseyed, and he sketched a benedicite over her
head. "Lord Richard?"

"Come, Father." She led him to the body, and withdrew a
little way off. She slumped down on one of the long benches
that lined the walls of the hall and watched as the priest bent
over the body, holy water in hand. The serving women whispered amongst themselves and stole furtive glances in her
direction. She knew what they whispered. She, too, doubted
there was anything he could do to save her husband's soul.

The priest's shout startled her out of her detachment. "My
lady!" He was standing upright, one bony hand against
Richard's chest. "My lady, a miracle! Surely God has
wrought a miracle this day! Lord Richard lives, thanks be to
God! He lives!"

Hugh bolted out of his chair, and charged down the length of the hall. "You lying crow—he's dead. He's dead—or I'll kill him!" Before Eleanor or any of the others could react, Hugh was standing over the body, dagger raised.

Father Alphonse stepped in front of the pallet. "My son!" His deep voice boomed through the cavernous hall, echoed off the high roof. "You imperil your immortal soul with such threats! Have a care, lest you be damned."

Hugh hesitated and met the priest's unwavering eyes with raised chin and sullen mouth. When Alphonse did not flinch, Hugh dropped his arm, then turned away. Eleanor rose to her feet, feeling light-headed from shock and disbelief. Her voice shook. "Father. You say he lives?"

"Yes, praise be to God! Are you deaf, woman? Your husband lives and you stand gaping like a sheep? You, there—" Alphonse looked at Ursula. "Bring me wine—bring bandages—bring men to carry Lord Richard to his bed."

Hugh had come to stand beside her, his face flushed, his lips pressed together. He still gripped the hilt of his dagger in its sheath, and Eleanor reached for his arm, as much to steady herself as to restrain him.

"Don't worry, Eleanor. We'll rid ourselves of the bastard, I promise you. On our father's grave, I promise."

As though in a dream, Eleanor watched as the women scurried to do the priest's bidding, and Ralph directed the men carrying her husband from the hall. This was no dream, she reflected. This was a nightmare, and from it there would be no waking.

Chapter 3

PAIN. IT CAME in different intensities and shadings, like a hellish symphony that played across his body. There were the acute white-hot stabs, which radiated from his side and chest every time he tried to move, the rippling edges sharp as razors caused as his breathing drew air down his throat, and underneath it all, a dull ache throbbed steadily through his body like the beat of a great drum. Well, he guessed he couldn't expect to fall the equivalent of two or three stories and not be hurt. But couldn't they give him more morphine or Demerol or whatever they used for pain?

As consciousness returned, he gradually became aware of another sensation, a prickly, lumpish feeling under his back, as though the bed on which he lay was not the cool, firm hospital bed he expected. It almost felt as though he were lying on piled blankets full of straw. The sheet that covered him felt coarser than even the cheapest percale.

There was something else—a smell. A smell unlike anything he'd ever encountered in his life, a smell that made the memory of Mr. Powell's cows almost seem fragrant by comparison. This was a stench, of hairy, unwashed body, ancient perspiration, and human—there was no other name for the odor—sewage.

As his vision cleared, he realized that the flickering light was made by the candle placed by his bedside. Candle? What kind of place was this?

Richard shut his eyes tightly, and mentally counted to ten. He knew he had fallen on the stairs in the ruins—stupid thing to do, really. He should have had better sense than to try climbing eight-hundred-year-old stairs, which were so obviously unsafe. He could remember nothing of a rescue, which if his body hurt so much just lying still, it was probably a blessing he was unconscious when they'd moved him. But moved him where? Surely this was no hospital. This seemed more like a barn.

There was a sound from some darkened corner of the room as though someone—something—moved in the shadows. He held his breath to minimize the pain, and, careful not to move any other part of his body, he opened his eyes. The sight of the woman who bent over him as she lowered a pillow over his face shocked him into unconsciousness. His Lucy was trying to kill him.

"My lady, you mustn't!" Ursula seized the pillow out of her hand and wrenched it away, as Eleanor sagged against the bed, sobbing.

"Let me alone, Ursula, you don't understand—"

"Oh, yes, I do indeed, my dear." The older woman threw the pillow aside and reached for Eleanor, drawing her into an embrace as though she were a child. "I do, indeed. I know what Lord Richard is—believe me, he's not much worse than most men—"

"Then why won't you let me alone? Leave the room, just for a few minutes—" Eleanor knew she raved, but she was past caring. This was the solution to the problem.

"Because I love you as if you were my own, and I won't have you damned for all eternity." Ursula smoothed the fine, pale hair back from Eleanor's damp face. "There, there, child. There, there. Why don't you lie down in the solar? I told Mag to make a bed for you. I'll stay with Lord Richard. You go get some rest. Ralph is sending up the men in a little while."

"Men?"

"To hold him while I push the arrow through his side. It must be done that way, for there's no way to pull it out without causing more harm. But there's no need for you to stay for that."

Reluctantly Eleanor withdrew from the comforting embrace. She looked at the man lying still on the bed, naked and vulnerable beneath the bloodstained bandages and unbleached linen sheets. In the candle's wavering light, he looked more gentle than she had ever seen him, all the harsh lines smoothed away, the chiseled mouth relaxed, his long lashes brushing his pale cheeks.

"I'll be in the solar if you need me."

Ursula nodded her out of the room. Eleanor shut the door of the bedroom and leaned against the wooden frame. What had possessed her? Had she stooped so low that she would even contemplate murder? She shuddered at the memory of what she had nearly done. Thank God Ursula had stopped her. No matter what Richard was, or had done, he would not die by her hand. How could she have thought to live with such a deed on her soul?

A cold gust of wind blew through the hall, and the rush-light flickered. She shivered and went to seek refuge in the solar.

There she found a clean shift spread out before the fire, a pot of water steaming on the hearth, and a ragged linen towel beneath her brushes. Wearily she stripped off her grimy gown and underlinen, and stood shivering as she dabbed at her body with the rag and the warm water. If only she could have had a bath. If Richard were lying dead in the hall instead of sick in the bedroom, she might have ordered the heavy wooden tub filled with hot water and lavender. But the hour was late, and there had been enough demands made on the overworked servants for one day. Perhaps tomorrow. And besides, Richard was wounded so badly, he might still end up in his grave. But she would not even think of such a possibility. She would not have even the wish of his death on her soul.

She pulled the clean shift on, and wrapped herself in the loose robe that had been her mother's. The fabric was worn, the hem was ragged, but something of her mother's scent, roses and gillyflowers, lingered, and Eleanor fancied something of the feel of her mother's arms lingered as well.

She unbraided her hair, and the heavy mass fell straight almost to her waist. The strands felt lank and greasy between her fingers. Yes, tomorrow, she would bathe and wash her hair, and feel clean for the first time since her marriage. A knock on the door startled her. "Come in."

Hugh peered tentatively into the room. "Eleanor?"

"Come in. Are you all right?" In all the confusion, she had not had a chance to make sure.

"I'm fine. I was better when I thought the bastard was dead." He walked over to the fire and sank down beside her on the floor.

"We mustn't think like that, Hugh. Richard is my husband, no matter what, and he lives by the will of God."

"He lives by mistake. He was dead, Eleanor, admit it. It was no miracle brought him back. More like the devil kicked him out of hell."

"Hush. You mustn't say such things." But she grinned in spite of the wickedness of the thought.

"And spare me your convent prattle. You were glad he was dead."

Eleanor looked up into Hugh's hazel green eyes, the thick brows that swooped across his forehead so like her father's. He was built like her father, too, long and wiry. Her eyes filled with tears. "Oh, Hugh, what are we to do?"

"I don't know." He stared moodily into the fire. "I wish I were older—I wish I weren't a bastard. Why couldn't Father have married my mother, not yours?" At the stricken look on Eleanor's face, he was instantly contrite. "Oh, Eleanor, I'm sorry. I didn't mean that the way it sounded. I'd take care of you, you know that. But if these were my lands, de Lambert would never have come."

A hoarse scream broke the quiet of the night, long and anguished, a man's scream torn from ragged flesh. Hugh shuddered, and Eleanor closed her eyes, as though that could block the sound. In spite of everything de Lambert had ever done, she pitied him at that moment. Nothing living, no matter how cruel, should ever have to make such a sound.

"He still might die," Hugh whispered as the scream faded away.

"Hugh, hold your tongue! No one should suffer so. That

could have been you lying there with an arrow stuck in your side—by the grace of God, you weren't even hurt. Beware for what you wish." Hugh merely shrugged, and Eleanor sighed. "Even if you had been Father's heir, the king would still have sold your wardship. You're still a minor, even now. It profits us nothing to sit and wonder what might have been. And if it weren't Richard, it might have been someone worse—"

"That reminds me." Hugh sat back, arms clasped around his knees. "De Courville thought it was the Welsh who attacked us, because of the arrows. But I think it may have been Giscard—Giscard Fitzwilliam."

Eleanor stared at her brother, a pang of fear beginning to tighten in her stomach. "Why do you say that?"

"Because they let me go. If it really were the Welsh, they would have pursued me. I think it was Giscard's men—with orders to kill de Lambert."

Despite the warm fire, Eleanor shivered. Giscard was of the same breed as Richard, cunning and brutal, and, what was worse, the sworn enemy of her father. He was one of John's most loyal supporters, even before John had assumed the throne.

He had been vassal to William de Braose, the lord of Bramber, who, along with his wife, it was whispered had a hand in the disappearance of Arthur of Brittany. Arthur had been John's nephew, who some said had had a better claim to the throne of England than John himself. Although the lord of Bramber and his lady had fallen from favor, Giscard remained the king's familiar, and he had coveted the Barland demesne for as long as Eleanor could remember. He had approached her father for her hand when she was only ten, and Hugh St. Clair had scornfully sent him on his way, writing to her aunt at the abbey that he would never see his daughter wed to the king's lackey.

Giscard had bid for her wardship, and seemed like to get it, when Richard had bid higher. John, swayed as always by the need for money, promptly set aside his favorite. Eleanor remembered how glad she had been to learn that Giscard was not to be her guardian. Until, of course, she'd met Richard. "But you have no proof?"

"No," admitted Hugh. "No proof. Just a feeling." He turned to face his half sister. "You know, Eleanor, if de Lambert does die, we may be vulnerable to Fitzwilliam. He will most assuredly go to the king and petition him for your hand—"

"No!" Eleanor leaned back. "What if he does? He cannot force me—the king himself cannot force me—"

"Not in theory, perhaps. But in reality . . ." Hugh let his voice trail off.

"We must appeal to the marshal." Eleanor wrapped her arms around herself as though to ward off cold. William the Marshal of England, Earl of Pembroke and Striguil, was one of the most powerful men in England, and one of the most honorable. The Barland demesne was part of his fief. "Father was his vassal. . . ." It was her turn to fall silent. The marshal might not even be in England, and who knows how long it would take to find him? Meanwhile, Giscard could attack the keep, kidnap her, force her to marry him. . . . She quivered. If it really were Giscard's men who had attacked Richard, it was better that Richard lived. At least for a while.

Another knock on the door ended further speculation. Before Eleanor could respond, the door opened a crack and Ursula peered inside. "My lady, it's Lord Richard. He's awake, and I think he's calling for you."

"Me?" Eleanor glanced at Hugh. It would never do for Hugh to learn what she had attempted. He might take it as tacit permission to end Richard's life, and she had no wish to see her young half brother punished in this life or the next. And she was no longer so certain she wanted Richard dead. Yet.

"Will you come?" Ursula held the door open wider.

"All right." She gathered a shawl around her shoulders and followed Ursula back down the short corridor and the winding stairs to the bedroom below. The candle by the bedside flickered in the draft. A bowl of bloody water and a pile of bloody bandages lay discarded beside the bed. "How is he?"

"He's very bad, my lady. I thought when I pushed the arrow shaft through, I might have killed him, but he only swooned from the pain. I don't think the chest wound is so very bad, but I doubt he'll be able to speak much until his throat heals."

Eleanor looked down at her husband, and was struck once more by his vulnerability. His hands rested on the coverlet, and she noticed for the first time how long the fingers were. The hands looked far more sensitive than their owner. He stirred, and his eyelids fluttered open. In the flickering light, she caught a glimpse of his eyes, bright with fever. Automatically she touched his damp forehead, and smoothed the dark waves back from his face. "I'll stay with him awhile, Ursula. You rest. I'll call you if I need you."

"My lady, you won't . . . ?" The older woman let her voice trail off.

"No," Eleanor shook her head as she drew a chair beside the bed. "I may live to regret it, but he'll not die this night by my hand."

She sat down beside him. A low moan escaped his lips, and she dampened a rag in clean water, and held it to his lips. He sucked gently, then turned his head away. She saw the pain cross his face as he turned his head. He opened his eyes and looked at her. His mouth worked, and his breathing made a harsh noise in his throat. She leaned closer, trying to understand.

His voice was a rasp over injured flesh, less than a whisper in the quiet room. "Don't try to talk," she murmured, more to herself than to the wounded man.

He plucked at the blanket. This time the look in his eyes was so intense it took her breath away. She bent her head almost to his mouth. He gasped out two syllables with an urgency that astounded her. Who in the world was "Lucy"?

Chapter 4

THE PAIN EBBED and flowed like a tide, sometimes diminishing, sometimes intensifying, always present. The voices that filtered through his fogged brain said nothing he could understand, although sometimes he picked up a cadence or two that sounded familiar. It was as if he had fallen from the ruined tower into a looking-glass world like Alice's where nothing made sense and yet rationality was always hovering on the borders of his mind, maddeningly out of reach.

He must be crazy, he thought, or hallucinating. The woman who looked like Lucy came and went with predictable frequency, replaced or sometimes joined by an older woman dressed like a nun. Lucy herself, if that's who she was, was dressed like a nun, too, he noticed, when the pain had dulled enough to allow him to notice such things. He was still puzzled by the lack of drugs and intravenous equipment, the rudeness of his surroundings. He was fed things that tasted like broth and wine and herbal tea of some sort, his bandages changed, his body bathed. But for the most part, he drifted in and out of consciousness, incapable of wondering about anything for very long.

More than a week had passed since Richard had been carried back to the keep. Eleanor marveled at the tenacity with which he clung to life, although he was either asleep or unconscious much of the time. Sometimes he raved, muttering in a language she could not understand, but assumed was some obscure Arab tongue learned in the years when he had been on Crusade in the Holy Land with the Lion Heart. Once in a while he woke, and his eyes followed her, staring at her with such intensity it made her shiver. Did he remember that she had tried to kill him? If he did, it was not something he was likely to forget. Or forgive.

On a cool morning when Eleanor was sorting clean bandages beside the bedroom hearth, Ursula knocked on the door, and entered with Geoffrey de Courville at her heels. "What's wrong?" She knew de Courville would never have invaded the sickroom unless the matter were extremely pressing.

"You'd better come, my lady," Ursula began, twisting her hands in the fabric of her gown.

"Giscard Fitzwilliam is in the hall, my lady." Geoffrey cut Ursula off brusquely. He wore a leather jerkin over his tunic and hose, and she realized he had come from the courtyard where the men-at-arms were in the midst of their morning drills.

The bandages tumbled from her lap as Eleanor got to her feet. "I'll come at once. Ursula, see that our neighbor has some refreshments after his journey." Ursula opened her mouth to protest, but the look on Eleanor's face stopped her. "Will you come with me, Sir Geoffrey?"

The knight glanced once at the man on the bed, and grimly offered Eleanor his arm. Ursula hastened down the steps with a reproachful glance. On the steps, still out of sight of the main Hall, Eleanor paused. "Sir Geoffrey?"

"My lady?" The knight's voice was impassive. His dark eyes were hooded, his forehead beaded with sweat. His cheeks and neck were flushed with his morning exertions, and the muscles of his heavy arms and chest strained against the ragged tunic he wore for the drills.

Eleanor shivered and reminded herself that this man was sworn to Richard—that in matters pertaining to the defense of the demesne, she could trust him implicitly. "We must not let Fitzwilliam know how serious my lord's condition is. If he were to believe that Richard might die—"

"I understand, my lady." De Courville was only slightly less brusque with her.

"Then lead on, sir knight." Eleanor raised her chin and picked up her faded skirts, painfully aware that Fitzwilliam was not likely to overlook the shabbiness of her dress, and the general neglect of the manor.

In the hall, Giscard lounged by the fire, munching the oatcakes set before him. He was holding his goblet up as Ursula poured wine from a heavy skin.

Eleanor's mouth tightened involuntarily, then she deliberately arranged her face in what she hoped was a smile of restrained welcome. "My lord." She curtsied when de Courville had led her to Giscard's bench. "We are honored."

Giscard smiled as he swallowed. "Indeed, my lady de Lambert, the honor is mine."

She rose from her curtsey and stared. Giscard Fitzwilliam was some twelve or fifteen years older than her husband, and despite his name and his lineage, looked more Saxon than Norman. His thinning hair was blond, and his face was broad and would have been fair skinned had years of hard living and constant exposure to the elements not reddened it. His little eyes darted up and down her body in a glance that made her want to cross her arms over her breasts. He took another oatcake, and munched as he gestured for her to join him.

Deliberately Eleanor seated herself on another bench and waited.

"Come to bring you some news," he said with a mouth full of food. "Old Prince Rhawn is dead, and his heir, Llewellis, has sworn revenge upon your lord for the treatment he gave their vassal, Owen Ab Hoell, last summer. But now I understand he may have already accomplished his goal."

"Oh, my lord?" asked Eleanor. "And just how do you understand that?"

Giscard snorted, and waved at de Courville, who stood like a Goliath just behind Eleanor. "Heel your hound, lady. It's no secret your lord lies close to death. I come to bring you a warning, to guard your walls and your borders—"

"Indeed, we must alert our men." Hugh's young voice rang out down the length of the hall. "They were lax enough to let you in."

Eleanor flinched. Although she understood the reason, Hugh's blatant display of antagonism was unwise.

Giscard quaffed the whole goblet of wine, and set it down with a thud. "Still haven't been forced out of the den, young puppy? Never mind." He leered at Eleanor. "If de Lambert should die, I am quite certain His Grace will hear my petition to wed the lonely widow."

"My sister won't have you." Hugh had come to stand beside Giscard, thumbs hooked in his belt. "And not even the king can force her."

Giscard leaned back. "It would be for her own good, and the good of the kingdom. These lands are too close to the border of Wales for so lovely a woman to hold. And now, with the situation made even more dangerous by this rampaging Welshman—"

Hugh opened his mouth, but de Courville forestalled any more words with a heavy hand clapped on the boy's shoulder. "We shall certainly take all care, my lord, to ensure the safety of Lady Eleanor while Lord Richard heals. You need have no worry."

Giscard met de Courville's eyes with a measuring stare. "My worry is only in the event of Lord Richard's death."

"You need have no worries on that score, either, my lord." Eleanor rose to her feet, and smoothed her skirts with hands that shook. The men were like coiled springs, she could feel the tension between them. Suddenly she was confused, beset by fears of a future she did not care to contemplate. She longed to escape to the quiet of the sickroom. "My husband mends quickly."

Giscard took the hint and pulled himself to his feet, slinging his cloak around his shoulders as he did so. "For your sake, my lady, I hope so. I know something of this Llewellis—he's savage in the fight. I've seen him slay women and children with no more thought than he might a louse. And Welshmen have no honor—though of course you know that." This he addressed to de Courville, who only nodded expressionlessly. "Well, I'm on my way to join the king at the hunt. I shall give him your good wishes, my lady, and will be sure to mention Lord Richard's unfortunate state of health, as well as your precarious position. Good day, my lady. Sir knight." He gave them all a brief bow and stalked away.

When the heavy doors slammed behind him, Eleanor turned to Hugh. "Are you mad? Are you trying to provoke him? He's one of the king's favorites—"

"Do you fancy yourself wedded to him?" Hugh spat back. "Why not give him Barland now—why wait for de Lambert to die?"

"Richard's not dead."

"Not yet." Hugh would have said more, but de Courville picked him up by the scruff of his collar and shook him as though he were an ill-behaved puppy.

"You've the manners of a stable boy." De Courville looked at Eleanor. "By your leave, my lady, it's time this brat exercised more than his jaw." He gave Hugh a little shake, and dragged him off without a backward look, Hugh kicking and shouting in protest.

Eleanor watched them go. She knew that Hugh only wanted to watch out for what he perceived to be her best interests, and that of the estate, but he was much too impetuous. It was not only foolish to antagonize Fitzwilliam, it was dangerous as well. He was too close to the king, and the king was too greedy, too unpredictable. Besides, John had the reputation of seducing ladies no matter whether they willed it or not. She shivered. Unless the marshal could be induced to intervene, it was possible that John could command her favors, then pass her along to Fitzwilliam, like an unwanted bratchet hound.

Slowly she made her way back to the bedroom, where Ur-

sula was brewing a batch of willow-bark tea. She watched
impassively as Ursula worked. Perhaps the abbey in Rouen
was the answer. What sort of life could she hope to have
here, between the Welsh and Fitzwilliam and de Lambert?
Better a life as a bride of Christ than the bride of a devil in
the guise of a man.

She sank into the chair, and picked up a pair of hose that
needed mending. Perhaps she would write to her aunt
tonight.

The snap and hiss of the fire roused Richard from sleep. He
opened his eyes. Afternoon sun streamed through the one
narrow window, and a strong wind wailed outside the walls.
For the first time in what seemed like a long time, his mind
was clear and unclouded by pain. He felt the coarse linen
bedclothes beneath his hands, and tried to speak. His voice
was a rasp, and pain flooded his throat. He touched his neck,
and was amazed by the thick wad of bandages.

Instantly a woman was by his side. In the clear light of
day, he stared at the face bending over him. It was Lucy's
face—the same heart shape, wide across the high cheekbones, narrowing into a little pointed chin. Her eyes were
that same shade of blue that made him think of cloudless
summer skies, and her mouth was the same delicate pink
bow. But her hair was covered by some sort of scarf that fell
over her shoulders, and her gown—he blinked and shook his
head. So he hadn't been dreaming. She was dressed like a
nun—and a poor one at that. Her skirt bore evidence of
many mends, and her patched apron was a uniform shade of
pale yellowish gray, as though the detergent she used wasn't
very effective. "Lucy?"

"Shh. *Paroles pas.*"

He frowned. That almost sounded like French, though not the French he'd learned so many years ago in college. Why wasn't she speaking English? Or was he brain damaged in some way? Was he going to have to learn to talk all over again?

Carefully she raised his head with one arm, and held an earthen cup to his lips. The familiar, bitter taste of the herbal tea made him gag. That hadn't been a dream, either. This was all real—more real than his fevered mind had imagined.

The older woman he'd come to recognize peered over Lucy's shoulder, and said something to her. Richard listened closely as Lucy replied in the same tongue. There—that word—wasn't that the old French word for "you"?

He made as if to raise himself on one elbow and winced as the pain in his side flared again. The woman stood back, as though afraid. "Help me, will you?" He tried to speak as clearly as he could, but the injury to his throat mangled the words beyond recognition even to his own ears.

They looked at each other and Richard saw fear in their eyes and complete confusion. Biting back a curse, he pushed the sheets out of the way, and rolled over onto his good side, pushing himself up to a half-sitting position. He stared down at his body, shocked beyond words.

This was not the body he'd known, the body of an aging American grown soft with long hours sitting behind a desk, and too much food too well cooked. This was the body of a man in the very prime of his life—surely no more than thirty—in the very peak of physical condition. Even in his twenties, Richard didn't think he'd ever looked like this. Now he lay naked beneath the covers, his skin covered with a thick pelt of dark hair, heavily muscled across the chest, the thighs thick as young trees. The belly was flat and ribbed

with muscle—a washboard stomach, his son would call it. A
long scar puckered the pale flesh here and there. A long
piece of cloth ran around his midsection, holding a thick
bandage in place against his left side. Another bandage ran
over his right shoulder and around his chest. He brought his
hand up to his face, and stared. This hand was not the hand
of an attorney who had spent most of the last twenty-five
years writing briefs and poring over law books. The back of
this hand was covered with more of the coarsely curling
black hair, the skin hard with calluses and disfigured with
scars. The littlest finger was misshapen, and the very tip
looked as though it had been hacked off long ago. He
touched his face, feeling the rough growth of many days'
beard.

He gazed around the room, seeing for the first time the
great bedstead on which he lay. The posts were squared, the
canopy was of red-and-blue wool, and at the sides, heavy
curtains of wool were looped back by thickly woven braids
of what looked like yarn. The walls of the room were whitewashed, the floor covered with what looked to be some sort
of long leaves. He looked over his shoulder at the two
women who stared at him with what could only be fear. He
tried to say something, but his throat flared with pain.

The older woman patted the younger on the arm, and
leaned toward him, beckoning as she spoke. Although the
words eluded him, he understood she wanted him to lie back
flat. Slowly he complied, and the younger woman—Lucy—
looked over her shoulder.

"Ursula, tais. Nel dire."

This time he understood the name. Ursula. The older
woman's name was Ursula. And they were not speaking any
language he knew.

The older woman replied, and again he caught the word that sounded like *tei*, which, if he remembered the poetry Lucy used to read, meant "you." In medieval French. He decided to try it. "*Tei*," he rasped.

The effect on the women was electric. Both of them jumped, and Lucy looked at him with that obvious fear. She asked him something he could not understand, and he shrugged, even as he hoped that was an appropriate response.

He settled back against his pillows and stared at the bottom of the canopy. The women spoke medieval French. They wore costumes like those worn in Lucy's—his Lucy's—history books. But their dresses weren't costumes. They were too worn, too shabby with the look and smell of use. And the room—it looked like no room he had ever seen outside of a film.

The older woman, Ursula, approached, a steaming goblet in her hand, and a clean cloth on her arm. She spoke, and this time he caught the words "*Sire de Lambert*." Not "*Lambert*," the modern pronunciation. But "duh Lom-*bear*." Medieval French again. Where the hell was he?

He pushed her arm away gently, and rolled over on his uninjured side. He pulled the sheet across the bed, awkwardly wrapped it around his lower body, all the while ignoring the Ursula's squawks.

Lucy dashed around to the other side of the bed, hovering, and he motioned her forward. Careful to keep himself modestly shielded, he staggered out of bed, and would have fallen if she had not been standing by his side. His head swam with dizziness, and he clutched at the bed. Lucy said something that sounded like a plea, but he shook his head "no."

He pointed to the window. Ursula rushed to his side, and together, the women helped him limp to the window. Another wave of dizziness threatened to overcome as he clung to the rough wooden sill. He hung on to the window frame with all the strength he could muster as he stared out over the landscape.

England stretched before him, another England nothing like the country he remembered. This was an England of rutted, unpaved roads and darkly forested hills, stretching on to the horizon as far as the eye could see beyond the high gray walls of what could only be a castle. A castle? And where were the cottages, the barns, the pastures? Movement in the lower corner of his eye got his attention, and he looked as straight down as the thickness of the wall would permit.

In a courtyard, cobbled with stones and scattered with straw, thirty or forty men armed with swords faced each other in two long lines, performing what looked like some complicated military drill. From a low building off to one side, smoke billowed, and a row of horses swished their tails and stamped impatiently. Three or four boys dressed in ragged smocks swarmed between the horses, and a barrel-chested man wearing a soot-stained apron roared orders and gestured with hands like slabs of meat.

On the other side of the courtyard, women stirred giant pots hung on huge iron tripods, and the wind fanned the fires beneath into long orange tails. A child of indiscriminate sex burst out of the shed, chasing a squealing piglet.

As Richard stared at the unbelievable scene before him, one of the men-at-arms caught sight of him, and gestured to his fellows. The men looked up at the window and cheered, shouting incomprehensible encouragement.

Another man, who stood a little distance apart directing

the rest, bowed. Obviously he was in charge of the rest of the men. Richard nodded slowly in acknowledgment.

Lucy said, *"Droit à cel lit iras, mon sire?"*

This time he recognized the word "bed." *She wants me to get back in bed,* he thought.

As the two women slowly propelled him across the weed-covered floor, understanding slowly dawned. This was all real. This was no dream. He remembered his last thought as he'd fallen from the tower. *Let me find Lucy.* Well, he had found her all right. In England. In the Middle Ages.

They settled him back into bed, and he winced, almost glad for the pain, because it kept him centered in this unbelievable reality. He had transcended time. He looked down at the body—his body, now.

He lay back against the pillows and listened to the women bustling about the room. He had fallen from the tower. That last snap he had heard so distinctly—had that been his neck? But he hadn't died. At least, this was like no afterlife he'd ever imagined.

This body was material, with all its aches and pains and needs and wants. This place, this time, surely this was real. He remembered dim sayings from his physics classes so long ago. Space and time are one. We only perceive time as linear.

Then if time were not linear, was there some way to return to the twentieth century? His thoughts were abruptly interrupted as Lucy held a goblet of hot wine scented with tangy herbs to his lips. He touched her hand, and she startled back like a frightened rabbit.

He caught a hint of her fragrance. She smelled good, like wild roses blended with something like cinnamon. Her eyes were that same clear blue he'd loved. And suddenly he thought, *Would I want to?*

The thought surprised him. What would it mean to stay here—to give up everything he'd ever known—all the people he'd ever loved? The idea of such a loss staggered him. Lucy's loss had been awful enough—what if he never saw his children and his grandchildren again? And the way of life—all the comforts of the twentieth century—his mind reeled in defiance of what his senses told him had happened.

Things happen for a reason. Richard closed his eyes, and tried to breathe slowly. Every breath still hurt. Why had he come here? What purpose could there be in his sudden appearance in another man's body—in another man's time and place? Was his muttered prayer enough to bring him here? Or was there something else?

What had he left? His children were grown—even the youngest had graduated from law school just a year ago with honors. The family firm he'd begun so many years ago as a single lawyer striking out on his own was doing well. He had been thinking of retiring and naming his eldest daughter managing partner. There were his grandchildren, of course—but they were happy and healthy, well cared for by loving parents. They didn't need him.

And this girl who looked so much like Lucy, why did she look at him as though she were afraid of him? He could surmise fairly easily, judging from the seriousness of the wounds, what had happened to the original occupant of this body. What sort of man had he been?

He reached out and touched her face, tentatively, and she froze like an animal caught in the headlights of an oncoming car. Beneath his fingers he felt her tremble. Their eyes met and held, and he was puzzled by the obvious animosity in her expression. This Lucy didn't love him. She didn't even like him.

"Ma dame Eleanor." The older woman's voice broke his reverie. The girl turned and answered, relief stark on her face.

So her name wasn't even Lucy. It was Eleanor—which was the same root word, if he remembered his Latin and Greek. Both names meant "light." As he watched her, moving efficiently about the room with that same peculiar grace Lucy had, he realized that for whatever reason, he had been given a great gift.

He had found his Lucy. In another time and in another place. And wherever he was, or whenever, perhaps he could be of some use. Perhaps he had accomplished whatever he had been meant to do in the twentieth century. He had always thrived on challenge. Perhaps it was time to accept another.

He looked up into Lucy—or Eleanor's—eyes, and was startled once more by the expression in them. *She hates me,* he thought. *She hates me and I don't belong here, and it isn't going to take very much for them all to figure it out.* But until he himself could figure out a reason why he should have come here, and until he could figure out a way back—if there was a way back—he would do all he could to show her what love, even if it were only the semblance of love, between a man and a woman was like. Perhaps, after all, that was the reason he was here. He wouldn't expect her to love him. But perhaps, just perhaps, with enough time, she would be his once and future love.

Chapter 5

IT WAS THE intensity in his eyes that confused her, thought Eleanor, the piercing way his gaze followed her everywhere she moved. Three days after the day Richard had insisted on getting out of bed, and showing himself to the men at arms—a foolhardy gesture of brazen heroism if she had ever seen one—Geoffrey de Courville presented himself at the sickroom door, and asked Ursula for admittance.

The older woman sniffed suspiciously as she looked over her shoulder to Eleanor where she sat pounding a salve with her mortar and pestle by Richard's bedside. Eleanor saw that he was sleeping again, his breathing deep and even, his color better than she had seen it in many days. None of his wounds had opened up when he'd risen from the bed. But the worst wound was the one in his throat, and she thought it would be many weeks before he could speak normally again. And the rest of his wounds continued to mend—what a constitution the man must have. Now he gulped the broth she brought him, although he still winced as he swallowed.

What was he thinking when he watched her, she wondered, as she gazed down at his sleep-slack face. Was he gathering up transgressions, storing them away in his memory, to punish her for them on another day? Or was he thinking of something else? His eyes burned into her brain, roaming over her body again and again. It made her uncomfortable that he was naked beneath the heavy woolen blankets. Did he miss her lying beside him, her body responding of its own volition to his every touch? Her fingers trembled a little as she pounded the mixture under the pestle.

"My lady?" Ursula repeated. "Did you hear me? Sir Geoffrey wishes to speak to Lord Richard—"

With a little shake of her head, Eleanor roused herself. "Sir Geoffrey?" She glanced at Richard, and set the little clay implements aside. "I don't think so. Not yet, he's sleeping so soundly." She glanced down once more, and saw with a start that those blue eyes had opened and were staring at her with the same ferocious intensity. *He looks like he wants to eat me,* she thought, and blushed. "Richard? My lord?"

At the sound of his name, Richard shifted on the pillows as though he would sit up. He glanced to the side, and saw Geoffrey's face peering into the sickroom. At once he looked back at Eleanor.

"My lord, Sir Geoffrey wishes to speak with you, concerning the manor defenses. There's been trouble with Welsh—are you feeling well enough?"

He did not wait for an answer. He raised his left arm from under the covers and beckoned. Obediently Geoffrey entered, throwing the women a triumphant glance. Of course,

thought Eleanor. The defense of the manor was always para-
mount in Richard's mind. Of course he'd speak to Geoffrey.

Though listen was a better word, she thought, as de
Courville settled his broad bulk in the chair she had abandoned. He leaned forward, speaking rapidly and sparingly,
and she saw Richard staring with that same frightening concentration. It didn't seem to bother the knight, though, for he
continued on and on, describing the current state of the
manor forces, the precautions he'd taken since the attack on
Richard, with words as rapid as sword strokes.

From her place at the hearth, Eleanor watched Richard's
face. He was concentrating very hard on everything de
Courville said, and a thin line had appeared between his
brows, as though he wasn't very pleased with what he was
hearing. Finally de Courville paused, and it was plain to
Eleanor that he, too, was trying to assess his lord's reaction.
"And so what do you think, my lord? Our scouts have reported that Llewellis has withdrawn into the mountains beyond the river. If he has holed up there for the winter, we
might do well to continue our raids on the villages he has
left undefended. It will keep them unsettled, and will un-
doubtedly weaken his position in the spring."

Richard's gaze flickered over to Eleanor, and she was
struck by the sudden thought that he was asking her for help
somehow. Confused, she got to her feet and tapped de
Courville on the shoulder. "Sir knight, my lord can only nod
or shake his head. He's not yet up to speech. You must
phrase your questions so that he answers them yes or no."
Eleanor watched Richard's face. He had closed his eyes, but
she could see his eyes moving beneath the lids. He seemed
to be thinking.

With an impatient huff, de Courville placed both hands on

his knees, and spoke again, slowly and deliberately. "The raids, my lord. Shall I continue?"

Richard glanced at Eleanor, almost as though, she thought, shocked, he wanted her to answer. She met his gaze calmly, trying to show no sign of her own confusion and concern. Finally Richard shrugged, a noncommittal gesture that made de Courville swear beneath his breath. "But, my lord, if we continue to harry the Welsh—"

Richard turned his head away, and Eleanor understood her cue. "I'm sorry, Sir Geoffrey. My lord must rest. Although he doubtless understands your concerns, his first concern must be for his own health. If he doesn't recover fully before he takes up his arms again, there is a very real possibility that the Welsh may accomplish their goal without having to raise their hands."

De Courville stared up at her, his mouth twisting beneath his thick beard. She knew he wanted to argue, but Richard had opened his eyes and was staring at them both with the expression he wore whenever he expected to be obeyed without question. Eleanor knew exactly what he wanted of her. "You must let my lord rest, Sir Geoffrey. You may speak with him again tomorrow, if you will. Surely there is nothing so pressing that it cannot wait?"

With a sigh of resignation, the knight rose to his feet. He inclined his head briefly in a gesture of obeisance, and with another bow to Eleanor, left the room. Eleanor looked at Richard, who had closed his eyes. "Rest, my lord," she murmured, as she resumed her place by the fire.

Reeling, Richard shut his eyes tight, and pressed his head back into the pillow. What had just happened was only the briefest taste of what could happen if he didn't learn the language and quickly. This was no film, no made-for-TV movie where the hero and the heroine, who were destined to live happily ever after, were bound to solve all their problems in two hours and fifteen minutes. The grizzled warrior who had sat beside his bed looked to him—to *him!*—for leadership, and he would know it in a moment if Richard were any less than the man he remembered. The thought of military leadership made his mind spin dizzily out of control, and with only the greatest effort, he pushed those thoughts out of his head. He forced himself to breathe calmly. Lucy used to tease him, saying that the law really was a different language from the one ordinary people spoke, the words just sounded familiar. If he had learned one obscure and convoluted language, surely he could learn another. And he knew that Norman French was one of the two great rivers from which modern English flowed. In the past days he had listened closely to Lucy—no, Eleanor—and the old woman talk. "Yes" and "no" was plain enough. Names and titles he understood, as he did all the nouns that had a similarity to the French he remembered from school. The total of those could probably fill up all of one page in a Middle French-English dictionary.

But how did infants learn to speak? They listened. All the time. At this point the best thing would be to listen to them all speak as much as possible. To immerse himself in the sounds and the rhythm and the cadence of the language. At least, he thought, the poor fellow whose body he'd stolen was probably illiterate. He wouldn't have to learn to read and write to carry out his charade. But eventually—surely at some point, if he were going to stay in this time and this place he would have to learn to read. And write. But not yet. First he had to get them to talk to him. His mind raced.

Talk—how did one say that? In modern French, the verb was *parler*. And in modern English, Parliament was the place where people met and talked.

He opened his eyes and raised his head, wincing in pain. "El—" he rasped, before the pain made his throat close in protest.

Eleanor looked up, wearing the same startled-rabbit expression she always did whenever he looked at her. Immediately she set down her sewing and hastened to his side. She touched his forehead with the back of her cool hand and gazed at him, concern and fear mixing on her face. "My lord?"

She was completely bewildered when he beckoned for her to sit in the chair by his side. She looked back at Ursula. "Ursula, what do you think he wants?"

Ursula shrugged. "Offer him wine."

Eleanor picked up the goblet, and raised it to Richard's face. He shook his head vehemently.

"See if he's cold," suggested the old woman.

Eleanor reached for the woolen blanket folded at the bottom of the bed. Again Richard shook his head violently, gesturing once more for her to sit. "Talk," he rasped.

Aghast, Eleanor sank into the chair. Talk? she wondered. He wanted her to talk? About what? The manor, she decided. Of course. Geoffrey couldn't tell him everything. Slowly, haltingly, she began, twisting her fingers in the rough woolen fabric of her skirt, hoping he wouldn't notice. Like any other common bully, obvious fear always whetted his appetite. As she went on, Richard settled back against his pillow with the barest sigh. Gradually her voice grew stronger and she couldn't help but notice his hand lying upturned and vulnerable on top of the coverlet, close to the edge of the bed. It almost seemed as though he invited her to hold it.

Hugh crept through the undergrowth, his soft leather boots making no noise at all. The day was a rare one for late October—the sun was warm, and the sky, for the first time in weeks that he could remember, was clear. Beneath the flame-colored leaves, the forest was quiet. At the perimeter of the remains of the little village, Hugh paused. Before de Lambert's vicious attack, it had been a forlorn enough little place, and now in only a matter of a few weeks, the forest looked as though it would claim it once again. He looked over his shoulder. It would never do for someone to find him here. Richard's men would drag him back to de Courville, who would punish him severely for abandoning his tasks. De Courville was strongly lobbying against him, petitioning Eleanor to send her brother away to the house of some greater lord, where he could learn the skills of knighthood and win his spurs. But Eleanor, fearing to hand Hugh into the clutches of someone like Richard, hesitated. Surely, she reasoned publicly, it was for William the Marshal to do that. Which was utter and complete nonsense, as Hugh and everyone else knew, but Eleanor had enough on her hands these days.

That's why he had come, risking the wrath of de Courville and his elder sister, to see if he could find some clue, something that might link Giscard Fitzwilliam to the attack. De Courville wouldn't listen to him without proof. But what? Arrows, perhaps, some scrap of clothing, some tangible evidence that the feeling in his gut was true. The bracken scratched his face as he crouched in the underbrush, and the

musty odor of the damp leaves belied the horror that he remembered.

But the evidence of that awful day was gone, buried in a
mound in the center of the village. He got to his feet and
started through the trees, certain that no one was about,
when he heard horses breaking through the forest, and he realized that someone was coming.

Instinctively he ducked down, then slowly straightened as
he saw two horses break into the clearing. Two women—
girls, really, for they were no more than his own age—sat
upon the horses' backs, the one clinging for dear life, the
other riding with the easy, comfortable seat of the seasoned
horsewoman. Her dark hair blew about her face, her riding
dress billowed behind her. She turned around and gabbled
something incomprehensible that Hugh realized at once was
Welsh, reined her horse abruptly, and slid to the ground.

The other girl awkwardly managed to induce her mount to
stop, and half rolled out of the saddle, speaking in frantic
whispers, clearly terrified.

Hugh peered through the trees, hoping to get a better look
at the tall dark-haired girl. The two went to the mound in the
center of the village. He saw the one in charge gesture impatiently to the other. The other drew a wreath of fading
wildflowers from her belt and offered it to her mistress. She
bent, placed the wreath in the center of the low mound of
raw earth, and bowed her head. Immediately Hugh understood. This was a grave, the grave of all of the villagers de
Lambert had slain in his fury against the Welsh.

He knew that de Courville had never returned to finish the
wretched work, and he realized that the Welsh chieftain
must have seen to his people in death as he had not done in
life. As they stood with bowed heads, Hugh shifted on his

knee and a twig snapped beneath his ankle. At once the taller girl looked up, grasping her companion's hand. Hugh expected them to bolt for the horses and flee, but the dark-haired girl only turned in the direction of the sound, and, drawing a slim dagger from a sheath on her belt, peered suspiciously in Hugh's direction.

At the first real look he had at her face, Hugh was struck by two things—one, the girl had a wild elfin look about her that suggested to him forest glades and mountain heights, and two, that there was no fear on her face. She handled the dagger as though she understood its uses very well. The other girl was pulling back and trying to tug away, but her mistress held her firmly by the hand, and spoke in Hugh's own tongue: "Show yourself."

Curiosity got the better of him. Hugh gingerly parted the trees and stood up. "How do you know my language?" he asked, as he stepped into the village clearing.

She drew herself up and met him with a haughtier stare than any Norman lady he had ever seen. "Do you think we can't learn the language of dogs? Get out of here, Norman, go back to your stone cess pits. Leave us to mourn in peace."

She was about his age, he thought, or maybe younger, and he raised his hands to show he wasn't armed. "Who are you?"

"Your death, if you don't leave us now." The wind whipped her tangled hair across her face.

He raised his hands to show he meant no harm and took a single step closer. This girl had the bearing of a queen, he thought, and he wondered if she knew anything of the events of the day Richard had been wounded. "I mean you no harm."

"As you meant these poor souls no harm?"

"It wasn't my fault!" The memory of that day sickened him, the reminder of de Lambert's face as he spitted the innocent child with his sword.

"I suppose you came to mourn them, too?"

"Not exactly," he admitted.

"Then what do you want? Get out of here—before my brother's men find you, and give you the fate you deserve."

"I told you I had nothing to do with what happened here." Hugh paused, as the full import of her words struck him. "You're Llewellis's sister?"

"Prince Llewellis," she corrected him. "And you're Hugh St. Clair's bastard son, whose guardian lies close to death. I hope the devil takes his rotting soul to hell."

"Your brother nearly managed to send him there," said Hugh, wondering if there were some way to get information out of her.

She frowned as if she didn't understand what he'd said, and in that moment, Hugh wondered if he had the proof he'd sought. "He'd like that," she answered slowly, as though she weighed his words, and found their meaning obscure.

Hugh narrowed his eyes, wondering how to phrase his next question, and just as he opened his mouth to speak, three armed horsemen burst into the clearing, longbows slung across their backs, quivers of arrows at their sides, long sheathed daggers slapping against their thighs. Hugh turned and bolted, speeding through the forest with the speed of fear, and an arrow thudded past his ear. He dodged behind the broad trunk of a great tree, flattened himself against it in anticipation of a deadly volley. He waited, heart thudding visibly, straining to hear the sounds of his pursuers. The forest was quiet. Only a bird twittered, scolded in the branches above his head, and a squirrel scampering across the forest floor paused and looked at him, as if assessing whether or not it was safe to cross. As the animal bounded away, Hugh eased a peek around the tree. No one had followed him. The minutes sped away, and Hugh realized that no one intended to pursue him. He had only to return home and face Sir Geoffrey's anger.

Cautiously he started off, and paused when he came to the tree where the arrow was imbedded. He pulled it out of the trunk. He ran his fingers over the tip, down the shaft, and examined the fletching. The Welsh arrows were legendary; there was no parallel in all of Europe. He remembered the day of the attack and he realized he had what he had come looking for. Now if only he could convince Geoffrey de Courville to listen to him.

Then a heavy hand fell upon his shoulder, and he turned, startled, to see a Welshman who grinned at him as if he'd just captured a prize. Or dinner.

Chapter 6

"SHE WAS WONDERFUL," stammered Bronwyn, her face red with the unaccustomed attention. She glanced at Angharad as she fingered her long black braids, chewing thoughtfully on one end.

"She was foolish," answered the young man beside the hearth. The resemblance between the brother and sister was striking. Llewellis, the heir of old Rhawn who had died in the summer, glared at his sister with a look of exasperation. "How many times have I told you not to venture so close to the border? What if that young puppy weren't the only one there? What if de Lambert himself were waiting?"

"De Lambert's dying," replied Angharad, her tone reflecting nothing of the incipient quarrel.

"So you hear."

"That's not the only thing I hear, brother." Angharad raised her chin and stared at her older brother.

Llewellis made an impatient noise. "So he blames me for the attack? What else is new? Do you expect me to be surprised by that?"

"Don't you see?" Angharad rose to her feet and held her hands out over the fire. The day was fading behind a blaze of purple and red clouds, and the warmth of the flames felt good. "They quarrel amongst themselves—perhaps there is a way to turn this to our advantage."

Llewellis turned to her with a start, and she pressed on. "Think. If de Lambert believes that we were the attackers, he has another enemy he doesn't know. And that means that this enemy may do for us what we would so dearly like to do for ourselves, and rid us of this Norman nuisance once and for all."

"And replace him with himself, no doubt," said Llewellis.

"But think of it, brother," pressed Angharad. "Surely you see."

Llewellis looked down at his youngest sister. Last of all old Rhawn's children, the only one unmarried, Angharad had been their father's favorite. A smile played on his lips behind his beard, and he glanced at the men lounging by the long hearth on the opposite wall. Angharad's clear voice had carried, and they were pretending not to have heard. But he knew more clearly than they did what they were thinking. He exchanged a glance with his second-in-command across the hall. "Yes, little sister. I do."

When the men had gone to their feasting, and the women had retired to their quarters above the hall, Bronwyn crept up to Angharad, who sat before the fire, where her old nurse, Nesta, was brushing out her tangled braids.

"Lady." Bronwyn twisted the fabric of her gown between her fingers. "What will they do with him?"

"With whom? That young Norman viper?" Angharad shot her companion a look bordering on contempt. "Do?" She cocked her head at the same moment that the brush went the other way. "Ow! Nesty, watch what you're doing."

As the old woman murmured an apology, Angharad looked back at Bronwyn. "My brother will hold him for ransom—he's the old lord's son. And his sister is wed to de Lambert. He has some value, that's certain. And doubtless he'll let something slip that will be of use to us. He didn't seem like he was a complete fool, but if you keep a man bored long enough, they'll talk just to hear themselves."

"He seemed as though he was quite taken with you, Angharad," Mairedd, Llewellis's wife put in. "I saw him at dinner—he didn't take his eyes off your face. Even when the prince himself spoke to him, the young Norman kept his eyes on you." She giggled and Angharad sniffed. Mairedd was pretty, an empty-headed nuisance who kept Llewellis warm in bed at night, but otherwise had not the brains of a hen.

Angharad snorted. "Leave be. I'd cut my own throat before I'd let one of them touch me." Mairedd laughed, that empty, silly titter of hers, and turned away to the other women, brandishing a length of new-spun wool. Angharad stared moodily ahead. Llewellis would linger long in the hall this night, discussing the situation with his men. But as far as she could tell, it mattered not at all which Norman vassal held the lands over the border. She sighed. Wales needed a strong leader, a high king, who would unite all the parcelings under one banner. She remembered the tales of Daffyd the bard, of Arthur and the Pendragon. Would the day ever come when the sleeping dragon of Wales would wake?

She realized with a start that Nesta had finished with her

hair, and was waiting for her to stand and undress for the
night. Instead she shrugged the old woman away, and
reached for her shawl.

"Angharad," called Mairedd from her cluster of women,
who were discussing the finer points of the new woolens,
"where are you going?"

"Out," she answered. "I find the air in here very close."

She did not wait to hear the babble of protests. She threw
the shawl over her head and dashed from the chamber. On
the landing she paused. From the hall she could hear the
loud jumble of the men's voices, rising and falling in endless
argument and boasting. The mead was flowing freely by this
time, a maid who ventured into the hall would likely find
herself not so soon a maid, and even Llewellis might be
powerless to protect her. No, she thought, better the clear of
the cold night. She gathered up her skirts and climbed to the
roof, emerging into the cold night air, with a sense of relief
and escape. The mountains of Wales loomed like black
shapes against the star-studded sky, thickly forested, rolling
onto the horizon, stretching to the west. The air cooled her
hot cheeks and she leaned against the battlements, watching
the stars.

"It's a pretty night," said a voice from the shadows.

She jumped, and turned to see the young Norman
hostage. "You! What are you doing up here?"

"Your brother's not a cruel jailer," answered Hugh as he
walked to stand beside her, "he said I might have the run of
the roof. I suppose he figures I have little chance of escape
up here." With a wide sweep, he indicated the sheer three-
hundred-foot drop to the ground below.

She favored him with a brief nod and turned away.

"Wait!" he called. "Don't go."

She looked back at him, knitting her brows together. "What makes you think I'd want to stay and talk to a murderer like you?"

"I'm not a murderer," he said, holding out his hand. "I had nothing to do with de Lambert's actions—it wasn't my idea to raid your villages."

She looked at him up and down, considering his words. Who knew better than she that often younger sons and daughters were caught in cross fires not of their own making? As the wind blew harder, and she pulled her shawl tighter across her shoulders, she shrugged. "What were you doing there?"

"I told you. I was looking to see who it was who attacked de Lambert. I know it wasn't your brother."

She leaned back against the stone. He was guileless, still a boy, she thought, to tell her so much. Didn't he realize they were enemies?

"Who do you think it was?"

He shot her a quick look, a rueful grin. "I don't know. De Lambert has lots of enemies. Like your brother. Isn't that the situation with the Welsh?"

How neatly he had turned the tables. She admitted his rightness with a smile and a little bow, and she turned back to the battlements. "It does my brother no good to think that he can banish your people from the land," she said.

"No," he admitted, "we're here to stay."

"There's only one way for the Welsh to win this war with the Normans," she said, "and that's not likely to happen in my lifetime."

He looked at her with a question in his dark eyes.

"There has to be a leader—one man—who can unite all the Welsh under one rule and so make us strong."

"Like Duke William," said Hugh, "who led the Normans here."

"Who led the Normans into England," she corrected. This time it was his turn to bow. "You don't like de Lambert," she said, watching his face.

"I hate him." Hugh could not control the savagery in his voice.

"And yet you're both Normans."

"He's not like my father, he's not like the Lion Heart, or even William the Marshal, who is—was—my father's overlord. I would do anything to get away from him—anything to get Eleanor away from him."

"Anything?" Angharad raised one questioning eyebrow.

"Anything," said Hugh. And she marked well his tone of voice.

Chapter 7

"DAMN THE PUPPY," swore Geoffrey de Courville as he flung the parchment message to the floor. It snapped back into its original shape and came to a rest beside the hem of Eleanor's gown. She pressed her lips together and glanced at Richard.

"If he hadn't gone off, this would never have happened. He deliberately shirked his duties—deliberately flouted my commands—how dare the wretched boy think that his hide's worth so much as a chicken's?"

"Please, Sir Geoffrey—" began Eleanor.

"Oh, no, my lady, you wouldn't listen to me when I told you the time had come and gone for him to be sent away. You wouldn't listen when the lord of Bramber himself sent for Hugh—"

"The lord of Bramber is no better than those marauding Welshman!" Eleanor stood up and faced the knight. "I will not see my brother turned over to some scoundrel simply because it is inconvenient for you. Hugh is the son of the lord of the manor—"

"The bastard son of the old lord," Geoffrey spat back. "And so was I and so are a hundred, no, a thousand like him. And he'd best be sent to learn to earn his keep, for he'll not eat otherwise."

From the bed, Richard coughed, the strangled, hoarse noise he made when he wanted attention. He pointed at de Courville, and motioned him to leave. "Not—now," he managed to choke out. Geoffrey shot Eleanor another murderous look and left the room. The door slammed with a dull thud.

Eleanor stared at Richard. The expression on his face was inscrutable. He struggled to sit up, and gestured for the scroll lying discarded on the floor. With a trembling hand, she stooped and retrieved it, handing it to him automatically. He opened it, scanned it almost as though he expected to read it, and made an impatient little noise. He thrust it back at her. "Read," he said, "slow."

She took a deep breath, sat in the chair beside the bed and obeyed. The words were simple enough. Llewellis Ab Rhawn was holding Hugh for hostage in retaliation for the raids of the last months, until Richard ransomed him for five thousand gold marks.

Eleanor sighed again. Five thousand gold marks was more than all the worth of both her manors put together. There was no question of such an amount being raised.

Five thousand gold marks was the ransom of a prince. Llewellis offered them six months to raise the money—very clever, with winter coming on and the fighting likely to cease anyway. She put down the parchment and raised her eyes reluctantly, afraid of the anger she would see in

Richard's face. She expected at the least derision. Hugh was lost.

The expression on his face made her draw back. He was looking at her with a mixture of what could only be concern and sorrow. He looked as though he cared, and cared deeply, about her brother's fate.

"What—do?" he managed.

She laughed, a little hysterically and got to her feet. "Do, my lord? Do? What is there to do? We no more have five thousand marks than we have wings to fly. We have six months in which to raise it, but we will sooner grow wings." She paced to the window and gazed out over the November landscape. The heavy clouds massed over the trees, and wind was rushing through the bare branches. Even the courtyard was deserted, except for the fire in the smithy and the odd scullion here and there engaged in their miserable occupations.

"El—," he began, the closest approximation to her name he could manage, she supposed, since that was what he always called her. She turned back to see him holding out his hand. "Come—" He beckoned.

Like a woman in a dream she stared. Surely this couldn't be true. This wasn't her Richard, the Richard who had ridden out that September day, eager for conquest and the joy of the kill. This man's eyes were soft, his expression kind, and his hand was raised, not in anger, but almost in supplication, as though he invited her to allow him to help her. She shook her head as if to clear it and took one wary step backward, her hip flat against the windowsill.

There was a sharp knock and Ursula peered into the door. "My lady, my lord," she said, when she saw Richard sitting up. "Giscard Fitzwilliam has just ridden up to the gates and

asks for admittance. He brings a message so he says from
His grace, King John."

The change in Eleanor's expression was startling, thought
Richard, as he watched her reaction flicker across her face.
Giscard Fitzwilliam—the name meant something to her,
something she didn't like. He saw the revulsion, the terror,
flicker across her features as clearly as it had when he had
beckoned. *So,* he thought, with a grim sort of satisfaction,
someone she hates more than me.

He understood the words King John. There was one certain way to find out who this Giscard was and why Eleanor
was so frightened of him. He beckoned to Ursula and nodded. "Yes," he managed. "I see."

As he fell back against the pillows, he thanked God that
the neck wound prevented better speech. The arrow that had
wounded his throat must have caused severe damage to his
vocal cords, he reasoned, and was thankful that no one appeared to think it odd that what few words he did utter were
ungrammatical. He heard the heavy feet on the steps, and in
the corridor, and as Eleanor took a chair by the fire, the door
opened once more, and Ursula curtseyed as she admitted the
newcomer.

"Giscard Fitzwilliam, my lord."

Eleanor got up to leave, and Richard looked at her. "Stay."
He glanced up to see what could almost be a walking pig.
He had to control the urge to laugh. The man who strode into
the room looked like a cross between Friar Tuck and one of
the Three Little Pigs.

And then he realized that the look in the man's eyes was
as dangerous as anything he'd ever seen on the face of a con-
victed felon, cold and flat and dead. Only once before had
he ever seen eyes like that—in a youth who had been

charged with the rapes and murders of three women, one of them a fifteen-year-old girl. In a fit of misguided compassion, he had agreed to represent the youth at his trial, since he couldn't afford counsel, and no one else in the county had volunteered. Richard had regretted that decision every day of the trial, and the look in the youth's eyes as he was led away burned itself into his brain, and haunted his dreams twenty years after the fact.

Now another man, with eyes just as hard, just as cold, stood over him. The reek of his stale body made Richard want to gag, and he controlled his reaction with only the greatest effort.

"So, my lord," drawled the newcomer, his voice a high-pitched whine, which immediately set Richard's nerves on edge, "I see you mend against every expectation."

Richard met the newcomer's gaze evenly. This was an enemy—Eleanor, and her younger brother, had been right. There were no good intentions on the part of this man, he had come solely to satisfy his curiosity. He glanced at the dagger hanging from the belt, at the sword in the sheath. Giscard carried his weapons with the same calculated insolence street-wise youths did—or would, in the far-distant future.

Richard inclined his head in a gesture of greeting, never breaking eye contact. He was gratified when Giscard dropped his eyes and turned away, under the pretext of accepting the goblet and plate of cakes Ursula offered.

"Our royal master bids you heal quickly—I shall be certain to assure him you heed his command."

Richard smiled, pulling his lips up, keeping his eyes steady.

"But I hear, my lady," Giscard looked at Eleanor, who automatically took a step backward, holding her hands out of the way as though she feared contamination. "I hear young Hugh has purchased a mort of trouble. Will you meet the ransom, my lord?"

He slid his gaze back to Richard. Richard shrugged, spread his wide-fingered palms wide.

"The puppy's not worth the trouble, really, bastard son and all that he is. But to please you, my lady, perhaps I could be of assistance in raising the ransom. I hear it's quite high."

Eleanor made a little sound that sounded like a hiss, and Richard nodded gravely, as though he might consider such a thing. Eleanor's face was white, and her mouth was pinched tight. Two spots of color had appeared on her cheeks. *Poor thing,* he thought, *she looks as though she's trapped.* It only gratified him a little to think that here was someone she hated more than him.

"Well." Giscard took a long quaff of ale, and wiped his mouth across his sleeve. "I only came to offer my good wishes, my lord, and those of our liege. I was at the hunt— I've brought you a fine stag."

"You're most kind, my lord," murmured Eleanor. She kept her hands clenched in her skirt, and Richard understood that she would rather starve than accept Giscard's meat.

"I look forward to riding out with you, my lord." Giscard got heavily to his feet. "And don't forget, my offer of assistance with the puppy still stands."

As Ursula ushered Fitzwilliam from the sickroom, Richard looked at Eleanor. She was staring into the hearth, as though thinking. "El—" he managed. "Please—"

She raised her head. Never, in all the months of their marriage, never once in all the time since Richard had come to

Barland had she ever heard him use the word "please." Never. It simply wasn't a part of his vocabulary.

"Hugh—" he croaked. "Fitz—" He nodded toward the door. "You must—talk."

"Talk, my lord?" She shook her head as if to clear it. "You want me to talk to Fitzwilliam, about ransoming Hugh?"

"No," he shook his head violently, although the word was no more than an emphatic whisper. He hit his chest with his thumb. "Me. Talk me."

Angharad paused at the stable entrance, listening. Above the stamp and pawing of the horses, she could hear her brother's voice as it rose, berating one of the grooms for treating his prized stallion carelessly. The thought crossed her mind that perhaps now was not the best time to discuss the matter that she had in mind. But the cold wind gusted hard about her skirts, and she shivered. Better to do it now, while they had privacy. There was no point in discussing such a thing before any of her brother's men. She would only make herself the laughingstock of the entire castle.

Heavy footsteps pounded down the long row of stalls, and Angharad saw her brother's dark head over the high rails. He was frowning, and his mouth was pressed tight in the expression he wore when it was best to stay away from him. But he was alone. She held her ground.

He was almost upon her when he spied her, standing in the door, and his expression changed from annoyance to surprise. "What are you doing here, Angharad? Riding again?"

"No," she shook her head and clutched her shawl more tightly about herself, more from sudden nervousness than from cold. In all the years she had spent listening to the men speak beside the long hearths, she had never taken so much upon herself. "I wanted to talk to you."

His expression changed back to annoyance. "Now what?"

"It isn't anything bad," she said, feeling mildly annoyed herself. Why did so much have to depend on whether or not the men were in a good humor?

"What then?" He didn't pause in his stride, only gestured with his head to let her know she should follow him out the door and across the wide yard.

"I wanted to talk to you about Hugh—about St. Clair's bastard," she corrected herself and wondered if he had heard her use the boy's Christian name.

Of course he had, for he stopped short, and stared down at her, suspicion curling his lip and narrowing his eyes. "If that young bastard has made any improper advances—" Llewellis put his hands on his hips and swore softly beneath his breath.

"No." Angharad was disgusted. And why did men think of improper advances before anything else?

"Angharad, I'm busy." Llewellis glanced impatiently about the yard. Just beyond the walls, she could hear the shouts and the thuds as the men at arms practiced their archery.

"I've spoken with him," she began, wondering how to convince her brother that the Norman bastard might be of some use.

"Oh? And have you made improper advances?"

"Brother!" Angharad was shocked.

"Say on, little sister." He grinned down at her, and then glanced up, as though eager to be away.

"I—I was thinking he might be of use to us."

Llewellis raised one brow. "St. Clair's bastard? Other than for ransom?"

Angharad nodded. "Yes, of course other than for ransom. After all, you've asked for such a high price, it's unlikely you'll ever see it. You'll have to kill him, and you know it, but I think he might be of use in other ways."

Llewellis tapped his booted foot impatiently on the ground and rubbed one hand across his bearded chin. "How?"

"He hates de Lambert. Hates him more than even you or I or any of us do."

Llewellis narrowed his eyes at her once more, as though he doubted such a thing were possible, but she could tell he was listening. Angharad went on. "And anyone who hates de Lambert—and distrusts Fitzwilliam as much as Hugh does—" She broke off, letting the thought sink into her brother's mind. She didn't even notice that this time she had used his Christian name again.

Llewellis raised his head and nodded, staring off into the distance, and Angharad knew he was turning the idea over in his mind. She had been right to come to him when he was alone and relatively unburdened by the expectations of the household as to how he should behave.

"I am not certain. . . ." His voice trailed off, but he continued to stare into the distance.

"Maybe not," said Angharad. "Maybe you don't see a way in which this can be helpful to us. But you should speak to him yourself. If you see and hear for yourself how much he hates de Lambert, you'll know he means it. And anyone who hates someone as much as he hates de Lambert—"

Llewellis shrugged. "That might be, little sister. But an enemy of de Lambert is not necessarily a friend to us. Remember that." He turned on his heel as if to go, then paused. "But you might speak to him—from time to time. Garner as much information as you can—about the keep, about de Lambert's men. Tell me everything he tells you—who knows what we might find to be of use? After all," he smiled as a gust of wind blew dead leaves across his boots, "we've time. A winter's worth of time."

Chapter 8

ANOTHER WEEK PASSED. No word came from the marshal, and Eleanor fretted silently every time she found herself thinking her little brother in the clutches of the Welsh. Fitzwilliam paid no more visits, and de Courville subsided into a grim silence, speaking to her only when absolutely necessary. But was that so very different from the way it had always been? she wondered. Or had the change in Richard made Geoffrey's disdain of her all the more clear?

The changes in Richard—changes that at first she thought only she had noticed—were increasingly apparent, and she soon realized that Ursula had marked it too. Who would ever have believed that now every evening, as the room grew dark, Richard insisted upon candles—a dozen or more—so that the room was lit so brightly it seemed nearly day. Or that he seemed to expect her to spend her time with him, sewing, or reading, or simply talking to him about the day's events? He seemed insatiably curious, about every aspect of the castle life. He asked halting questions about the sorts of things she had never thought to tell him, or would never have thought he would have noticed or cared about.

And it even seemed, to her complete astonishment, that he was interested in learning to read. Eleanor wondered if such a change ever came over other men who found themselves close to death and yet lived.

As if hearing the echo of Eleanor's thoughts, Ursula leaned forward on the other side of the hearth. Richard slept, snoring softly, the rasping breathing evidence of his healing wound. In his sleep, a long lock of dark hair had fallen across his face. His mouth was slack, his hands relaxed by his side. Eleanor watched him, entranced in spite of herself, by the contrast between the implicit strength in the heavy muscles of his chest and arms, and the soft, full curves of his lips. How was it possible a man so beautiful could be so cruel? She jumped when Ursula said, "He's very different now."

"Yes," answered Eleanor, flushing a little and telling herself it was the heat of the fire that made her cheeks red.

"Who knows what he saw, in the time he lay as if in death?" Ursula glanced from Eleanor to the bed.

"Saw?" Eleanor frowned. "What do you mean?"

"Perhaps he was dead, my lady. He had no signs of life. Perhaps he went to hell, and met the devil"—here Ursula crossed herself—"or even met the Lord and learned the error of his ways."

Eleanor smiled in spite of herself at Ursula and her beliefs, which amounted to little more than superstitions. Although she wanted to believe that a miraculous transformation had occurred, she couldn't quite bring herself to do so. And yet . . . She cocked her head, watching him sleep. There was something undeniably different about him—in his eyes, in his expression, something she had never seen before. It was especially noticeable when he looked at her. He clearly wanted her to spend time with him—it was almost as if he wanted her to like him.

But that was impossible, thought Eleanor, even as she gazed at his face. No one changed so dramatically. Richard was too cruel, too demanding, too harsh. And even if some miracle had occurred, and he had changed overnight from a beast to a veritable prince, how could she ever forget or think of forgiving everything that had gone before?

But even as her mental resolve strengthened, the memory of Richard's mouth on hers, his hands on her breasts, his lips on her nipples stirred her body's desires. The very thought of those long nights, when he'd reached for her time after time, using her until every fiber of her body drooped with exhaustion and satiation, made her body stir once more. She pressed her lips together in a firm line, but she could no more will herself to forget such dark pleasures than she could will herself not to breathe.

"Stranger things have happened, my lady," whispered Ursula, over the snap of the flames. "When did Lord Richard ever ask for so much light in the evenings before?"

Eleanor bit back a chuckle, lest she insult Ursula and her good-hearted beliefs. "Are you saying he tasted the darkness of hell, and now is afraid of the dark?"

"No, my lady," said Ursula with a little sniff. She knew Eleanor wasn't taking her seriously. "I'm saying he tasted the darkness of hell and now wants no more part of it. I'm saying he's not the man he was when he rode out that day. And you, my lady, will be the first to know it."

"Me?" Eleanor stared at Ursula. "Why me?"

"I've seen how he looks at you—follows you with his eyes as you move about the room. He listens for your step in the hall, and his face lights up when you walk into the room. Mark my words, my lady—he looks like a man in love."

"Love?" This time Eleanor had to laugh. "What did Richard ever know of love?"

Ursula shrugged and rose to her feet. "It must be close to noon. I'd better fetch Lord Richard's dinner. You laugh now, my lady—but you'll see." Shaking her head and still muttering, Ursula left the room, closing the door firmly behind her.

Eleanor shook her head and went back to her sewing. The foolish fancies of an old woman. Who would ever have thought that Ursula of all people would entertain such hopes? A little sound made her look up. Richard was awake, his eyes a brilliant blue in the sunlight. Her heart did a little jig all its own in her chest. There was no question that Richard was the fairest man she had ever seen in her life. She remembered how her body had responded the first time she'd seen him pull his shirt over his head. The massive muscles of his chest and shoulders had flexed and rippled beneath his skin, and in the glow of the firelight, a sheen of sweat had made him gleam like some pagan god. How she had trembled when he'd reached for her, and how her heart had pounded as he'd kissed her. He'd reached beneath her modest virginal nightgown, and begun a slow exploration of every inch of her body. . . . She startled.

With effort, she dragged herself back to the present and looked back at the sewing on her lap. She was falling into

Ursula's trap. The woman wanted her to be happy so much that Ursula was willing to fit her faith to hope. From beneath her lids, she glanced back at him.

He beckoned her, and she was shocked to see a little smile lift the corners of his mouth. Or was it a grimace of pain? She rose and walked to stand beside him. "My lord? Is there anything you require?"

He shifted on the pillows, and reached for her hand. This time he caught it, and held it, not tightly, but gently, as though he thought she might snatch it away.

Almost of their own volition, she felt her fingers begin to curl around his, and she stiffened, forcing her hand to remain loose and limp in his. "My lord?"

"Thirsty," he managed. "Please."

There was that "please" again. She had heard him use it so frequently in the last few weeks, it nearly sounded natural for him to say it. She dropped her eyes, unwilling and somehow unable to meet the intensity in his. She gently extricated her hand and poured water from the pitcher into the goblet by the bed. He sat up, took the goblet she offered, and drank it down, with noticeably less difficulty than he'd had before. She noted his color was much better and that he moved restlessly. Soon he would be up and about. And then, she wondered, would the old Richard return? He did not slump back against the pillows as he had before. "Must dress."

"Now?" she asked, startled by what seemed to be the silent communication between them.

"Tomorrow. Dress tomorrow. In bed too long. Am weak."

Ah, she thought, of course. Richard would feel the lack of exercise, the lack of activity. Last winter he cursed and chafed when the heavy snows made it impossible for him to ride out. "Would you like to sit by the fire, my lord?" She gestured to Ursula's abandoned chair, where the light of the late autumn sun pooled on the seat, making the warmth of the fire doubly pleasant.

Richard glanced at the chair, and then at her, as though uncertain of her meaning. Finally he nodded. "Why not?"

She reached for his robe at the foot of the bed, and helped him slip it on over his shoulders. She kept her gaze averted from his long, muscular body, and he seemed almost shy, as though he had forgotten he had once strutted before her naked, his erection jutting before him. She felt an unexpected twinge of tenderness for his weakened condition.

She stepped back and watched as he walked slowly to the chair. He sank into it carefully, as if feeling his way down into it, and looked up at her. This time, to her astonishment, he smiled unmistakably. "Sit?"

Wondering, she sat down in the chair opposite. His dark hair curled in unruly locks about his face, but his eyes were bright with health, not fever, and he gazed eagerly about the room as though seeing it for the first time. There was nothing of his usual customary disdain. His eyes met hers and she dropped hers under that intense scrutiny. What was he thinking when he looked at her that way?

Someone knocked on the door, startling her out of her reverie. "Come in, Ursula," she called, forgetting that Ursula was unlikely to knock.

It was Geoffrey de Courville who stepped into the room. He barely glanced in her direction, but he smiled broadly upon seeing Richard sitting by the fire. "My lord. My lady." He spoke directly to Richard. "A message has come from the marshal."

"From the marshal?" Eleanor cried. Perhaps Hugh would be home by Christmas.

"Yes, my lady," said Geoffrey. "I brought you the message, my lord. His messenger awaits a reply in the hall." Geoffrey proffered a sealed scroll.

Eleanor took the scroll, and looked at once to Richard. He gestured to her. "Read," he rasped.

Geoffrey's dour face brightened considerably when he heard Richard speak. "You sound much better, my lord."

Richard nodded. "Tomorrow. I dress. Go down—" he hesitated, as if groping for a word.

"To the hall, my lord?" Eleanor supplied. "Join us in the hall for dinner?"

Richard was listening carefully. "Yes," he said finally. "Hall. Dinner."

Geoffrey beamed. "That's truly good news, my lord. The men will be glad to hear of your improvement."

Eleanor, meanwhile, had broken the seal and scanned the parchment letter. A pall of disappointment fell over her like a shroud and she had to struggle to hold back her tears. Nothing in the letter spoke of Hugh, or of their situation. It was addressed to all the barons who owed the marshal fealty. She controlled her emotions with difficulty and managed to look up at Richard. "Shall I read it, my lord?" When he nodded, she said, "It's to all those who owe fealty to the king through William, Earl of Pembroke and Striguil, the Marshal of England. He says that the Archbishop of Canterbury and other barons are fomenting rebellion in the realm, and he bids you remember your oaths you swore as his liegemen. He calls you to meet with him or his appointed representative at Pembroke Castle a fortnight hence, to take counsel. Any grievances that you may have against the king he will hear at that time. And he bids you stand fast, and to trust in the Lord, and not in the force of arms against your

king." Eleanor looked up at Richard when she finished reading. His brow was furrowed, and he was staring into the fire.
He seemed to be deep in thought.

"Of course we'll stand fast," said Geoffrey. "What does
the marshal take us for? I will tell him so when I see him.
'Twould be best for us to forget that puppy and muster the
support we can so that we are ready for whatever the spring
brings us."

Richard did not react. His eyes were fixed on the leaping
flames, and his expression was grim.

"My lord?" said Geoffrey. "Shall I tell his messenger that
I will answer in your place?"

Richard turned to look at Geoffrey, shaking his head no.
"Must think first."

"What is there to think about?" Geoffrey stared at Richard
with disbelief, and even Eleanor was surprised. Richard discussed everything with Geoffrey.

"Enough now." He shook his head. "Must think. Tomorrow. Talk."

Geoffrey narrowed his eyes and glanced at Eleanor as
though he held her personally responsible for the change in
Richard, but the custom of obedience was too strongly in-
grained for him to challenge Richard outright. He said nothing more, but squared his shoulders and bowed stiffly from
the waist. "My lord."

"Tell Ursula to be sure that the messenger is to be treated
with all courtesy," said Eleanor.

Geoffrey paused with his hand upon the latch. "Yes, my
lady." With another dark look at Richard, he was gone.

Richard had turned back to the fire. A lock of hair fell
across his forehead, and the flames danced across his narrow

face, his roughly shaven cheeks. He drew a deep breath, and turned back to Eleanor. "Read. Again."

Eleanor fingered the thick parchment, and read the message again, slowly, carefully. Although the words themselves were simple enough, there was a world of meaning in the message. Could it be that Archbishop Langton intended to incite a rebellion among the barons against the king?

Richard rubbed his hand across his chin and stirred in his chair as she finished. He looked at her as if waiting for her to say something.

"My lord?" she asked finally, baffled by what he could be waiting for.

"You—what you think?"

Eleanor's eyes flew open. HE was asking *her* for her opinion? She drew a deep breath, hoping to cover her confusion. "W-well," she stammered, hoping to buy a few minutes to collect her thoughts. "The archbishop is no friend to the king. And John has ever been in a mort of trouble with the Church—"

Richard looked down at his hands as though seeing them for the first time. "King John," he muttered. A line creased his forehead, as though he were trying to remember something. He looked back at the bed, almost longingly, and Eleanor anticipated his need.

"To bed, my lord? Do you grow tired?"

He shook his head. "Go. Leave me. Must think."

With a puckered little frown, she rose. He held out his hand for the parchment, and a little surprised, she handed it to him. He turned away, his eyes fixed once more on the flickering flames. He leaned his chin upon one hand. He looked so troubled, so lost and alone, she found she had to stifle the urge to speak a word of comfort. But Richard had never brooked unnecessary words from her, and she was the last person whose opinion he would have sought. But what was he thinking? she wondered as she quietly withdrew.

The flames danced with maddening unconcern. Richard tightened his fingers on the parchment, feeling the thickness of the material, the rough texture. How could this be real? he wondered. And then again, how could it not? Delusions didn't come with their own sets of complexities, did they?

He unrolled the parchment scroll and stared down at the writing. The neat script flowed across the page, and here and there he discerned letters and what had to be words, all in French. Old French, he thought. The language he was slowly learning to speak. He fingered the wax seals, the pale blotch with which the message had been closed, and the red one that carried the imprint of a rough symbol. He stared closely at the signature, the clumsy penmanship of a man who had spent his life fighting, to whom books and paper and pens were the domain of the priests and the scribes, whose duty it was to support the men who fought.

What did he remember? He racked his brain. John was King of England. John—called Softsword and Lackland. The most hated of all England's kings—the one of whom Lucy had told him it had been said: "We'll have no more kings named John." And there hadn't been, he knew. Never again had a king named John reigned on an English throne.

So, he thought, taking a deep breath, scanning the words over and over. Where did that leave him? In the early thirteenth century—but what was happening in England? Something rang a bell, tantalizing him, something he ought to know, something important, something so important even schoolchildren in the United States were taught it. 1213— 1214—what had happened in the early thirteenth century?

The barons and King John—John had been challenged by his own barons, and what had been the result? The recollection burst from his memory. The Magna Carta. The Great Charter—the foundation of English law, and the very earliest beginning of what would one day give rise to the American legal system. Now the memories came flooding back. The Magna Carta had been signed in 1215. In actual fact, it was less than the sweeping document it was sometimes purported to be, but what was more important than the individual parts of it was the concept that had created it—that by implication, it reflected the rudiments of a coherent political philosophy. The barons sought not to exclude the royal government, as similar charters of the period had, but to influence it—to make it act in their interest and respect their customary rights. Incorporated into the charter was the concept that the king is limited by tradition and by custom in his relations with free men of every class, not just the knights and the nobility. It was the first time that the concept of the common law, overarching and circumscribing the power of the king, had been in any way expressed.

Well, thought Richard, as a log split and the shower of sparks brought him back to what was now the present, it was all well and good that he remembered so much legal history. But what was the situation in England in the years prior to the signing of the Great Charter, which gave rise to it? What led to the meeting at Runnymede in June of 1215?

He closed his eyes and tried to think, fitting current information with that which he dimly remembered. John was an autocratic king, he remembered, not necessarily a bad king but one who lacked a crucial attribute—he didn't know how to get people to do what he wanted them to do. He lacked political savvy. He didn't have the charisma to make people follow him because they loved him, as they had his brother, Richard the Lion Hearted, and he somehow managed to antagonize many around him.

But not William the Marshal, thought Richard, musing. Who was this William, who held so much sway and influence over, Richard realized with a sudden start, his own life? William the Marshal—he searched his memory. A great warrior, a man respected by all who knew him, including John. Otherwise he wasn't much more than a footnote of history.

Richard slumped in his chair. He'd better come up with more information on the political situation in which he was obviously expected to play a part, albeit a peripheral one, but a part just the same. He turned what he knew over and over in his mind. The Welsh had Eleanor's brother, and expected ransom—or maybe they didn't. Maybe they expected him to invade. Giscard Fitzwilliam was involved in some way—his one meeting with Giscard was enough for him to know that the man was not to be trusted. If he was the sort of man the king kept in his confidence, maybe the Archbishop of Canterbury was correct in his grievances.

Richard pressed the tips of his fingers together, and gazed into space. Giscard coveted what Richard had. That was easy enough to understand—he wanted Eleanor, and the lands that were her patrimony. And in order to acquire them, he needed Richard out of the way.

If only he knew, thought Richard ruefully. If only Giscard knew that the Richard he now faced was a man who had little knowledge of the language, and even less of anything else that had value in this time and place. He was going to have to win as many friends as he possibly could, learn as much about the allegiances here as possible—and judging from the way everyone looked at him, from Eleanor on down, that wasn't going to be easy.

And there was Sir Geoffrey, the captain of the guard, or whatever his title was. Geoffrey knew there was something different about the man he called his lord, which jeopardized Richard's own position with a man he would have to trust implicitly. Eleanor sensed it, too, he was sure of it. Abruptly Richard forced thoughts of Eleanor out of his mind. There was too much at stake right now for him to indulge in pleasant daydreams. Not only was the situation at hand tenuous and fraught with uncertainty, there was a greater drama developing, one whose implications would reverberate down the centuries.

It was obvious what the answer had to be. Loyal as Geoffrey might be—might be, for Richard suspected that if Geoffrey knew the truth, he would be less than faithful—Richard knew he couldn't trust Geoffrey to handle matters as he would. Geoffrey might not even mention Eleanor's brother at all. In fact, Richard was sure he wouldn't. Geoffrey didn't care about the fate of a nameless, landless bastard son. The "real" Richard obviously hadn't. But he was the real Richard now, the only one there was, and not only would the meeting give Richard the opportunity to try to learn where matters stood in the nation. It would give him the chance to prove to Eleanor that he was not the man she had married.

There was simply no other solution. He would have to appear at Pembroke Castle and learn all he could from the marshal. Perhaps he would even be able to speak to the marshal himself, though it was lucky the throat wound prevented clear speech. He just hoped he'd be able to make himself understood and, what was even more important, to understand what was said. He closed his eyes as a wave of exhaustion overtook him. He straightened up with an effort. He'd been weak long enough. He had to learn just how matters stood, or he might make some mistake, a mistake for which in this brutal time and place he and all those around him were likely to pay with their lives.

Chapter 9

IT WAS NOW or never, thought Richard, as he walked slowly and carefully down the narrow staircase—the same one from which he had fallen from his present into the past. A chill ran down his back as he leaned against the rough-hewn stone. His body was still stiff and sore in many places, his throat ached if he forgot to chew his food carefully and thoroughly. Talking hurt, too. But the time was coming— had come—for him to begin to try and fill the role of the lord of the manor. The magnitude of the task sometimes made him wake in the middle of the night in a cold sweat. He took a deep breath, and deliberately banished all doubts from his mind. He would never win Eleanor otherwise, and besides, whether she liked it or not, he knew that she had come to rely upon him. Otherwise, her choices were Giscard, some-one else of the king's choosing, or the Welsh.

As he reached the bottom of the steps, he saw Sir Geof-

frey across the hall. The man was watching him closely. Geoffrey would have to accompany him to Pembroke. There
was no doubt about that. Richard didn't even know the way.
He raised his arm and beckoned.

At once Geoffrey broke off his conversation with one of
the other men at arms, and hastened to Richard. "My lord?"

Richard paused, taking a moment to assess the burly warrior who stood before him. Geoffrey was tall and barrel
chested, his shoulders and upper arms huge hams of muscle. Richard gazed thoughtfully into Geoffrey's eyes. Beyond the surface suspicion, Richard read abiding loyalty.
This man took his oaths to his lord very seriously. He wondered what history these two men shared. "Must talk about
the journey. My horse—" He broke off, hoping he had a favorite horse. And then he chided himself. Favorite probably
wasn't the right word.

But Geoffrey was talking, with an eagerness that told
Richard he was anxious for his lord's complete recovery.
"I've seen to his exercise, my lord, but he's eager to be out—
a journey will suit him well. Would you like to see him?"

Richard nodded. What better time than the present, he
thought, as Geoffrey called for their cloaks. He thanked God
he'd had some experience riding, and hoped that this body
had some memory of its own. He followed Geoffrey out of
the hall, realizing that this was the first time he'd ventured
so far. The cold air was refreshing, although many odors,
some good and some not, blew by on the cold gusts. His
boots crunched over the gravel in the courtyard. Everyone
they passed paused and bowed as he walked by. He nodded
here and there, and a few smiled tentatively, fearfully at him.
The original occupant of this body must have kept absolute
control of the entire household, he mused.

In the stables, the astonished grooms bowed and stammered, staring with open mouths, and Geoffrey cuffed one on the side of the head. "Get to work, boy, before Lord Richard makes your face uglier than it already is."

From the way the boy bolted away, Richard wondered just exactly how formidable a threat that was. They continued down a row of stalls, until Geoffrey paused at the end. The huge black head of the occupant of the last stall swung in their direction, whickering a greeting. "He's glad to see you, my lord."

Richard nodded and reached for the bridle. He stroked the animal's nose. The beast was huge. Richard gulped inwardly. He hoped he remembered enough horsemanship to control the animal.

"Will you ride, my lord?" The high-pitched voice of a young groom interrupted his thoughts.

"Tomorrow," answered Richard. He'd been up nearly all day—he didn't think he should push himself too much. "Early. Have him waiting for me—"

"After drill, my lord?" asked Geoffrey. "The men will be eager to see you."

Richard gave Geoffrey a dubious glance. Somehow, judging from the cowed looks of the people he'd seen so far, he doubted that the men would be any happier to see him than anyone else appeared to be. But maybe not. Maybe someone as obviously brutal as Richard de Lambert would only attract soldiers as brutal as he. Richard shivered a bit inside. To become the leader of a pack of rapacious opportunists—armed opportunists—had never been one of his life's ambitions. "After drill. You accompany me."

"Of course, my lord."

Richard turned away, and Geoffrey fell in step beside him.

"I must say, my lord, I admire your determination to see the marshal, but I—"

"You question whether I am ready to travel?" Richard raised one eyebrow.

"I've never minced words with you, my lord." Geoffrey met his stare evenly, and instinctively Richard knew why. He was probably one of the few skilled enough to challenge Richard in a fight—and have a chance to win.

"You have no need to mince," Richard said, hoping he got the sentence construction correct. "Say what you will."

"It could be foolish for you to go, to risk your life, your health—"

Richard held up his hands. "You have good concerns." He frowned a little. That sounded awkward, even to his ears. "Is not only the marshal I go to see."

"Oh?"

"Fitzwilliam—"

"He'll not be there—he owes no fealty to the marshal."

"No," Richard shook his head. "But he will hear. These past weeks—is clear what he wants. He wants Eleanor and these lands."

Geoffrey gave him a long look. "He is the king's man—his lands border these to the north."

"It does not prevent him from wanting—" Richard hesitated. It occurred to him he didn't know how to refer to this place. The landlady at the pub—eight hundred years in the future—had called the place Barland Castle, but how was he to know if this was Barland for sure? People who behaved strangely in the thirteenth century were thought to be possessed.

But Geoffrey hadn't finished speaking. "Life on the

marches is hard, my lord. These lands require a strong hand to hold them. This isn't like life in London—or in Paris."

To what was he alluding, wondered Richard. Some shared past episode? He took a deep breath. "Life on the marches will become harder still," he said. "Clouds gather, trouble comes, even as we watch." He gestured to the leaden sky, watching Geoffrey's reaction. How should he explain to this suspicious knight what Richard knew was coming? Geoffrey followed his gaze with a wary look. "If Langton incites a rebellion among the barons—and I believe it is possible— the kingdom may fall to chaos. And if that happens, we will have a difficult time holding the Welsh back. And you know Giscard will try to take advantage as well."

"Giscard may try and take advantage as it is," replied Geoffrey. "Young Hugh thought it was Fitzwilliam who ordered the attack upon us that day."

"Why?" demanded Richard. "And why wasn't I told?" He could well believe that Fitzwilliam was at the back of the raid, and it seemed completely in character for the lord of the manor to demand to know why he hadn't been informed of something so potentially threatening.

"But you were, my lord." Geoffrey was watching him carefully. "I told you several weeks ago—perhaps you were in too much pain to understand."

"Perhaps." Richard turned away, feeling his cheeks grow warm. He clutched the thick cloak around his shoulders as the cold wind gusted through the courtyard, fanning the blacksmith's open flame. "There's too much I don't recall. . . ." He let his voice trail off, hoping to plant in Geoffrey's mind the suggestion that if he seemed different, it was because his injuries had been so severe, he lacked memory of the attack. "No matter now—what matters is that Fitzwilliam know that I am well again."

"I agree, my lord. But what if he—or the Welsh—attack while you are on the road? Can you defend yourself, do you think?" Geoffrey was staring at him, his eyes narrowed to little slits and Richard read his expression.

"You must come with me."

"And what of Barland? What if Giscard—or the Welsh—attack here?"

Richard stared off into space, thinking furiously. Would it really be in Giscard's best interest to attack while he was gone? "Giscard won't attack—not while I am at Pembroke, in the house of the marshal. Even if he won Barland, how would he hold it? You know as well as I that Lord William will send men to our aid. No," he said as decisively as he possibly could, "the danger to Barland is not from Giscard. And as for the Welsh—" He stroked his chin, and wished Geoffrey would stop that ferocious stare. "I doubt they will attack so long as they hold Hugh. And even if the Welsh attack, they, too, will have to face the marshal's men. What do you think?" He looked Geoffrey straight in the eye, as if daring him to nay-say his words.

Finally the other man lowered his, and made a little sound of assent. "You take a long risk. But doubtless you are right, my lord. Your words make sense. If you truly believe all is well enough to leave Barland—" He broke off and shrugged. "You will join us in the morning for the drill, my lord?"

"I will be there," Richard said carefully. The wound in his side was nearly healed; it was time he concentrated on learning to use the weapons he would have been expected to know. This body was fit and strong—although he had many qualms, he was confident he possessed the strength and agility to learn to fight. If he didn't, it wouldn't matter, he re-flected grimly. He'd be dead. "And I will like to fight with you—practice with you," he said.

Geoffrey nodded with satisfaction. "I'll go easy on you, my lord—something just to get the blood moving again?"

"Yes," Richard said. Inside his body, of course. A cold chill went down his back and he forced the fear out of his mind. He had to learn these things, he had no choice. He would never survive in the thirteenth century otherwise. He glanced up. The sun was high in the sky. It was nearly time for dinner. A sudden wave of exhaustion washed over him, and he stifled a great yawn. He grinned awkwardly at Geof-frey. "I'm weak as a new—" he hesitated. How did one say "lamb"? What was it Geoffrey always referred to Hugh as—puppy? "Puppy," he finished, feeling a bit lame.

"Better rest, then, my lord." Geoffrey paused and glanced moodily at the lowering sky. "Soon there'll be no time for rest, no time at all."

"Has the man gone mad?" Eleanor demanded of Ursula. The older woman only pursed her lips and shrugged, as she con-tinued to fold linen. "What in the name of the Virgin can he be thinking? He's only just up from his deathbed, and now he thinks he can go riding out—with winter approaching—and make a journey of over a hundred miles? How can he even think of leaving us?" She placed her hands on her hips and stalked to the window. The sky was gray and cold; she wouldn't be surprised to see snow flurries before dusk. And Richard was adamant about leaving.

"He sees it as his duty, my lady," said Ursula softly.

"I understand that," Eleanor spoke without turning. She gazed out over the trees. Their bare branches groped for the sky like claws, and abruptly she turned her back on the window. "But doesn't he understand how fragile his health is? How close he came to dying? Doesn't he understand he risks—"

"My lady," Ursula said with a puckered smile, "you almost sound as if you'd miss him when he leaves."

Eleanor drew herself up. "Certainly not." She felt the color rise in her cheeks. She knew she blushed and cursed herself for it. "It's just—it's just—he has responsibilities. He owes it to us all to stay alive."

"It's just you're getting to know him all over again, and this time, you rather like what you are learning?"

Eleanor took a deep breath, opened her mouth, and closed it. Of course Ursula was right. But she wasn't about to admit that, not to Ursula and most certainly not to herself. "That has nothing to do with it. You know as well as I that if Richard dies now, Giscard will swoop down on Barland like a crow on carrion."

"My sweet child." Ursula walked over and hugged her tightly. "It isn't up to you to decide if Lord Richard should go or not. That is his decision, as the lord of the manor and the sworn man of Lord William."

"That's not what I mean." Eleanor spoke from the comfort of Ursula's shoulder. She pulled away, and sank down on the floor beside the hearth, wrapping her arms around her knees. "You're right, Ursula. He's so different now, it's as if he were another man altogether. To tell you the truth, it almost frightens me. He's not at all like he was before, he's—" She broke off, unwilling to say the words which came to her mind. Kind. Gentle. Who could ever have thought of applying those words to Richard? "All that time we've spent nursing him, it will all be for naught if he leaves and dies on the road."

Ursula patted the top of her head, as she used to when Eleanor had been very small, saying nothing. "And yet," Eleanor continued, "when he said he was going and Geoffrey challenged him, I could see that same look in his eyes he used to have—the one that meant he was going to have his own way or none at all. So has he changed, or hasn't he?"

Ursula made a little soothing sound in her throat. "Only time will tell that. It's best that you not interfere. These are men's affairs, it isn't for either you nor I to question."

Eleanor moved restlessly under the gentle hand. "It would be just like him to die after all we've done to try and save—" The door opened and she broke off. Richard stepped inside, his face pale, his lips blanched. "My lord, are you all right?" She leapt to her feet.

He nodded, waving her away. "Only tired."

"Come and sit. Would you like some wine?"

He sank into one of the chairs beside the fire. "No wine. Talk—you and me." He looked at Ursula and immediately the old woman curtsied.

"Of course, my lord. I will see to the rest of the laundry, my lady." With a step that was practically a scamper, Ursula hastened from the room, carefully shutting the door behind her.

Eleanor sat down in the chair opposite Richard. She knotted her hands in her lap to keep from trembling. This was how it usually began—he'd seem so calm, and then little by little, his voice would change, until she could hear the sneer, the sarcasm and then the anger, long after she dared look up. And yet, try as she would to deny it, she sensed something entirely different in the tone of his voice. She dared a peek beneath her lashes, and the intensity in his eyes took her breath away. A tingle of anticipation ran down her spine, and deep in her belly, a low heat began to burn.

He took a deep breath, and frowned a little, but he looked more confused than angry. "El—" He stopped and began again. "Eleanor. I know you—" he cleared his throat. "Not want me to go. But Geoffrey won't tell the marshal about Hugh. I trust only me to do that—" He paused again, as if struggling for the words, and Eleanor looked at him in amazement. Richard was concerned about Hugh's welfare enough to risk his own life?

"You do this for Hugh?" she repeated wonderingly.

"Geoffrey won't say to the marshal the whole—" He paused again, clearly frustrated. He looked as if he might be getting angry, and Eleanor swallowed hard. "Do you understand?"

She blinked, forcing herself to exhibit a calm she didn't feel. "Forgive me, my lord—I don't know what to say. I—I never knew you held Hugh in any regard at all."

"The Welsh are a threat to us all."

Ah, so that was it. It wasn't really her brother's welfare that concerned him so. Eleanor got to her feet and straightened her back. "You have a responsibility to Barland—to this demesne. Is there nothing I can say to convince you otherwise? What if you fall sick while you are gone?"

Richard rose. He towered over her, nearly a foot taller than she, and she thought he looked as though he wanted to touch her. Involuntarily she shrank back, even while her heart pounded harder, and something else made her wish that he would take her in his arms. She saw an unreadable expression cross his face, the very flicker of a frown. He walked away from her to stand beside the window. With his back to her, he gazed out over the countryside. "I understand my—responsibilities." The word was mangled nearly beyond recognition, but she understood the sense of it. "I know what I must do. I have decided. If there is any hope for your brother, I must go to the marshal myself. I know Geoffrey. And I think you do, too." He turned to look at her, and she felt herself pinned by those compelling azure eyes. Her heart skipped a beat. She said nothing. Richard was in all likelihood correct—Geoffrey probably wouldn't mention Hugh at all. And Richard—the possibility that he wanted to get to Hugh himself, to punish her brother occurred to her for the first time. She met his eyes with a blank expression. It was never wise to argue with Richard.

He let out a deep breath, and shook his head. "I said what I must. In three days, I will go. You must make ready."

"Of course, my lord," she curtsied as an obedient wife should, head bowed, eyes downcast. "Of course. Everything you require will be prepared for you." *And a shroud for you on your return,* she thought. *If you return.* Hugh might get his wish yet.

Chapter 10

THE LONE CANDLE flickered mournfully, the old bronze holder so covered with runnels of wax, the metal was totally obscured. Eleanor cocked her head and laid the brush down beside the hearth, her fingers sorting her long hair into sections. She rocked back on the lumpy little pallet. She had been sleeping on it for so long she scarcely remembered what the big bed felt like. She braided her hair, the long strands twining like silk through her rough, work-worn fingers, catching here and there in the roughened fingertips.

Lumps or not, she preferred the privacy of the solar to Richard's intrusive presence. At least, she told herself over and over that she did. Since his bandages had been removed, and his wounds were clearly healing, there was no reason, she supposed, she should not return to the bed they had shared as man and wife. And yet, Richard had made no move toward her—not like that—and she saw no reason not to leave well enough alone. If his memory truly had been affected by the accident, perhaps it was best she didn't bestir any memories until she had sorted out her feelings. This new Richard left her puzzled and unsure. He seemed so clearly vulnerable—something the old Richard never was—and yet, at times, there were flashes of determination, of courage, and the same familiar will.

She finished braiding her hair and plumped the one pillow, pulling the worn quilt up to her shoulders. With a sigh, she lay down, staring into the red embers of the dying fire. It certainly was warmer in the big bed with Richard, she thought, as she drifted off to an uneasy sleep, curled in a tight ball against the cold that seemed to seep up through the thin pallet from the floor.

Her sleep was fitful. In her dreams, dark horsemen, dressed in the colors of both Richard and Fitzwilliam hunted her through a black wood where the branches reached down like fingers, catching in her dress, and tearing the coif off her head. She ran and ran, clutching the torn white fabric in her fingers, frantically holding her skirts to her knees. She tripped over roots, her ankles twisting painfully as she tried to escape, knowing that if she could only reach her destination, she might be safe. She dashed through the trees, hearing the crash of horses' hooves, knowing that both her pursuers were hot on her heels, and the hanging limbs caught and twisted in her hair like skeletal fingers. She stumbled, her foot caught in the hem of her dress. She heard the fabric tear, and a heavy hand fell upon her shoulder. She turned, screaming.

"Eleanor, wake up—"

She opened her eyes. Her whole body quivered from head to toe, and she was breathing hard. For a moment, she was confused and disoriented, and then she realized it was Richard who was staring down at her, wearing an expression that could only be concern.

"My—my lord," she managed, her breathing caught in her throat.

"Are you all right? I heard you calling—you must have had a bad dream." He shifted his position, and she saw he knelt above her on one knee. Through the open collar of his bed gown, she saw the hair that curled in black clusters on his chest.

"Yes," she said. "I'm fine. It was only a bad dream."

He said nothing, and in the dim moonlight, she saw his eyes run down the length of her body, hidden as it was beneath the shift and the quilt. "Come," he said, at last. "You're cold."

Without waiting for a response, he picked her up as easily as if she were a child. His arms were warm, his body gave off a radiant heat. She could feel his heart beating in his chest, and realized hers was pounding hard.

He eased the door open, and carried her to his—their—bed. He placed her gently on one side, covered her carefully, and got in on the other. She watched him, scarcely daring to breathe. Their eyes met and held, and for the space of one brief moment, time hung suspended. In the moonlight, the white linen glowed and the bed smelled of him—of masculine sweat and horses and leather and that indefinable scent that was uniquely him. Her blood rushed through her veins, and between her thighs, she felt the first trickle of moist heat. Beneath the long linen shirt, she saw the outline of his erection.

And then, almost at once, the two of them reached for each other. He wrapped his arms around her, and buried his tongue in her mouth, his fingers twining eagerly through her hair. He raked through the heavy braid, and the long locks tumbled free about her shoulders, as her breasts were crushed against the hard muscles of his chest.

She lashed his tongue eagerly with hers, sucking and tasting the deliciously soft flesh of his lips. She felt him tug at her shift, and she shrugged away from him, long enough for him to tear it over her head. She knelt naked before him on the bed, her body glowing in the silvery light. For another brief moment, he stared at her.

Then he tugged his own shirt off, and before she could even take in the sight of his long, lean body, the heavy muscled frame, he was on her, his hands cupped around her breasts, his mouth encircling one nipple so delicately it made her moan. He laid her back against the pillows, stretching out so that his body was pressed against hers, and she felt the hard length of him against her thighs. Of her own volition, she spread her thighs, moaning against his ear. She wrapped her arms around him, her fingers tugging at his thick, black curls, pressing him closer. She arched her back as he engulfed her nipple, and flicked the other with his thumb.

"Please," she panted, as he lifted himself up and settled down in the cradle of her hips. She felt him press against her wet flesh. "I've missed you so." Involuntarily she moaned once more.

He looked up at her, and his eyes were bright in the silver light. "Tell me you want me," he said, his voice harsh and ragged.

"I do, I do," she crooned, arching up against him, so that the very tip of him caught in the folds of her flesh. With one swift thrust, he buried himself inside. He bent his head, catching her mouth with his, and they strained together, as if each would engulf the other whole.

She moved her hips back and forth, searching for release, and with a low chuckle, he matched her rhythm. "It's been so long," she whispered, as the heat built between them, and the pleasure grew to unbearable heights.

He paused then, and drew back. She stared up at him. Had she said something wrong? But his answer surprised her even more. "Oh, my lady," he said at last, "you have no idea how long."

And then there was no more space for words, for he caught her up in the driving force of his lovemaking, and swept her away on a tide of passion so intense she was left breathless in its wake.

From the windows of the bedroom, Eleanor watched the little party disappear down the road. She had waved them out of the courtyard after a breakfast, of bread steeped in broth for Richard, and coarse brown bread and ale for the men at arms who were to accompany him on the journey. She sighed, and Ursula, who was pulling the linen off the bed where Richard had lain for so long, raised her head and gazed at her mistress with sympathy. "He'll come home, child."

Eleanor smiled sadly. "I wish I could be so sure, Ursula." She gazed at the western mountains, and a wave of longing swept through her. Where was Hugh? she wondered. Was he warm, well fed? What if Richard failed to keep his promise to speak to the marshal about the ransom? And yet, a small voice whispered, deep in her mind, she didn't think he would break a promise to her. And yet—doubt raised its ugly head and danced a maddening jig in her mind. How could any man change so completely? Their lovemaking last night had held an element of tenderness she had never encountered before in Richard's arms and certainly had never expected to experience. But was that enough to entrust him with Hugh's safety and welfare?

She stared out over the countryside where the thickly forested hills rolled all the way to the horizon. Just over the last rise lay the little manor that had been her mother's. With a sigh, Eleanor realized it had been nearly two months since she had thought to ride over and see to the men and women who tended the lands. There hadn't even been a manor court since Richard had been wounded. She should go there, she thought with a twinge of guilt. The people who tended Rhuthlan were as much her responsibility as the ones who tended Barland. And the castellan of the keep was her father's old captain of the guard, a grizzled old veteran nicknamed John Longshanks for his long limbs and extraordinary reach. He had been her father's loyal servant for as long as Eleanor could remember, and had guarded her and Hugh with a father's care, until Richard's coming had banished him to the smaller manor.

Memories of Longshanks flooded her mind, and as she stared into the distance, an idea occurred to her. Perhaps it wouldn't be necessary to rely on Richard after all. Perhaps there was another way to rescue Hugh. It was a long shot, but maybe—maybe, she thought, just perhaps.

Chapter 11

"THAT'S CHEATING," CRIED Hugh as Angharad deftly scooped up his pawn from the chessboard.

"Is it?" she asked with wide-eyed guile. "Perhaps the rules are different in Wales—we know the way the game is supposed to be played."

Hugh snorted in derision. "I doubt it, lady, I doubt it very much." He pushed away from the table and rose to his feet. Restlessly he paced the room. The life of a captive was dull and confining. He had never realized how much he'd enjoyed all the endless drills in the practice yard, nor how much he'd relished the freedom to come and go. De Lambert was a devil, but even he never restricted Hugh's freedom.

Angharad watched him pace back and forth, occasionally pausing to look outside the tiny window. Winter was coming on in the high mountains, and they could ill afford the loss of warmth even the smallest windows allowed. But

Llewellis had never been a cruel man, and so the room in which Hugh was confined had a small window set high in the walls, where he could see the outside world if not be a part of it for more than an hour or two at a time.

Angharad cocked her head, considering. She had spent a fair amount of time with Hugh—anything so she didn't have to listen to Mairedd's endless twittering. "De Lambert left Barland this morning."

"Left?" Hugh spun on his heel and stared at her in astonishment. "You saw him riding out?"

"I didn't, obviously—my brother's scouts did."

"How did he look? What direction did he ride?"

"They took the southern road. De Lambert looked alive, I suppose. He didn't die of his wounds. He looked uncomfortable in his saddle, though—I hope they weren't going far."

"Was de Courville with him?"

"Yes, I think so. He's the big one, right, who's always by de Lambert's side?" Hugh nodded and Angharad went on. "As far as they could tell, I believe."

Hugh sank into his chair, staring into the fire. "I wonder where they've gone. . . ." His voice trailed off.

"We've heard rumors of a gathering at Pembroke Castle," said Angharad. "De Lambert is the marshal's man, isn't he?"

"Yes," said Hugh, nodding slowly. "But I can't believe de Lambert would leave Barland undefended."

"The garrison is there—and your sister. She would see to the defense of the manor, if she had to, would she not?"

Hugh shrugged. "Eleanor is convent bred. She knows nothing of war, of siege." He sighed and looked worried. "Do your scouts tell you anything of Fitzwilliam?"

Angharad shook her head. "Do you think it's likely

Fitzwilliam would attack Barland, even with the winter upon us?"

Hugh nodded, his mouth set and grim. "I wouldn't put anything past Fitzwilliam. He wants Barland, and I think he won't hesitate to take it if he thinks he can."

Angharad nodded, smiling secretly to herself. She would have to be sure to hear the news the men who watched Fitzwilliam's keep brought home. And alert her brother to Hugh's fears. It was quite possible the situation could be turned to their advantage very nicely.

"He's right," said Llewellis as Angharad listened by the hearth, her arms around her knees. He glanced in her direction and she smiled tentatively. So far he hadn't ordered her up to the solar when the rest of the women had gone, and she hoped he wouldn't take notice of her presence until after the war council was done.

Nearly a week had gone by since de Lambert's departure from Barland, and in that time, the scouts had reported increased activity within Fitzwilliam's keep. It was more than likely that Fitzwilliam intended to attack Barland in just a few days.

Fleetingly Angharad wondered what would happen to Hugh's sister, with her convent-bred sensibilities. It was more than likely that Fitzwilliam would rape her given the opportunity—well, such things happened to women in war. But the plan now was to interrupt Fitzwilliam, to attack him hard on his heels as he faced the defenses of Barland. Timing was everything. She leaned back and listened as Llewellis discussed the battle plan with his men. From across the room, she saw Hugh slip into the hall. Llewellis allowed him to stay in the hall in the long winter evenings—

he knew his captive was bored. Or was there another reason, she wondered, as she saw her brother glance in Hugh's direction. Llewellis made no attempt to lower his voice as Hugh sidled closer.

"But the keep is well defended nonetheless, sire," Pwyll, Llewellis's second-in-command, was saying. "There're more than enough men in residence to not only defend, but to repel an attack by invaders. And with winter coming on—" The big man broke off and shook his head, his dark eyes somber above his dark beard. "Tempting as it may be—" Here he looked around at the men who surrounded them both and glared. "I say the time is not yet to attack the manor."

Llewellis, his brow knitted in concentration, glanced once more at Hugh. He touched the tips of his fingers together and gazed down, as if considering.

"But what's a better time?" asked Rhonan, a younger, more impetuous version of Llewellis. He was one of the many bastards their father had sired, and Angharad disliked him intensely. She was tempted to answer him, and bit her tongue hard. If she spoke her mind now, Llewellis was sure to send her away. And away was the last place she wanted to be, with Hugh moving ever closer as he pretended to study the fire.

"We'd be making a big mistake—with de Lambert on his way back. If his lady got word to him, he could arrive with reinforcements. And then we'd be trapped—between the walls of his keep." Pwyll wagged his finger at the younger man.

Llewellis glanced once more at Hugh. Angharad followed her brother's eyes. Hugh leaned over the hearth as close as he dared, his face flushed. She wondered if it were the heat of the fire that brought the color to his face, or if he'd over-heard the men talking about Barland. Finally her brother sighed. "Enough. The hour grows late."

"But—but—" Rhonan rose to his feet. "What of the plan? How much time do you think there is, brother, before de Lambert returns? Don't you think that we'd better—"

In answer, Llewellis stood up. Although Rhonan was as tall, Llewellis's shoulders were broader. His eyes were narrowed dangerously. "I said 'enough.' And I mean it." He glanced once more at Hugh.

"If you think to toy with us, brother—" Rhonan stalked away and out of the hall.

Pwyll let out a long sigh as the other men dispersed. "I don't like that one, my lord. He's too rash. I'm afraid some-day he'll act before he thinks."

Llewellis shrugged. "You may be right, Pwyll. That's why I trust you to watch my back." The two men exchanged a grin.

Angharad glanced at Hugh. The boy's ears were red, and his shoulders were rigid. So he had overheard, and he understood enough Welsh to know that the discussion had centered around the possible invasion of Barland. What would he do?

His next move didn't really surprise her. He was as rash and impetuous as Rhonan in his own way. The only difference was that he posed no threat to her brother.

"My lord Llewellis," he said, his voice shaking with suppressed tension. "I would have a word with you."

Angharad tried to shrink back. The last thing she wanted now was for her brother to notice her.

Llewellis smiled at Hugh. "Of course, young lord. What can I do for you?"

She saw Hugh swallow. "I couldn't help but overhear, my lord. Tell me the truth—do you mean to attack my sister in her keep?"

Llewellis raised an eyebrow. "Such things are none of your concern, young lord."

"My sister is my concern," Hugh said. He drew himself up. "I may be much younger than you, my lord, and my sister may be the wife of a monster, but she is most certainly my concern."

"Which does you credit, young lord." There was a lazy lilt in Llewellis's voice, and Angharad leaned closer to see what Hugh would do next.

"I would not want her to be harmed."

"It is not my intention to make war upon a woman."

"But if you attack," said Hugh, "that is exactly what you will do!"

Llewellis appeared surprised. "And if you were in my position, my young friend? What would you do?"

Hugh spread his hands. "I beg you, spare my sister. She's endured enough at his hands—"

"As have we all."

Hugh wet his lips. "My—my lord. Perhaps there is another way."

"Oh?" Llewellis looked even more surprised. "Well?"

Hugh drew a deep breath. "You know you can never hold Barland. And while you might kill de Lambert, another will come to take his place—you know that. But perhaps there is another way."

"And what way might that be?"

"You and I—together—we could reach a peace between us. We could make a treaty—one that would hold even in the baronial courts. Even before the king."

Llewellis glanced around and his gaze swept over Angharad. "What kind of a treaty?"

"In exchange for my help in killing de Lambert, give me your sister's hand in marriage."

Angharad gasped. The very audacity of the boy shocked her. How dare he even suggest that she—or her brother—would consider a marriage to a Norman dog? But Llewellis was looking around the hall.

"Which sister?"

"An-Angharad," Hugh stammered out.

Angharad leaped to her feet, but before she could speak Llewellis took her brother's arm and drew him from the hall. "Tell me more, young lord. Tell me more."

She was left, staring speechless at the two of them, as they walked off.

"I won't, I won't—" Angharad stormed into the solar, where the other women were in the midst of their nighttime preparations. Bronwyn looked up fearfully, and even Mairedd paused in braiding her hair. "You can tell him so, Mairedd, do you hear me?"

"Tell who what?" The older woman yawned.

"Your husband. My brother. I won't have it, do you hear me? I will have nothing to do with that Norman knave—nothing."

All the women stared. At last old Nesta spoke. "What's wrong, my lady? What Norman knave?"

"Young Hugh—that's who. He's proposed a marriage—I cannot believe the audacity—I cannot believe he would dare such a thing—as if I—"

Heavy footsteps sounded on the steps and with a little

shriek from Bronwyn, Llewellis strode into the room. "Ladies."

Mairedd rose to her feet, smiling vapidly. "My lord—I didn't expect—"

"Of course not," he said. "Angharad, a word if you will."

"You can have a word right here," she snapped. "Hell can freeze before you'll wed me to Norman scum. I'll have nothing to do with him—nothing, do you hear?" She stamped her foot for emphasis.

"Yes," said her brother at last. "I imagine the whole keep has heard. However, I would like a word with you. If you can keep from interrupting me long enough?"

Angharad gave her brother a smoldering stare. With rigid shoulders, she swept out of the room. On the stairs she paused. "Well?"

He took her arm and guided her down the steps to the room he shared with Mairedd. "Now. I understand you are upset. I understand you want nothing to do with him—"

"Less than nothing!" she spat. "Just because I've played chess with him—been civil with him—doesn't mean I want anything more to do with him. How dare he presume—"

"He's in love with you." Llewellis was grinning.

Angharad stared at her brother in horror. "That can't be true."

"I assure you, my dear little sister, it is. And I also assure you I have no intentions of selling your hand to a landless Norman bastard—so rest easy and stop your squawking. But I do need your help."

"To do what?" Angharad scowled at her brother.

At the look on her face, he laughed outright. "Spare me and save that for your lovelorn suitor, Angharad. I need your help to encourage the young Hugh. I think we can turn this to our advantage—as long as he thinks I'm willing to help him rid himself of de Lambert, he's willing to help me. And there's too much he can tell me—too much he can tell us all. He knows the lay of the land, the manor defenses like the back of his hand—and he's right, of course. There will be another who takes de Lambert's place, but if it happens, on the off chance, to be him, what does it matter if he's well disposed toward us?"

"There's a world of difference between being well disposed to you, and wanting to marry me."

Llewellis shrugged. "Play along with me, right now, do you understand? There's more at risk here than you understand, little sister. And if young Hugh is so distasteful to you, perhaps you'd prefer the privacy of the cloister. He's willing to take you dowerless—how's that for love?"

"Is he a complete fool?"

"He's a man in love." Llewellis grinned again. "And men in love will do almost anything, anything at all, for their ladies. Just remember that, will you? And play along."

Angharad straightened her shoulders and sniffed. "As you will, brother." The thought of the cloister frightened her not at all. She was quite sure she could arrange to be sent home in less than a week. But in the meantime—"And if I do go along with this?"

Llewellis laughed. "I'll send you to a cloister that allows the nuns meat and wine, how's that?"

Without dignifying that answer with a response, Angharad stormed back up the stairs to the solar.

Chapter 12

"OF COURSE IT'S possible, my lady." Old John Longshanks leaned back in the chair and sipped his wine reflec-
tively. His long legs were sprawled out before him, and his
hose bagged at his ankles. His gray beard spilled over his
chest, but in the light of the leaping fire, Eleanor could see
that the old man's eyes were bright as ever. "They will not
be expecting an attack—especially so late in the year."

She nodded. "But?"

He met her eyes evenly. "What you propose is a risk, my
lady. What if we fail? What will Lord Richard's reaction to
that be?"

Eleanor stiffened. She preferred not to think about what
Lord Richard's reaction to failure would be. "I think you and
I both know what that would be, Sir. John. But if we think
of nothing but failure, surely we are doomed to fail."

Sir John sighed. He placed his goblet carefully on the

table beside him and stared into the fire. "It would be better to wait for Lord Richard, my lady."

"But who's to say when he'll come home, Sir John? You know yourself—the roads are well nigh impassable by this time of year—it was a dangerous, foolhardy thing he did. If there's a snowfall in the next month, he could be delayed till after Christmas. And if he doesn't come home at all—" Eleanor broke off as her gut twisted. Somehow, she no longer wished that Richard would never return. The memory of their last night together was seared into her very flesh, it seemed. "And if he doesn't come home, and we must wait till spring . . ." Her voice trailed off. "Sir John, you know as well as I that the Welshman asked the ransom of a prince for Hugh. We have no way to raise such a sum. And in the spring, even if Lord Richard returns well and healthy, they will be expecting an attack—you know that."

Sir John heaved another sigh. "Or a challenge."

"But, Sir John—" Eleanor leaned forward, her hand stretched before her in supplication. "You know that Hugh could be killed. You know it's possible they would do that. You know that that could well be the reason for the huge ransom—they look for an excuse to kill him. And I can't let that happen to him. I can't." A tear spilled down her cheek.

Sir John's grim face softened. "My lady, my dear lady, please don't weep. I know how much you love your brother. And there is truth in what you say. The whole thing stinks of a ruse—a ruse to kill either him or Lord Richard or both. And I swore to your father on his deathbed I would protect the two of you, though it seems to me I've done a poor enough job of it so far." He gave her a crooked grin.

"Please, Sir John." She waved her hand. "You have no need to think my father would find your service wanting in any way. But you do understand? You do see why I think we had best not wait for my husband—" She broke off. How easily the word slipped off her tongue. "For my husband to return. Even if he were to bring reinforcements from the marshal—"

"There are no guarantees of that, my lady." Sir John shook his head. "I wouldn't expect that at all."

"I don't." She smoothed her skirts over her knees. "What do you say, then?"

"I must think on it. This isn't something we can enter upon lightly, or without great forethought. At least we know where Hugh is. And we know he's not going anywhere. That gives us one advantage. As for the rest . . ." The old man rose to his feet. His back was as straight as a broadsword. "Let me think on it. There must be some way to divert them from their keep—if we can surprise Llewellis, even as Hugh himself was surprised—we may be able to arrange an exchange, which will shed little blood, and cost nothing."

Eleanor rose as well. For the first time, she felt as though there was some hope, as if the nagging doubts of endless waiting were about to be assuaged. Action was always better than simply waiting for the worst to happen. It kept her thoughts from wandering too often to Richard—which they had an annoying habit of doing, lately. "I thank you, Sir John, from the very bottom of my heart. And I know my father would thank you as well."

"I am still his sworn man, my lady. That oath will only die when I do." He gave her a brief bow and walked with aged dignity out of the room.

"I want the scouts posted on the southern road night and day, do you understand me?" Giscard Fitzwilliam paused long enough in his chewing to gesture with the chicken leg. "There's not to be one minute of the day or night that the southern road goes unguarded, do I make myself clear?"

"Perfectly, my lord." The captain of the guard bowed.

"Then what are you waiting for?" With a snarl, Giscard waved a dismissal. He grinned at the man who lounged on the other side of the fire. "You have to keep the fear of god in them, you know, Guillaume. Once they lose that, there's no telling what you can expect to happen."

Guillaume laughed, an unpleasant sound like a rasp deep in his throat. "So you've decided to attack him from the southern road?"

Giscard stretched. "For the moment, yes. Unless something else occurs to me. And that, brother, is why I asked you to come here." He gestured to the hide map pinned to the table before the fire. "You see the way in which the land lies. What think you?"

Guillaume shrugged. "The southern road makes sense. De Lambert's mind will be on returning to his hearth—he'll have little thought anyone might lie in wait for him. But here"—he pointed with one long finger, its dirty nail tapping on the rough hide—"this is by far the best place for an ambush, and it's perilously close to de Lambert's own lands. Are you certain you want to risk discovery?"

"Discovery by whom? The bastard whelp got himself captured by the Welsh. The delicious Lady de Lambert will have more important things to worry about than posting guards to ensure her husband's safe return. Who is there to discover us?"

"Us?"

"My men and I. I am not about to entrust this venture to the same buffoons who mismanaged the last. This time, when de Lambert dies, he's going to stay dead. And if the whole retinue is killed, who will tell the tale?"

Guillaume frowned. "It sounds likely enough, brother. But you know as well as I that our royal master thinks little of his barons murdering one another. He won't be pleased if he finds out—he might even refuse to allow you to wed the grieving widow."

"By the time he does find out—if he finds out—I shall have wed the grieving widow long since. It will be too late for him to do anything about it. He won't even be able to strip the lands away. And what will he care, really? He has no personal attachment to de Lambert."

Guillaume shrugged. "Maybe not. But if even one of them escapes . . ." He let his voice trail off. "You know you play a dangerous game. And what if your own men are spotted, even as they watch? Think you the Lady de Lambert is so naive as to suspect nothing?"

Giscard shook his head, contempt plain on his face. "She's convent bred. So a few men are spotted in the forests. Who's to say for certain they are mine? Do you think I'm so foolish as to send them in their colors? I might as well knock on the manor gate and ask permission to slit de Lambert's throat while he sleeps." Giscard chuckled at the thought. "No, brother. Surely you know me well enough to know that I will take every precaution. Every precaution possible."

Guillaume reached for the wineskin that rested on the floor by his chair. He tipped the wineskin over his goblet, and dark purple liquid splashed into the cup. "So you thought in October. You managed to kill neither Hugh nor de Lambert."

"But no one suspected me. The Welsh were blamed."

"And I suppose it's possible to blame them once more."

Guillaume replaced the skin on the floor and sipped the wine. "Excellent vintage." He raised his goblet to Giscard. "To success, brother. In all you do."

The two men exchanged nasty smiles. Then Giscard raised his own goblet, and the two men drank.

"A letter?" Eleanor wiped her hands on her dirty linen apron and looked up eagerly. She was up to her elbows in greasy soap. The last batch of soapmaking before the coldest weather made such outdoor activities well nigh impossible was in full swing. All around her, servants bustled here and there, carrying bundles of firewood, stirring the huge pots of smoking tallow. There had to be enough soap to last the entire manor through the cold winter months ahead.

On the other side of the yard, Ursula supervised the cutting of the huge slabs of new-made soap into bars.

"Aye, my lady." The young servant dipped another awkward curtsey.

"I'm coming." Eleanor craned her head. "Ursula! Come here and take my place—there's a letter."

The older woman looked up, surprise and then worry creasing her face. Letters were so few and far between.

"Where is the messenger?" asked Eleanor as she followed the girl across the yard.

"In the hall, my lady. Sir John told him to wait there while I came to fetch you."

"Thank you." Eleanor nodded and smiled and continued on her way. Could it be from Richard? Suddenly a cold chill went down her back. He'd been gone nearly a month. Surely it was time for him to return, unless—Her mind refused to shape the troubling thought. Unless he was sick or reinjured.

Biting her lip, she made her way into the hall. A tall man,

younger than Richard but older than Hugh, sat before the fire. A serving woman set a plate of oatcakes and apples before him while he sipped from a cup. With a start, Eleanor recognized his livery. He was a servant of William the Marshal, the great Earl of Pembroke. "Greetings, sir," she said, feeling oddly embarrassed by her workday clothes, her stained apron and untidy coif.

Instantly the man was on his feet, bowing. "My lady de Lambert. I bring a letter from your lord, and greetings and best wishes for your continued health and happiness from Lord William."

"Thank you," she said. She flushed a little, for his eyes lingered on her body.

He handed her the letter, and eagerly she broke the seals. The message was brief: "Greetings, my lady. I hope this message finds you in good health. I shall arrive less than a fortnight after this message reaches you, so long as the roads and the weather hold good. Richard."

Eleanor stared at the parchment. The letter itself was penned in a monastery-bred hand, which was to be expected, since Richard himself could neither read nor write. But the signature puzzled her. It had been signed, as was customary, by the writer, and next to it, was a large letter R and a seal. The seal was unmistakably Richard's own, for she'd seen him use it time after time in the manor courts. But the letter R was not the shaking scrawl she was used to seeing. This was a large, sweeping letter, drawn by the hand of one who was clearly practiced in writing. With a troubled frown, she looked up. "Lord Richard sent this?"

"Aye, lady, he handed it to me himself in front of Lord William, and bid me bring it posthaste."

"And how did Lord Richard look?"

"Well, lady. He seemed in good spirits and excellent health when I left him, and he told me to tell you to allay any fears you might have of your own in that regard."

Eleanor looked at the initial again. Could he have been practicing? "He did not write this?"

"I believe one of Lord William's scribes penned it, lady. Is aught amiss?" The messenger was looking at her with a puzzled expression on his own face.

"N-no, of course not," she answered. "'Tis only a relief to have news at last—I thank you, messenger. Will you stop here tonight?"

"No, my lady. I am directed on to Hereford. There is other business for Lord William that awaits."

"Then enjoy your refreshments, and Godspeed."

"Thank you, my lady."

Clutching the paper close, Eleanor went to find Sir John. If anything were to be done about Hugh, it would have to be done soon.

Chapter 13

THE ROAD WOUND down through the trees, the narrow graveled track barely more than a path. Someday, mused Richard, this path might well be a highway. He wished he knew more about the topography of modern England. But, he wondered, looking around at the dense forest that closed in on all sides, even if he did, what good would it do him?

His muscles ached and his back was sore from the long ride. A hot bath, and a warm meal, and then—his thoughts turned to Eleanor. In the last weeks she'd had an annoying habit of creeping into his consciousness at every waking moment, even the most inopportune. A color, a scent, a glint of light across a woman's face, and there she was, her memory filling his mind, momentarily obliterating everything else. She was so different from Lucy. Memories of their lovemaking surged through his mind, and he felt a hot rush suffuse his body. Lucy had been sweet and accommodating in bed, eager to please in every way. But Eleanor had amazed him with the intensity of her passion. He'd never expected her to react with such—such hunger. And in turn, she'd ignited a fire in him unlike anything he'd ever felt in his life.

Perhaps it was the uncertainty of life in this century in general, he mused, as his horse picked its way across the rutted road. An ordinary cold might turn into some deadly fever, a bout of flu could be the deadly beginning of pneumonia. Poor harvests meant less food, a bitterly cold winter meant that all would be forced to huddle around inadequate fires. He was lucky to have landed in the body of an ancestor who possessed some wealth and standing.

A wave of longing swept over him for the life he'd left behind. There'd been no time in the last few weeks to try and ascertain if there were any way to return to his own century. He thought of all the things he'd taken for granted and accepted without thought. Central heat, refrigeration—these were the least of them. He'd settle for underwear that didn't itch, socks that didn't bunch irritatingly around his toes, and razors that didn't make him wonder if every morning he might slit his own throat. And roads that didn't cause pain in every fiber of his body when he traveled over them.

Nothing was likely to happen in the next few months as the winter settled in. Perhaps he could find a way to return— once Eleanor's brother had been ransomed. And then he remembered that if he went back, he would not see her again. A pang went through him. She looked so much like Lucy, though she clearly wasn't Lucy. And yet, the thought of leaving her caused him . . . he tried to identify the emotion. It was regret, he realized with a start. Despite all the depri-

vations of the time in which he'd found himself, he still felt
a distinct regret about returning to his own time.

The dozen men in his retinue jogged along in silence. The
last few weeks had been trying, to say the least. But the obvious wound in his throat had excused him from most
speech, and listening to the other men speak had improved
his own skills. At times, he had even begun to think in
French. And William the Marshal had impressed him, more
than he'd ever thought possible.

There were great men in every age, he realized, men who
inspired confidence and hope and belief in something better.
He'd rasped out Hugh's story in his halting French, and the
marshal had listened gravely, all his attention focused upon
Richard. And then he'd asked the one question Richard himself had forgotten to ask.

The marshal had pinned those penetrating eyes of steely
gray on him. "Why?" he asked. "Of course we will see you
have every aid for the safe return of your wife's brother. But
why was the boy over the Welsh border? What was he doing
there?"

Richard had stared back. He didn't know. What had Hugh
been doing over the border? He tried to think back to con-
versations he'd overheard between Geoffrey and Eleanor
when Hugh had first been captured, and he realized that his
poor command of the language interfered with what he'd
been able to remember. He was about to shake his head
when Geoffrey de Courville stepped forward.

"May I speak, my lord?"

The marshal nodded. "Please."

"Young Hugh believed that the Welsh were not the ones
responsible for the attack upon Lord Richard. He was trying
to find a way to prove that another was guilty."

Richard looked at Geoffrey, surprised. The man returned his gaze evenly. There was no doubt that Geoffrey viewed him with suspicion, and knew that something was very different about the man he had sworn to serve with his life. He had expected Geoffrey to allow him to flounder before the marshal, and yet here was Geoffrey stepping forward, speaking for him. But in Geoffrey's eyes he saw something that could only be acceptance. At some point in the last weeks, Geoffrey had decided that, changed as Richard might appear, he was still his sworn overlord. And that could only be a good thing.

"And who might that other be, Sir Geoffrey?"

Richard was not surprised to hear the answer.

"Giscard Fitzwilliam, my lord. He has ever coveted the Barland demesne. It abuts part of his own holdings, and Fitzwilliam has made no secret that he was bitterly disappointed when my lord won it instead."

"Purchased it," drawled the marshal.

Richard raised one eyebrow, refusing to be intimidated. He'd spent too much time of his twentieth-century life before judges on power trips. Of course, this man wielded more power than any judge ever had in his wildest dreams, but any show of weakness could not be wise. "A man needs a wife, my lord."

At that the marshal looked surprised and an unreadable expression crossed his face. "Point scored, my lord." He chuckled. "Go on, Sir Geoffrey. So you think young Hugh had the misfortune to run into the Welsh while searching for some evidence against Giscard?"

"Yes, my lord."

"Then it was most fortunate that he didn't meet one of Fitzwilliam's minions, instead."

Richard nodded. "But we are left with the question of the ransom, my lord. We don't have that sum, nor any hope of raising it."

William sat back, stroking his chin. His eyes were set deep in their sockets, his thin hands were thick with calluses and patterned with scars. "Then there is only one way, my lord. You must open negotiations with this Welsh princeling. I can send you extra troops if you like, but I would prefer that this matter be resolved as peaceably as possible. You don't agree, Sir Geoffrey?"

Richard had turned to see the knight's glowering expression. "Of course, my lord. I bow to your wisdom."

Inwardly Richard had sighed. William was in some ways ahead of his time. The greatest fighter in all of Europe, he could afford to take the path of peace. But for men like Geoffrey, fighting was not only their way of life, it was the only one they knew.

But, he had decided, fortunately it was not the only one he knew. There had to be some way to open negotiations with Llewellis. But he'd accept the marshal's offer of troops, just in case.

They had been promised from the marshal's holdings near Hereford, and would arrive within the month. And Richard had understood that he was being given an opportunity not to need them.

Geoffrey leaned forward, interrupting his thoughts. "My lord, we're another three hours from Barland, and night will be upon us in two hours. I don't think it's wise to press on."

Richard glanced around. The roads themselves made for slow going. Riding in the dark would be treacherous. "You're right, Geoffrey. We'll stop at the first likely place."

Geoffrey nodded, and without replying, flapped at his reins. He cantered past the rest of the men.

A sharp crack from a splitting log roused Angharad from her doze. The afternoons were long and dull and dark in the winter, and in the gathering dusk there was little to do but sew and spin. The idle talk of the other women bored her to tears, and the heat of the fire lulled her to a fitful sleep. She started awake, and glanced around. The women were still clustered around the hearth, bent over their sewing. In one corner, Nesta braided Bronwyn's hair into intricate plaits. Angharad stretched and rose to her feet. She ignored the other women and gazed out the window. In the courtyard below, men and horses were milling around in every direction. It looked as if they made preparation for a raid. "What's going on down there?" she asked over her shoulder.

"Down where?" asked Mairedd.

"In the courtyard, ninny." Angharad could hardly contain her contempt. "Didn't you hear anything? It looks as though Llewellis is riding out."

"Riding out?" Mairedd blinked and yawned. "Surely not. It looks as though it's about to snow."

"It does, but he's definitely going somewhere. Come see." Angharad stood aside. With another sigh and a huge yawn, Mairedd heaved herself to her feet. She peered out the window, and frowned.

"But where could he be going? At this hour?"

"There's only one way to find out." Without waiting for a response, Angharad ran out of the room and down the steps to the hall, where she found Hugh pacing back and forth in front of one of the hearths. "What are you doing here?"

"He knows I'm not going anywhere," he said, gesturing with his head toward the doors.

"But where's *he* going?"

"The scouts came in less than an hour ago. There's a troop of Normans moving through the forest—Llewellis thinks it's another raid."

"Now?" She blinked.

"Such things have happened." Hugh stared at her. "He won't let me go with him."

"And why should he?" She shook her head in exasperation. "You're a Norman. Why trust you?"

"He's willing to trust you with me." Hugh took a step closer.

Angharad raised her chin. "Don't count on anything, young Norman. You're landless and have very few prospects. And—"

"You're dowerless, and have as few prospects as I. You live here by your brother's sufferance and you know it."

"And you live by de Lambert's."

"But if he's out of the picture—" Hugh came closer. She raised her eyes to his. His chin was shadowed with the very faintest haze of beard, and his eyes were dark in his pale face. An unruly lock of hair spilled over his high forehead.

"If he's out of the picture, that's another story completely." Angharad was confused. She liked Hugh, that was undeniable. He was amusing and fun to play with at chess— at least he didn't dismiss her out of hand and send her off to languish with the women the way her brother did. And he didn't try to take liberties, either, the way some of the other boys did.

He gave her a crooked grin. "The old marshal wants

peace. And if our union gives a measure of peace to the marches—"

"Our union—" Angharad sputtered, shaking her head. This was all too confusing. She gathered her skirts, spun on her heel, and ran out of the hall, retreating to the safety of the solar as quickly as she could.

"Llewellis is on the march, my lady." Sir John's face was grim.

Eleanor raised her head from her sewing and stared. Without having to contrive anything, the Welshman was moving? "Truly?"

"Aye, my lady. We've no idea why, though. But if we want to have a prayer of capturing him—I say we move now."

"As you say, Sir. John." Eleanor got to her feet. The old knight bowed and turned to leave, and in that moment, Eleanor came to a decision she had been toying with ever since she'd decided to engage Sir John's help. "I'm coming with you."

"My lady?" He turned back to her, clearly uncertain he had heard correctly.

"I said, I'm coming with you. I've but to change out of these clothes. I can ride as well as the next man."

"But, my lady, you cannot fight."

"I'll stay out of the way."

"This is madness, lady, I cannot allow—"

"This is not a question of permission," Eleanor said with all the authority she could muster. "This is the decision I have made. I am the lady of the castle, and I will not wait behind these walls while my brother's fate is undecided. I will be down in the courtyard directly. Make the preparations." She ignored the astonishment on his face and swept out of the room. No one would prevent her from doing everything possible to save her brother. No one.

The shadows were slanting across the road when at last Geoffrey called a halt. Richard slid out of his saddle eagerly. He was used to riding by now, but they'd been on the road for three days, and he was stiff and sore, and the muscles in his abdomen ached. The scars from the wounds would probably plague him for a long time.

Geoffrey cast an appraising eye on him. "Are you all right, my lord?"

He nodded. "I'm fine. More road weary than I thought I'd be, that's all."

Geoffrey nodded. "Rest, then, my lord. The men and I will see to the setting up of the camp."

Richard sank to the ground and leaned against a tree. He felt slightly dizzy, and exhaustion seemed to seize all his limbs. He closed his eyes, cursing his weakness. It was one thing to be faced by the limitations of a time and a place he knew virtually nothing about, it was another to have to also face the limitations of his own body. He would have to practice harder with Geoffrey as soon as they returned to Barland, or he would never command the respect of the men who were sworn to serve him. Unless, of course, he could find a way to return to his own time and place.

He accepted a flask from one of the other men, and allowed his head to rest against the rough tree trunk. Lifting the flask to his lips, he drank. The mead stung all the way down his throat, but the warmth that spread through his limbs revived him. His companions worked silently and efficiently. There was a noise in the forest, and suddenly, like dogs pricking up their ears, the men were instantly alert.

Geoffrey unsheathed his sword, and Richard struggled to his feet. Geoffrey glanced in his direction, motioning him to silence. Richard gazed around, but in the falling dark, there wasn't much to see within the thick forest.

And then the sound came again, and this time, Richard recognized it. It was the sound of a horse whinnying a protest. At once the horses tethered to the trees around them stamped and pawed the ground. Geoffrey motioned for the others to draw their weapons and Richard did likewise, the sound of his sword sliding from its sheath uncomfortably loud. His heart began to pound in his chest, and his eyes darted from side to side. They hadn't been attacked by the brigands he'd heard of so often in the tales the men told gathered around the campfires and the hearths. It seemed now as if that were about to change.

He raised his sword in what he hoped was a credible imitation of the others' fighting stances.

"Renaulf, Lanrac, guard the lord," murmured Geoffrey.

The sound came again. Richard heard another sound, the distinct sound of bodies moving through the trees, and the snap of booted feet across fallen twigs. And then they were upon them.

Later, Richard was never certain of the actual order of the battle. It seemed that first a company of Normans was upon them—Normans who wore plain armor without any kind of mark, but who carried weapons no brigand or outlaw would have access to. And then another company swept down upon them, men who rode shaggy, short-legged ponies, and whooped and sang as they fought. And then, finally, in the thick of the battle, as the darkness was closing all around them, and Richard swung his sword in desperate exhaustion, no longer knowing friend or foe, a hand came down, clad in mail, and he looked up into a vaguely familiar face. "Come with me, my lord," said a voice, and Sir John Longshanks swept Richard up and behind his saddle and galloped with him to safety.

A little way off they paused in the road, and Sir John whipped off his helm and wiped his face with the back of his sleeve. "Are you all right, my lord?"

"Yes," Richard managed. "What of the others? What happened back there?"

Sir John shook his head. "My lord, it was only great fortune that led me to you. Great fortune and—" he paused, as another dozen or so riders cantered up. In the dim light, it was difficult to see them, but one detached itself from the rest.

"Sir John?" Eleanor's musical voice carried through the dark night. "Sir John, is it you?"

"It's me, my lady. Me and—" He turned in his saddle as Richard slumped forward, at the very end of his endurance.

Chapter 14

THE RISING SUN tickled his lids and Richard opened his eyes. A small fire hissed in the grate, and in the chair beside the hearth, Eleanor leaned upon her hand. Her eyes were closed and she was breathing deeply, her head nodding gently back and forth. He raised himself on one arm and tried to remember the events of the previous night. He remembered little but dark and cold and confusion, the shouts of charging men, the crack of steel hitting armor and bone. He remembered the way the horses had screamed, the way the light had glinted off the edges of weapons. And he remembered the sickening thuds and the moans of the wounded and dying.

He shook his head as if to clear it. How had Eleanor come to be there? Where were Geoffrey and the rest of his companions? And who had attacked them?

He swung his legs cautiously around the side of the bed.

Once more he was naked, and he reached for the robe at the foot of the bed. He belted the cloth sash around his waist and knelt in front of Eleanor. "Lady?" he whispered, loath to wake her. Beneath her eyes, dark circles smudged her pale cheeks, and her hair was tousled and unruly without her customary coif. She wore only a shift and a ragged dressing gown.

She started awake. "My—my lord," she murmured.

He smiled. He really was glad to see her, he realized, gladder than he would have thought possible. She had been very brave to risk herself like that—brave and possibly foolhardy. But she had shown great courage. "How are you this morning?"

She straightened, pushing the hair off her face. "How are *you*?"

He gently pushed a single strand off her forehead. "I'm well. Wondering how I got here—but well. Can you tell me what happened last night? I—I'm afraid I—I wasn't very effective—"

"Effective?" she echoed. "Sir John said he'd never seen the like before. You killed at least a dozen of them by yourself. And when Geoffrey fell, you stood over his body until Sir John came—"

"Geoffrey fell?" He searched her face, a grim feeling of foreboding filling him.

She dropped her eyes. "I—I am so sorry to tell you, my lord. Sir Geoffrey de Courville is dead."

He rocked back on his heels and stared into the fire. Geoffrey was dead. He'd known him for such a little while, and yet he knew that Geoffrey had been a loyal knight. He sighed deeply.

"You must feel his loss deeply." She twisted her fingers in

the gown, and a scent, sweet and somehow familiar seemed to rise from the fabric.

Richard nodded. "But what happened? Who attacked us? Robbers? Outlaws?" Memories of Robin Hood ran through his mind. Wasn't it evil Prince John whom Robin had fought against?

Eleanor met his eyes, and in them, he read a kind of intensity he'd never seen there before, a courage and a determination. It had taken both to ride into the night the way she had, even if she had been surrounded by armed men. "It appears that you were attacked by a troop of men who were probably sworn to Giscard Fitzwilliam."

"Fitzwilliam?" He spat the name like a curse. "Are you sure of this?"

"No. They're all dead or run off. But the dead ones are clearly Norman men—it's clear by the very look of them, as well as their arms and clothes. And Giscard's men were attacked in turn by the Welsh, possibly for crossing into their lands and breaching their borders. And the Welsh—" She paused and looked down. Color rose in her cheeks and Richard raised an eyebrow.

"Go on."

"The Welsh were attacked by Sir John. And our men."

"Why?"

Eleanor squared her shoulders and looked him in the eye. "I wanted to rescue Hugh."

Richard got to his feet. He was much more steady than he'd been the night before. The rest he'd gotten in his own bed had done him good. "I'm afraid I don't quite follow you."

Eleanor pressed her lips into a thin line before answering. She looked so guilty he wanted to laugh. "I thought that if we were able to capture some of the Welsh knights, we'd be able to negotiate for Hugh's return."

"So you and Sir John and a troop of your men went riding out in the middle of the night and happened upon this band of Welshmen who happened to have followed a troop of Normans who were sent to attack me?" He could not help but hide a smile.

"Well. No. Not exactly."

"You didn't go riding out in the middle of the night?" He knew he was teasing her but she looked so uncomfortable he couldn't help himself.

"We planned this."

"Planned it? When you knew I had gone to the marshal, with one of the purposes being to get help for Hugh? Lady, are you mad?"

"I knew that, yes, and I thank you for it. But without a bargaining piece or two of our own, there's no way even the marshal could send us the money we need to ransom Hugh. And I couldn't bear the thought of my brother in the hands of those barbarians any longer than necessary." She leaped to her feet. "Richard, please, don't be angry. Please. I did what I thought was right. And it was lucky I was there—or that Sir John was, anyway. You would have fallen from sheer exhaustion. And it worked."

He stared at her, not sure whether to take her in his arms or to laugh outright. She looked like a rebellious child, her hands on her hips, her little chin raised, her shoulders squared. "It was most fortunate, I agree. But what do you mean, it worked?"

"We captured a bargaining piece of our own last night. A most valuable piece."

Richard raised his eyebrow again. This woman was more and more extraordinary. "Who?"

"Prince Llewellis Ab Rhawn. The very man who's holding Hugh."

At that Richard stepped back and began to laugh. He laughed and laughed until his eyes filled with tears, and he wiped them away. He looked at Eleanor. She was looking back at him as if he'd suddenly taken leave of his senses, which, he supposed, he had. He reached for her, and pulled her to him. "Oh, my lady," he said, still chuckling. "Are you always so full of surprises?"

"You—you aren't angry?"

"Angry? Why should I be angry? The marshal left me with a charge to make peace with the Welsh, and I return to find that my wife has provided me with the most fortuitous opportunity imaginable. Tell me, were any of the Welsh killed or wounded?"

"A few. But it's hard to say by whom. It's more likely they died fighting Giscard's men."

She was stiff in his arms, and he smiled down at her, pulling her even closer until she was pressed against his body. "Eleanor," he said, the word rolling off his tongue. "I thought of you while I was away."

At that a hot blush suffused her cheeks. "I thought of you too, my lord," she murmured.

He placed one finger under her chin and raised her face until she looked him full in the eyes. "Did you?" he whispered. His senses were inflamed with her closeness. She smelled clean and sweet, and her skin glowed in the early morning light. Her hair was touched with silver gilt. Without waiting for an answer, he bent his head and gathered her mouth to his. She resisted for only a moment, and then her lips parted and he felt her tongue twine around his, darting and probing, running along the edge of his lips, exploring his mouth as boldly as he explored hers.

He swept her up in his arms and carried her to the bed. He plucked at the sash at her waist. "Take this off," he said, his voice hoarse with passion.

She complied, as he stripped off his own robe. He reached over and helped her pull the shift off her shoulders. Her body was firm and white, her breasts high and rounded. She blushed when she saw his frank stare, and reflexively crossed her arms over her breasts, turning slightly away.

"Oh, no," he said, reaching to take her in his arms as he stretched out beside her on the bed. "Let me look at you—I imagined you so many times in the last weeks. Let me see you."

She turned back, shyly. He ran one finger down her shoulder and touched her nipple. She gasped, and the tip hardened into a pebbled peak. He drew her close, bent his head, and pulled the nipple into his mouth, tugging and sucking on it gently.

She moaned. Her fingers twined in his hair and he rolled on top, his erection hard and insistent against the soft roundness of her belly.

"Did you miss me, lady?" He raised his head, his fingers rolling her nipples and kneading her breasts.

In answer, she spread her thighs. "Yes," she gasped, as he pressed her breasts together and took both nipples in his mouth at once. "Yes!"

He raised himself slightly, positioning himself so that he pressed against her wet flesh. "Say you want me."

"You know I do," she moaned.

"Say it." He withdrew.

"I do, Richard," she said, raising her hips. "I do, so very much."

In response, he plunged into the soft sweet depths of her. Her body closed around him like a hot velvet sheath, warm and wet and silky. He thrust forward, pressing as deep as he could into her. She gasped and moaned against his shoulder, clutching him with small, rosy-tipped hands. And then he lost all sense of time or reason, for instincts older than time took over, and he rocked back and forth, until they shuddered together again and again.

It was much later when Eleanor finally opened her eyes. Richard still slept, her body nestled against his in a firm embrace. Her mind reeled when she remembered how he'd behaved when she'd told him what she had done. Was it possible that he was the same man who'd left Barland that wet October day, bent on ravaging the Welsh, and putting, as he said, the fear of something worse than the wrath of God into them? Her fingers brushed briefly over the angry red scars. They were so deep, so wide. It would be a long time before he had the same stamina, the same strength. And yet, Sir John had said he'd fought the way he'd always had, swinging the heavy broadsword as if it were an extension of his own body. But he hadn't been angry with her. He hadn't argued, he hadn't called her stupid and foolhardy and all the things she had wondered if he would all night long. Instead, he seemed almost admiring of her courage. There was a light tap upon the door. Eleanor gently disengaged herself from Richard's arms, pulled her robe around her body, and opened the door a crack.

Ursula stood outside. "My—my lady? Are you all right?"

"I'm fine, Ursula. Of course."

"Lady," Ursula spoke in a shocked whisper. "It's nearly noon. Father Alphonse is here to say a mass and shrive the dead, and the Welshman—the one who calls himself a prince—is demanding to speak to Lord Richard."

Eleanor blushed in spite of herself. "Go tell Father Alphonse I'll be down directly. Extend every courtesy to our guest the Welshman. Lord Richard is sleeping from his long trip and his exertions of last night." And this morning, she thought to herself with a stifled giggle. What was it about this man that made her feel like a giddy girl? She'd never felt so lighthearted in her life.

"Are you quite all right, my lady?" Ursula sounded suspicious.

"Absolutely, Ursula. I'm as all right as I can ever remember being." She gave the woman a little smile and pushed the door shut. "Oh—send some water to the solar—I'll dress there."

"It's waiting for you already, my lady." And with a little sniff, Ursula turned away, her heavy skirts whispering after her down the stairs.

Richard found the household gathered in the hall. He'd managed to dress himself with only slight discomfort, certainly less than he'd felt on other occasions. He stepped into the great room and saw Eleanor sitting by the fire, accompanied by the long-nosed, stoop-shouldered priest. Father—Father Ambrose? Richard groaned inwardly. In his long-ago and faraway youth, he'd been raised by parents who were casually religious at best. He knew only the barest rudiments of Catholicism. Talking to the priest made him nervous. Ursula bustled amidst the men crowded at the long tables eating and drinking, and Richard recognized a few of those who had accompanied him on his journey to the marshal. The rest must be the ones who'd come to his rescue last night.

Eleanor looked up and saw him. She beckoned and smiled. It was the first time he'd seen her smile at him in public. He smiled back, and started across the hall toward her. As he made his way through the rows of tables, the men nodded and called to him: "Greetings, my lord." "God's grace to you, my lord." "Your health, my lord." Goblets were raised and arms were extended in greeting. Richard nodded in acknowledgment, grasping arms, shaking hands, patting backs. These were the men to whom he owed his life. He remembered how he'd felt when he was a young attorney, an associate in a huge law firm. There was the same holiday air about the firm when a big case was won or settled to a client's advantage. But in this case, the advantage was their own lives—his and the other men's. And Eleanor's. He stood before her chair, reached down, and took her hand. With a gesture inspired by a hundred books and movies, he bent his head and kissed the back. Flustered, she started and colored.

"My lord!"

"You look well today, my lady. I hope you got enough rest?" He couldn't resist teasing her in front of the priest. She looked so pretty sitting beside the fire, her cheeks flushed rosy. Her hair was drawn back beneath her coif, and it emphasized her high cheekbones and little pointed chin. Her eyes were clear and very blue, and as he smiled down into them, he felt a wave of gratitude for her bravery, and a flood of desire in his veins. She was quite an extraordinary woman.

"I—I did, my lord," she said, as her color flushed even

deeper. "Father Ambrose has come to shrive Sir Geoffrey—and we shall hold his funeral mass tomorrow."

Richard nodded, turning to the priest. "My thanks, good Father." He wondered briefly, fleetingly, if there was a way to ask the priest about his situation. Could the priest be trusted? He thought of people in this time and place as superstitious, even the most well educated of them. But if he were ever to even hope of finding a way back to his own time, he'd have to take the risk. Perhaps after the service tomorrow. "Sir Geoffrey was a fine man. I'll miss him."

The priest sniffed, his thin nostrils flaring. "Perhaps, my lord."

Richard exchanged a glance with Eleanor. So the priest didn't think much of Richard's second-in-command. He didn't imagine Eleanor had either.

"Will you sit, my lord?" She gestured to the large chair beside the fire.

He sat down as Eleanor signaled to Ursula. Almost immediately a tray appeared before him covered with bread and cheese and slices of dried apples. He reached for the goblet of ale and drank, and tried to cover his grimace. He hoped he'd be back in the twentieth century before he had to get used to ale for breakfast. At least his body wasn't addicted to caffeine, although he still craved the scent and taste of coffee.

"And so, Lord Richard, will you speak to the Welshman?" The priest leaned forward. His black robes hung on his thin frame, and Richard was tempted to ask the man if he got enough to eat.

"Of course, Father. The marshal charged me with establishing peace along this section of the marches. I have no choice but to obey."

The priest narrowed his eyes. "Peace?"

"Is it so difficult to believe that there could be peace?"

The priest sniffed again, and Richard racked his brain for the man's name. Ambrose didn't sound right. "I don't find the possibility of peace difficult to believe, my lord. I find the possibility that the parties to the peace will adhere to any agreement difficult to believe." The priest gave Richard a pointed stare.

Eleanor glanced nervously at him, and Richard knew she was waiting for him to react the way her husband doubtless had reacted on many occasions. He paused, considering his response. What was there to say? Doubtless the priest was right, based on what he knew of the old Richard. And what if he were successful in his plan to return to the future? Would the old Richard come back? Troubled, he pushed the plate away from him and got to his feet. "I understand your concern, Father." He bowed briefly to Eleanor and walked out of the hall.

Eleanor stared at his retreating back. How unlike Richard—or was it? She'd expected some biting sarcastic remark, and apparently the priest had as well, for Father Alphonse was watching Richard with a look of surprise on his face. "Hm," the priest murmured. "Perhaps Lord Richard's brush with mortality has altered his way of living."

That's what Ursula had said. And yet—Eleanor gazed from Richard's disappearing form into the flames. He was so different. So very different. Even his way of lovemaking . . . She consciously pushed such thoughts out of her mind. But memories of this morning persisted. He did things he'd never done before, made love to her in ways she'd never experienced. Could his brush with mortality have made him a more sensitive, generous lover? Somehow, she doubted the priest would agree with her if she asked him. The thought of Father Alphonse's reaction to that made her giggle in spite of herself. She pressed a hand to her mouth and tried to stifle it.

"My lady?" he asked, his tone one of genuine concern. "Are you quite well?"

"Yes," she replied. "Quite well. I think I'd better go check on Richard, though. He was not at all well last night, and he was so tired this morning." With only the barest of curtseys, she excused herself and hurried off to find him.

The bedroom and the solar were empty. Puzzled, she retrieved her cloak from the hook behind the door, and, wrapping it around herself, she climbed to the battlements at the very top of the tower. She found him leaning against the stones, staring out over the wintry landscape.

He gave her a crooked smile when he saw her.

"My—my lord? Are you quite well?"

"Of course. Forgive me if I seemed abrupt with the priest." He turned back to stare across the landscape. If he left this time, and returned to his own, what would happen to Eleanor? What would happen to all these people who trusted him and relied upon him? Would the old Richard adhere to a peace he had no part in making? And what would the reaction of the people here be, if the old Richard insisted he had no memory of it? Would he be declared insane? Possessed?

Richard sighed. If only he had Lucy's knowledge, Lucy's insights. But all he had to go on were the bits and pieces he could remember, and his knowledge of human nature. Which, he believed, hadn't changed much at all. Loyalty was still loyalty, greed was still greed, even if the things that motivated such emotions had changed drastically.

"What troubles you, my lord?" Eleanor had come to stand beside him.

He glanced down at her. She seemed so fragile, so vulnerable in some ways, and yet, so strong in others. Her cloak was much patched and a pang of guilt went through him. Her robe had been ragged, too. In fact, all her clothes were patched and worn. "You must have some new clothes," he said, without thinking.

She blinked in astonishment. "Clothes?"

"Yes, new ones. All the ones you wear are worn and patched. Do you have any others? Or are these the only ones you've got?" He touched a patch on her cloak. His things were much nicer, and in a much better state of repair.

She flushed. "There is no need to spend—"

"Eleanor," he said, stopping her in midsentence. "It is not a question of expense. If we can't afford the finest of silks and velvets—well, you can still be dressed decently. Look how you're shivering." He wrapped an arm around and drew her close. "This cloak is scarcely enough in this cold."

He felt her yield against him, although she still stared up at him in surprise and something else—something that might be hope. He wanted so badly to change all that. What if he made her love him, and then he went back to the future? What would he leave her with?

"We—Father Alphonse and I—were concerned. Are you sure you're all right?"

He sighed. How to explain his general feelings of confusion? He was so torn. And she was definitely a factor in the equation. She was so lovely, so like Lucy and yet so unlike . . . "Eleanor," he began. "I—I know I seem different. But you

must believe that I do want to make peace with the Welsh—
it's not my intention to break any agreements we come to—
and I will see that Hugh comes home. Safely."

Her eyes filled with tears, and impulsively she hugged
him. "Thank you," she whispered.

He wrapped both arms around her. "You know—" The
words were poised on the tip of his tongue. It would be so
easy to tell her he loved her. But would it be fair?

She raised her face and looked at him. "Yes?" For the first
time, he saw trust and something else in her eyes. He
dropped his eyes. She was falling in love with him. There
could be no doubt. And if that happened . . . It had happened, he admitted to himself. It had happened, and if he
went back . . . *Then why go back?* asked a voice in his brain.
If too much depends upon you here and now, why even try?

But I owe it to my children and my grandchildren. . . . Or
did he? He pulled her even closer and buried his face in her
neck, nuzzling at the soft, white skin. He'd known from the
moment he'd first awakened in this new place that something drastic had happened. He remembered the sound of the
crack as he'd fallen. It all was so distinct—that sharp crack
and then nothing. Nothing until this. He turned his head and
kissed her. She responded immediately, arching up against
him, her body pressing close to his. Through the layers of
clothing, he could feel the heat of her flesh, and suddenly he
wanted nothing more than to be part of her. He looked
around. "Come."

"Where are we going?"

He grinned. "I'm tired and I need more rest."

"Rest?" She laughed out loud. "You hardly look as though
you have rest in mind, my lord."

He grinned. "Oh? And what have you in mind, my lady?"

She giggled. "I think we both need rest."

He pulled her close and whispered, before he kissed her once more, "We will need rest, my lady. I promise you, we will."

Chapter 15

"WHAT?" HUGH CRIED in disbelief. He stalked across the hall to the hearth, where the messenger stood impassively.

"Lord Richard de Lambert and Prince Llewellis Ab Rhawn have reached agreement, my lord. You're to be returned to the custody of your sister and her husband at noon on the morrow, and Prince Llewellis will be released." The messenger smiled. "You'll be home for Christmas, young lord. Doesn't that make you glad?"

Hugh ran his fingers through his hair. A feeling of desperation and disbelief swept through him. How could this happen? A treaty—an agreement of peace. The Welsh would stay on their side of the border, and Richard would stay on his, and he would most likely never see Angharad again. He looked over to the hearth, where she still knelt over the chess board. "I won't go."

The messenger glanced at Angharad and then back at Hugh. "I beg your pardon?" He spoke as if he wasn't sure he'd heard correctly.

Angharad leaped to her feet. "Go and tell your lord you've delivered your message and brought us good news indeed, sir messenger."

The messenger glanced from one to the other again. "As you will it, my lady."

"What's wrong with you, Hugh?" she whispered. She grabbed his hand and gave it a little shake. "What on earth do you mean, you won't go?"

"I don't want to leave you and go back to that—that monster. Do you have any idea what my life is like there? He treats me like a stableboy—or a dog. And that henchman of his, Geoffrey—" Hugh broke off. He stalked away to stand beside the fire. He slammed his fist into the mantel.

The few people in the hall looked at him curiously, and Angharad looked back at them and glared. "Hugh—" she said. "What makes you think things will be that bad?"

"Because they are that bad," he said. "And it's likely I'll be shipped off to some other lord's household, some place far away and then . . ." His voice trailed off and he looked miserable.

Angharad wet her lips. "And then what?"

"We'll probably never see each other again, Angharad. That's what." He met her eyes with a stubborn set to his shoulders. "Is that what you want?"

An unexpected pang went through her. Never see Hugh again? In the last weeks he'd become her friend, her companion. A saucy retort rose and died on her lips. This was serious. This was real. "No," she replied at last, her voice low. "It isn't what I want."

He caught her in his arms, heedless that anyone saw them. Angharad glanced around. They were alone. "Then come away with me. Come to France. We'll make our own way. It will be hard but I can fight—"

She pulled away. "Don't be ridiculous, Hugh. You know as well as I that will never work. Llewellis will hunt us both down—kill you and put me in a convent. And I most definitely don't want that." She shivered, thinking of her brother's rare yet formidable rages.

"Then what are we to do?" He stared at her in passionate despair. "I love you, Angharad. There. I've said it. And I don't care what anyone else thinks of that but you. Now. Do you love me?"

She drew a breath. Feelings raged through her. There was no one like Hugh. He was funny and kind and such good company. And good-looking too, in a young, half-formed sort of way. When he'd finished growing and his form finished filling out . . . "Well," she said. "Yes. I suppose I do. But what you don't want to understand is that that isn't going to matter. And you must return. For only then will de Lambert allow my brother to come home. And we need him—his people need him. He is our prince."

"And what of us?" Hugh pulled her close, so that she could feel the strength of his young body through the bulky clothes she wore against the cold. "What about this?"

Before she could stop him, his mouth came down on hers in a greedy kiss, a kiss made hard and demanding by desperation. She stiffened momentarily, and then a hot tide of passion swept through her, flooding all her senses, until she clung to him, limp, and returned his kiss with all the strength she could muster.

• • •

Richard glanced up as Eleanor came into the bedroom. Her hair was in the loose plaits she wore to bed, and she wore the ragged robe of faded silk. "Why do you wear that?" he asked.

"It was my mother's," she said, with a little smile of apology. "It's the one thing I have that always makes me feel her close to me. I hope you don't mind that I wear it."

"No, of course not." If it gave her some feeling of connection with a woman she barely remembered, he didn't mind at all. He only hated to see her dressed so poorly. The state of her clothes irked him more and more, but Eleanor said that until the spring fairs and market days opened once more, there was little chance of acquiring much in the way of fabrics. Except for those she made herself. "How is Hugh?" he asked, watching her face carefully as she continued to finger her hair. She wore a puckered frown.

"I'm not sure. He seems so upset. Not at all glad to be home. I can't understand it. Barland is his home."

The boy had been barely civil to them both. Richard guessed that there was a fair amount of animosity between Hugh and his brother-in-law, and hadn't allowed the boy's sullenness to bother him. He remembered dealing with his own sons' adolescence too well. But to Eleanor Hugh had been just as sullen, just as sulky. His behavior in fact had bordered on rude. And Eleanor had seemed hurt and shocked. Surely there was no reason to treat his sister that way. She'd risked much to get him back safely without crippling the manor that supported them all. For that matter, he thought, so had he. Hardy though his constitution was, he had risked his health to ride the distance to the marshal. And he could have died if Eleanor and Sir John hadn't shown up.

He sighed softly. "Boys are moody animals, my lady. I was one myself."

She shrugged. "Doubtless." She glanced at him with a flash of the humor he saw more and more. "But I don't understand why he acted the way he did toward me. He barely greeted me. And he said nothing at all at dinner."

Eleanor had gone to a great deal of trouble preparing a welcome feast. "It was delicious," he said, hoping to make her feel better.

"Thank you." She sighed and removed her robe. "I'm glad you enjoyed it, at least."

"We all enjoyed it," he said, moving aside in the big bed, and holding out his arms. "Everyone ate and ate—even Hugh. Didn't you notice he filled his plate three times?"

She smiled. "I—I don't think I did. I can't understand why he's acting the way he is."

"Perhaps something happened to him—with the Welsh?" Richard wondered if it was a possibility that the boy had been molested. Did such things happen in the thirteenth century? And then he realized grimly that in all likelihood they happened every bit as often as they did in the twentieth. Human nature hadn't changed.

"Like what?" She looked at him with wide, innocent eyes.

If they happened, he thought, it was likely Eleanor hadn't heard about them. "I—I don't know. Some unpleasantness perhaps? Something he doesn't want to talk about?" How else to put it delicately?

Eleanor sighed. "I suppose that could be. But Hugh is highborn—the Welsh would have had no reason to abuse him in any way. And Llewellis seemed like the sort of man who wouldn't brook any kind of mistreatment among his household. He was a good man—for a Welshman." She slipped into bed and blew out the candle on the table beside the bed.

Richard thought for a moment. "Why not give him a few days to settle in? And then try and talk to him. Perhaps he just needs a few days to get used to things here again."

Eleanor glanced at him. *Perhaps,* she thought, *he needs a few days to discover how different you are.* It had crossed her mind more than once that Hugh's displeasure was directly connected to the fact that Richard seemed so hale and hearty. He clearly wasn't going to die. "I suppose that is what we must do, my lord. And then we must discuss his future."

Richard frowned. "What about his future?"

Eleanor stared at him. "Well, where he is to go, for one thing. Geoffrey used to say it was long past time for Hugh to be sent away, and he was right. It is."

Richard lay back against his pillows, his mind racing. Here was something he hadn't been prepared for. He'd known in some dim way that boys of Hugh's class had been sent away from home. But how to arrange such a thing was beyond him at this point. Where was Hugh supposed to go? And who was he to approach? The marshal, he thought. Surely that was the logical place to begin. And with winter fast approaching, and the first layer of snow already on the ground—well, there was certainly time to find a suitable place for young Hugh to win his spurs. From the looks of him he was already a formidable fighter. He patted Eleanor's hand. "Don't worry. We'll find a good place for Hugh. Let's just get through the next few days with him, shall we?"

She smiled at him, relief plain on her face. Had she thought he was likely to turn the boy out in the cold? Probably. He put nothing past his counterpart.

"You are most kind, my lord," she said softly. "And I do appreciate it."

"Do you indeed?" he growled. "Then show me, wench. Come closer and show your appreciation."

She giggled. Their bodies molded together, flesh pressing against flesh. "With great pleasure, my lord. With the greatest pleasure."

Chapter 16

IT WAS ONE thing to imagine a world with no television, radio, or newspapers, thought Richard, and quite another to live it. He stared out over the gray wintry landscape. It had snowed in the night and now the world was covered with a soft white blanket. A soft white cold blanket. He pulled his cloak closer around his shoulders. A world without central heat was quite another thing to live in, too. A shout from below caught his attention. He peered straight down into the courtyard.

He saw a swirl of fabric. Eleanor and Hugh walked into the center of the courtyard. From the height, he couldn't hear what they were saying, but it was clear to him that Eleanor was attempting to talk to her brother. And Hugh was resisting all her attempts with an adolescent rudeness that made Richard grit his teeth. He'd tried to stay out of the boy's way since his return, thinking that he needed some space to get used to being with his sister again. As he watched, Eleanor reached for her brother's arm. Hugh shrugged her away, and stormed off in the direction of the stables. Eleanor followed, calling, struggling through the snow in her inadequate shoes. That's all he needed, Richard thought. Eleanor would catch her death of some fever or flu, and then he'd be left in the thirteenth century, all alone. As he said that to himself, he realized how important she was to him.

Hugh shouted something back, something brusque by his tone. Eleanor paused in the middle of the courtyard, looking after her brother. Richard could only guess the sadness and futility of the expression on her face by the slump of her shoulders. She hesitated a few seconds as Hugh disappeared into the stables. Then she gathered her cloak more tightly about her shoulders and turned back toward the keep.

A few moments later, Hugh rode out of the stables. As Richard watched, he galloped out the gate, and down the rutted road. He hoped the boy had enough sense to avoid laming the horse. He shook his head and decided to go and talk to Eleanor. Perhaps the time had come for him to intervene.

He found her by the hearth, staring into the flames, her hands held out. "Eleanor?"

She didn't turn around. "Yes, my lord? Is there something you require?"

Her distant tone of voice troubled him. "Not I, my lady. I saw you and Hugh in the courtyard just now. I wondered if there was anything you required?"

She drew a deep breath and gave a short bitter laugh. "I don't understand it. He's changed so much. I can't believe the way he acts. He behaves as if he hates it here. He says he'd rather be back with the Welsh—can you believe it?

Anywhere but here. And when I said we would discuss sending him away—to France perhaps—he shouted at me, and told me to mind my own business. But he is my business. I just don't understand." She shook her head sadly.

Richard stepped closer and wrapped an arm around her. "I'm sorry. But I think the time has come for me to say something to your brother. I haven't wanted to before now. But I've seen the way he treats you, Eleanor. And quite frankly, I haven't liked it."

She looked up at him. "What do you intend to say?" She sounded almost fearful.

"I intend to get to the bottom of this." He paused. It was on the tip of his tongue to say that no one changes in such a short period of time. But he of all people couldn't possibly say such a thing. "There has to be a reason, a good reason, for Hugh to act the way he has. We just need to discover what it is. And when we find it, we will address it. He may not like the outcome. But anything is better than this. I'm ready to send him away to France without a place in a household."

"Richard, no, please!" Eleanor clutched his arm and he realized that she actually believed him to be capable of such a thing. "He'd starve—be forced to fight as a mercenary—please—"

He shook his head and touched the tip of her nose lightly. He gave her a sad smile. "What a monster you think me, lady. I'm so sorry." He shook his head and turned away. He did not see her stare after him in disbelief.

Richard was waiting when Hugh stormed into the hall. He saw Richard in the big chair beside the fire, and stopped. "Where's my sister?" he demanded.

Richard paused in peeling an apple. He looked the boy up and down. "She's busy."

Hugh snorted and made as if to stomp off.

"Wait," Richard said. "I thought you and I might have a talk."

Hugh paused and momentarily, a look of pure fear flitted across his face. Then he shrugged in a gesture of bravado. "I don't have anything to talk about with you."

"But I have something to say to you. Sit down." Richard used the tone he used to use with his sons when they were at the same age and just as intractable. It was a tone they never disobeyed. It had a similar effect on Hugh. He gave Richard a sullen scowl, but sank down on a bench, as far away as he possibly could get. Richard peeled his apple.

"What do you want?" Hugh burst out finally.

"I want you to stop treating your sister as if she's done something wrong. I want you to start treating the people of this keep in the manner they deserve, which is with every courtesy you'd like to receive yourself. And I want you to tell me what's bothering you."

"When hell freezes first." The boy spat the words.

Richard raised his eyebrow but said nothing. "Very well. If you wish to be miserable, so be it. But I don't expect your behavior toward your sister to continue, do you understand? Nor do I expect to see you be rude to the servants. They work hard to do your bidding—there is no need to order them around as though they are slaves."

Hugh was staring at him with the same expression of disbelief Eleanor had worn when he'd first begun to interact with her.

"If I see that you are rude to anyone beneath this roof—anyone at all, from your sister down to the meanest scullery boy—I shall hand you over to Sir John to be punished. Do you understand?"

Hugh guffawed. "Some threat that is. Why don't you hand me over to your minion? Sir Geoffrey?"

Richard sat back. "He's dead."

"Good." Hugh got to his feet. "Are you finished?"

In one fast motion, Richard got to his feet. He picked Hugh up by the scruff of the neck, and spoke through gritted teeth. "I don't know what ails you, boy, but before God, I'll not have you speak that way of a brave and loyal man. Apologize at once."

Hugh looked down. "I'm sorry. Geoffrey was mean to me."

"And look at the way you've been treating everyone else," Richard said, as he let the boy go. "You're acting like a spoiled brat who won't get his way. There's no sense sulking about it. If you tell me what's wrong, I might be able to do something about it. But if you choose not to, I don't expect you to inflict your misery on us all. If you wish to skulk and scowl and act generally like a lout, feel free to do so. But you will give your sister all the courtesy she deserves. Do we understand each other?"

Hugh met Richard's eyes reluctantly. "Yes, my lord." He turned on his heel and fled. Richard watched him go, wondering how on earth he would ever deal with Eleanor's recalcitrant brother. Adolescents of any age were not easy to tolerate.

Hugh found Eleanor in her solar. She was sewing in the light of the fire, and at least two dozen candles, and Hugh blinked at all the light. She looked up when he peered into the room. "Hugh?" she said in surprise. "Come in."

He stood awkwardly just inside the door. "I—I just wanted to say I was sorry for the way I've been acting. I know I've been in a bad mood lately. I'm sorry. It isn't your fault."

"I accept your apology," she said, wondering what Richard had said to get through to him so effectively. "But can't you tell me what's been bothering you? If you tell me, maybe we can do something about it."

"That's what *he* said," Hugh said, with a jerk of his head. "That's exactly what he said."

"Richard?"

He nodded. "Since when do you call him that?"

Eleanor sighed. "Things are different since you've been gone, Hugh. Richard's different—changed. In some ways he's not the same man we knew. What did he say to you?"

"He told me to stop being rude to you and the servants. He told me he would try to help me if there was something wrong."

Eleanor sat back, her needle still in her lap. "And is there something wrong?"

Hugh shrugged. "Not really."

"But then what's been bothering you? You've been acting nearly as bad as Richard ever did since you came home. Did the Welsh hurt you in any way? Is there anything Richard should know?"

He shook his head. "They were fine to me. They gave me every courtesy. I was an honored guest, not a prisoner."

"Then what is it? I almost think you'd rather go back to them."

"I would."

Eleanor cocked her head, uncertain she'd heard her brother correctly. "Why?"

"There's a girl. Her name's Angharad. She's the most beautiful girl I've ever met, and she's brave and funny and so many things. And I don't think I'll ever meet her again."

"Who is she?"

"She's the prince's sister. His youngest sister."

"Oh." Eleanor gazed at her brother in sympathy. "I see."

He looked at her, misery clearly on his face. "Do you?"

"Of course I do."

"Then you understand why I can't bear the thought of leaving her? Knowing that there is nothing I can ever do—"

Eleanor held up her hand. "Hugh. I wish you had told me this earlier. The situation may not be as hopeless as you might think. She is the youngest sister, you say?" When he nodded, Eleanor continued. "I will speak to Richard."

"That monster?" Hugh snorted. "Since when would he do anything to help me?"

Eleanor sighed softly. It was going to be difficult to convince Hugh how much Richard had changed. "He has been charged by the marshal to make peace with the Welsh. A marriage with Llewellis's youngest sister would not be unheard of."

Hugh's face twisted in a bitter scowl. "Not unheard of if I had land. But I have nothing, Eleanor—nothing at all, and you know it. Llewellis would never entertain even the idea of a marriage to a landless nobody."

Eleanor pursed her lips and squared her shoulders. As much as she felt sorry for her brother, his self-pity was becoming exasperating. "Then we must see that that changes, Hugh. You must position yourself in a noble house—a place where you can win your spurs and make something of yourself. And in the meantime, I'm sure if Richard opens negotiations—the girl is how old?"

"Fifteen—sixteen—my age, I suppose."

Eleanor frowned. " 'Twould be better if she were a bit younger, but still . . ." She got to her feet. "I shall speak to Richard."

As she walked past Hugh, he caught her arm. "You really do seem to trust him, don't you?"

"Yes," she said, as she met his eyes fearlessly. "He's changed. You'll see."

When Eleanor entered the bedroom, she found Richard stretched out on the bed, his eyes closed. "My lord?" she asked, uncertainly. Outside snow swirled against the window, and the room was dark, despite the burning fire. "Are you well?"

He opened his eyes and yawned. "I'm tired. That's all. I spoke to Hugh. I told him to apologize to you."

"Ah," Eleanor stood beside the bed. "He did."

"Good." He held out his hand, and with only a moment's hesitation she took it. "I didn't like seeing him treat you that way."

She smiled uncertainly. *It was not so very long ago when you treated me that way,* she thought. But she said nothing, and he went on. "I've been thinking."

"Oh?" She wondered how to broach the subject of Hugh's love interest.

"About Giscard Fitzwilliam. If he in truth did send men to attack us on the road, and it seems likely from all the evidence that he did, something must be done about him. When the spring comes, if not before."

"And what do you think you should do?"

He pressed a kiss into the palm of her hand. "I'm not sure, lady. The marshal understands that peace is preferable to war, but sometimes war is necessary. It seems unfortunate that we must be at war with a close neighbor, especially if we can maintain our peace with the Welsh." He turned his head and frowned at the fire, gazing off into some unseen place. "But between the Welsh and Giscard . . ." His voice trailed off.

"Richard," she began, hesitantly. It still felt new to address him so freely, but he didn't seem to mind at all. "There may be a way to ensure a lasting peace with Llewellis."

"Oh?" It was his turn to look at her with surprise. "And what, my clever lady, might that be?"

He pulled her onto the bed beside him, wrapping his arms around her. She allowed herself to relax against him as a loud gust of wind rattled the glass in the window. "Hugh told me why he's been so upset. He fell in love while he was with the Welsh—Llewellis has a sister about Hugh's age. And the two of them, well . . ." She looked down and knew she blushed.

Richard chuckled, a pleasant little sound so different from the nasty one he used to make. "Ah. Now so much makes sense. But Hugh's only—fifteen? Too young to marry."

Eleanor shrugged. "But not too young to be affianced. Though that's not the problem. It might be that Llewellis would be willing to arrange a marriage for his youngest sister, but she's likely to have little dowry, and Hugh himself has nothing."

"What of the other manor?"

Eleanor stared at Richard. "You'd give it to Hugh? Break up the demesne?"

Richard frowned. Inwardly he cursed. He might have said something unheard of. There was too much about feudal land law he didn't know. "I—I'm only thinking aloud, lady.

It would seem that there is a solution here, if only we can find it. I would not take anything away from you—from us—but if it brings us peace, and peace to our children, then it might be worth it."

Eleanor blushed and dropped her eyes at the mention of children. Still there was no sign of pregnancy. "I—I can only hope there will be children, my lord," she whispered.

He smiled at her, brushing a wisp of hair off her face. "Have you anything that must be done right now?"

"Now?" She looked over her shoulder. "No, nothing that cannot be done later—or tomorrow."

"Good." He slid his arms around her, and pulled her closer, until their bodies were pressed against each other. "There are only a few things on a snowy winter's day that should be done . . . don't you think?"

She blushed again. What spell did this man weave? From the first, he'd conquered her body, and now it was clear he was close to having her heart. "What things are those, my lord?"

"Let me show you, lady. Let me show you at least some of them." He pulled her coif off her head and the white linen fluttered to the floor. He fumbled with the laces of her gown, and slipped it off her shoulders, exposing her shift. With a few expert tugs, he unlaced that garment as well. He laid her flat against the pillows, and pushed the fabric out of the way. Her breasts rose, round and rosy tipped. He gazed at them as though seeing them for the first time.

She felt the color rise once more in her face at his unabashed scrutiny. "R-Richard," she whispered, mortified.

"Shh," he said, placing one finger against her lips. "Don't you know how beautiful you are?"

She looked away, scarcely daring to believe him. "Do you mean that?"

For answer he bent his head, and slowly kissed each nipple in turn. She moaned, and clasped her hands in his hair, playing with the dark, unruly curls. He showered gentle kisses on both breasts, teasing her until she squirmed with pleasure. "Is there something my lady wants?" He raised his head and grinned.

She dropped her eyes. "Richard—" She hesitated.

"Yes?" he asked, puzzled by the seriousness of her tone.

"There are no children—not yet."

He shrugged. "But we've time, my dear." He caressed her face, and she smiled at the endearment. "A winter's worth of time. At least." He gathered her mouth to his, and then there were no words worth saying.

Chapter 17

"SO NOW WHAT?" Guillaume turned lazily on his stomach on the great bearskin and yawned. "Once again de Lambert escaped the trap you thought so cleverly set."

"Bah!" Giscard spat into the fire. "That was luck, nothing more."

"It seems like a mighty mort of luck indeed, considering that twice now, you've sent armed men after him. I suppose this means you'll give it all up?"

"Give what up?" Giscard reached across the table and speared another hunk of meat from the platter with his knife. He took a bite and grease ran down his chin to stain the front of his tunic.

"This obsession?" Guillaume yawned. "By God, you've got a miserable keep here, Giscard. Why not come back to France with me? Aquitaine is so much more pleasant, especially this time of year. Of course, almost anywhere is more pleasant this time of year."

"Oh, for God's sake, hold your tongue, Guillaume. If you prefer Aquitaine, go back there. I'll stay here and fight for what's mine."

"For what you'd like to have for yours, you mean." Guillaume got to his feet. "Why don't you give it up, Giscard? De Lambert's made peace with the Welsh—he's in the marshal's good graces. You've no excuse to wrest the lands from him legally, and if you persist in these attacks, you're likely to have no men of your own left. How many did you lose in this latest? Twenty?"

"Ten."

"If you want more lands, go kiss the king's backside. You've always been good at doing that."

Giscard finished chewing. He swallowed and looked at his brother. "I'm considering throwing this knife at you."

Guillaume got to this feet, laughing. "Do that, brother. If you wish to face the wrath of the King of France." He shook his head. "Perhaps there are worthier ways to increase your holdings—service to your king, and all that. John has need of good men around him, doesn't he?"

Giscard scowled. "And you know as well as I that John guards his favors selfishly, and dispenses them with an ungenerous hand. It's only luck that gave you our father's French holdings, and me the English ones. You'd be in the very same position as I if things had been different."

Guillaume waved a dismissing hand. "Oh, come, you don't believe that. Find yourself an heiress, a marriageable heiress, and wed her. Your obsession with de Lambert will be your ruin. He has his lands, you have yours. You've tried twice now to kill him. Either set aside your differences, or find some way to discredit him to the king. You've wasted enough time on this as it is."

Giscard stared at his brother. "Brother, you're a genius. Discredit de Lambert to the king . . . hm." He chewed thoughtfully on an oatcake. "But how?"

Guillaume shrugged. "That's your problem. But didn't I overhear your men saying how he was shouting nonsense during the battle? Perhaps you can make him out to be mad."

"Hmm." Giscard swallowed and reached for his goblet of wine. "Mad." He raised his glass to his brother, and smiled. "An interesting idea and one filled with possibilities. Who knows, brother? If something comes of this, I might finally forgive you for having been born first."

"Well, Angharad?" Llewellis gestured with the parchment scroll he held in his hand. "Would you be willing to wed the young Norman?"

Angharad drew herself up. Her cheeks were flushed red— from the heat of the fire, she told herself—and her shoulders were rigid. It was true she liked Hugh. It was true she'd found his company enjoyable, and their time together had made the long winter days and evenings far less dull than they were now. It was even true she missed him. But the thought of admitting that to her brother, not to mention her brother's wife and all the other women in the household, made her cringe. "Well, " she said reluctantly, "I suppose you could entertain the idea. At least long enough to keep him dangling."

Llewellis raised an eyebrow and shook his head. "Hm. No, little sister. I think you mistake my meaning. De Lambert is no untried boy. A marriage with his wife's brother, young though he might be, will go a long way—"

"Wait," interrupted Angharad. "This isn't exactly what you said to me when it was Hugh himself."

Llewellis shrugged. "He is a boy yet. His brother-in-law is another matter. De Lambert has the ear of the marshal of England—who holds quite a few estates in Wales, himself. It's in our best interests to take this suit seriously, far more seriously than when it was Hugh trying to hatch silly plots against de Lambert. And so, I ask you again, would you be willing to wed the young Norman?"

Angharad swallowed hard. "I—I suppose so. If it would help bring peace, of course."

"Of course," Llewellis grinned behind his dark beard. "Your concern for your country is duly noted." He rose to his feet. "I will respond to de Lambert immediately, then." He winked at her as he walked past her, leaving her feeling ridiculously happy for what she was sure could only be some very foolish reason.

"My lady?"

Eleanor looked up from her sewing in surprise. The morning sun slanted through the small window of her solar, and she smiled in surprise. "Sir John?"

The old soldier stood ramrod straight in the doorway. "If I disturb you, my lady—"

"No, not at all." She gestured with her needle. "Come in. What can I help you with? I think my lord is in the stables."

"So he is, my lady." Sir John looked acutely uncomfortable. "I wanted a word with you, if I may."

She nodded, curious. "Of course, Sir John. Come speak your mind."

The old man stepped into the room, glanced over his shoulder, and walked to stand before Eleanor's chair.

"Will you sit?"

He shook his head and pursed his lips. "It concerns Lord Richard."

She raised her brows. "Oh?"

He drew a deep breath, clearly uncertain how to proceed. "The other evening—when our men were attacked—Lord Richard acquitted himself honorably and with great valor. But—" He broke off and stared into the fire. "Several of the men have come to me since that night. They tell me that in the heat of battle, Lord Richard spoke words that they did not know. He shouted in a language not known to them. My lady, they believed he was possessed."

Eleanor stared at the old man, shocked. "You cannot be serious, Sir John. Richard is in full possession of all his faculties. How can you say such a thing? I will not hear any of this nonsense. It's well known he fought in the Holy Land. Perhaps there he learned words the other men know not. Perhaps in the heat of the moment, they misunderstood him. That is not unknown on the field, in the midst of battle, is it?" She drew herself up, her chin resolute. "How can you even dignify such a rumor by bringing it to me?"

The old man had the grace to look sheepish. He spread his hands. "Forgive me, my lady. I—I know how foolish it sounds. The men are superstitious louts for the most part. Forgive me for intruding upon your time." He bowed low from the waist and departed.

Eleanor drew a deep breath. She stabbed at the fabric in her lap with her needle, and realized her hands were shaking. How could such things be said? Richard was—her mind reeled in full rejection of what a voice whispered could be true. For Richard was altogether different from the way he'd been before last autumn's attack. There was no doubt, no question, that the man who was her husband now was a much more pleasant person, more fair and more just, than the man she'd married. How could that constitute possession, after all? Souls were possessed by demons—the old Richard was a demon. This new Richard, the man who gathered her in his arms every night, who'd made a peace with the Welsh, and now sought to strengthen it by negotiating for Hugh's love, he was the farthest thing from a demon one could imagine. But he had changed, she couldn't deny that. What could a change for the better mean?

She wrinkled her brow and chewed on her lip. If the men would not fight with him, that could be dangerous. And the fact that Sir John had come to her was troubling. She sighed. Should she speak to Richard or not? What could she say? It was likely he'd remember. And what would he say in response? *Yes, my lady, the devil is responsible for my miraculous recovery.* She shook her head and picked up her needle once more. The winter was long. There would be plenty of time to observe Richard and see if he exhibited any signs of demonic possession. And if he did, she would speak to Father Alphonse. She hoped such a thing was never necessary. With luck, this was the end of all such foolishness.

Chapter 18

IT WAS THE wind that changed first, Richard noticed. One day the air was cold and biting, with winter's unmistakable edge, and the next, there was a certain softness in it, like the back of Eleanor's hand as it brushed against his cheek. The calendar said March but in reality it felt as if the winter had lasted a year.

He shivered as he stared out over the still gray landscape. Although the temperature was noticeably higher, and the sunlight had the intensity of spring, the snow and the ice were slow to melt. The roads were still impassable, as his most recent attempt to venture outside the walls had shown him just a few days ago. Richard wondered what was happening in the outer world. It was impossible to imagine how many people had survived across the ages in such isolated hamlets as this. And, he thought ruefully, it was beginning to look more and more as if he were here for good. He could think of no way to approach the severe priest. Father Alphonse—he finally had the name right. The priest seemed to regard him as a necessary evil. He looked down his nose at Richard, and spoke to him mostly through Eleanor.

Perhaps it was the way he'd stumbled through the sacraments that made the priest so contemptuous. He'd managed to learn French, but Latin was proving beyond him. With a sigh, he shook his head and had decided to return to the warmth of the hall when movement outside the walls caught his attention. A horseman appeared and disappeared beneath the trees leading up to the gates. Richard took off down the stairs. Some news of the outer world at last.

He stepped into the hall just as a flurry of activity told him the messenger had been spotted by the guards at the gates. Eleanor came hurrying in from the kitchens, her cheeks rosy from the cold, but her eyes bright with anticipation. *We're all suffering from cabin fever,* he thought, and he felt a momentary pang for the twentieth century, when a snowstorm, even a blizzard, was usually nothing but a minor inconvenience.

Eleanor smiled when she saw him. "My lord," she cried, "a messenger is coming. The roads must be clear."

He smiled back. The change in Eleanor was remarkable. The scared-rabbit look was gone, for the most part, and only returned in fleeting moments when she thought she might have angered him. But those moments were few and far between, and the woman who stood confidently by his side, sending the servants scurrying for food and drink and more logs for the fire, was a very different woman from the one he'd seen when he'd first opened his eyes in the thirteenth century. She was cleaner, for one thing—her hair and skin glowing from the baths they often took together in the huge wooden tub before the fire in their room. And her clothes— although the long stretch of bad weather had meant that it was impossible to get anything like the silks and fine wools he'd like to see her wear, he'd insisted she use the best of the homespun for herself. At least she no longer looked like a poor nun. He reached down for her hand, squeezed it gently and raised it to his lips. He was about to press a kiss into the palm, when one of the outer doors opened, and a man strode in, accompanied by one of the manor guards.

His clothes were muddy and wet in places, and his face was rough with a matted beard. But he met Richard's eyes squarely. "My lord de Lambert?" he asked. He crossed the distance between them with the long strides of one who was accustomed to traveling with purpose. "My lady." He bowed to Eleanor. "I bring you greetings from William the Marshal of England, my lord. And a message." From his belt he withdrew a sealed parchment packet.

"Our thanks, sir," said Eleanor. "Will you please sit, and refresh yourself?"

"Gratefully, my lady. I've been on the road three weeks."

"Three weeks!" Eleanor signaled to the servant who stood beside the hearth, wineskin in hand, to pour the man a drink. The messenger sank down on the bench, and raised the goblet. "Are the roads so bad?"

"No," he shook his head, after a long drink. "I've had many messages to deliver. Great doings are afoot in England. The barons, led by the archbishop, are on the move. There's talk of rebellion from one end of the country to the other, but particularly in the South."

"You must tell us what you can, sir," Eleanor said, "but first you must eat and drink."

Richard was examining the parchment. He gingerly plucked at the seals, carefully opening them so that the parchment would not be damaged. He unfolded the letter and looked at it carefully. Although his French was vastly improved, and Eleanor had spent much of the last months teaching him to read, the uncial or minuscule script—whatever it was called—was beyond him. He scanned the letter with impatience, and handed it to Eleanor. "If you will excuse us, sir."

The messenger bowed. He was happily munching on oat-cakes and cheese. Richard drew Eleanor a little way off, and nodded to the letter. "What does it say?"

She wrinkled her brow. "To Richard de Lambert, Lord of Barland, greetings. We trust this letter finds you and your lady in good health and—"

"Yes, yes," he interrupted her impatiently. "What does the letter say?"

She frowned a little, reading quickly through a paragraph of formal courtly language. "It says that William is very pleased with the work you have done with the Welsh, and that he rewards you for your efforts with the gift of a manor—Bryn Addyn—" She paused here, and looked up at Richard in surprise. "This says—the manor's revenues are thirty pounds a year—my lord, he's doubled your wealth."

Richard nodded, surprised by the gift. Thirty pounds didn't sound like so much to him, but then, he had little idea how much things were worth. But the reward was welcome. "Where is it?"

"In Striguil—to the south. And he says he's arranged for Hugh to join his own retinue as a squire. He's to set out with the messenger for London, where he expects to be by the end of this month—" She broke off once more. "I didn't expect Hugh would go so far away." She bit her lip.

Richard smiled down at her. "Eleanor, perhaps it's for the best. If the country is as unsettled as our messenger tells us, it might be safer for Hugh to be with a man as powerful as the marshal. At least for a while. Does he say anything about my proposal of marriage between the Welsh princess and Hugh?"

"He says he supports whatever actions you feel necessary to maintain and promote the peace along the border. So, no, not really, but it does not seem as if he would disapprove."

Richard nodded, thinking. "Well, then, it would seem you'd better make sure young Hugh is ready to leave when the messenger does." He turned back to the messenger, who had polished off the food with relish. "Good sir, I understand my brother is to accompany you?"

The messenger rose to his feet. "I believe so, my lord. Can the young gentleman be ready to ride within a day or two? I have other messages to deliver on my way to London."

Richard looked down at Eleanor. "I—I shall see to it, directly." She bustled off, and Richard motioned for the man to sit once more.

"Tell me more about the unrest in the country," Richard said, as he settled into the chair opposite. "Would you like more to eat?"

The man shook his head. "Thank you, but no, my lord. This is more than enough. And as for the country—" He spread his hands. "My lord William is at his wit's end." He paused, as if considering what his next words should be. Then the messenger leaned forward, and in his eyes, Richard read concern. "I have another message for you, my lord. This one Lord William did not wish to commit to paper."

Richard was startled. What could be so important? "May I know your name, sir?" He had the feeling that this man was no lackey.

"Sir Walter of Banbury, sir." The messenger inclined his head. "I've been a member of Lord William's house for many years—since I was old enough to hold a sword. I was with Lord William in the autumn, though you perhaps don't remember me."

Richard shook his head, frowning. There had been scores of young men, all about Sir Walter's age in William's household, all eager, hardened men in the prime of their lives. "Forgive me."

"No offense taken, my lord. You made quite an impression on Lord William. Which is why he sent me to you."

Richard leaned back in his chair. He remembered little but his own awkwardness in front of the great earl. "Oh?"

"Forgive me if I speak frankly, my lord. But your reputation had preceded you—Lord William was fearful that your possession of the Barland demesne, so close to the border of Wales, would only precipitate war."

Richard nodded, saying nothing. No wonder he'd made an impression on William. The original Richard was a barbarian, he could see that by the way the people here at Barland had reacted to him. William must have been surprised, indeed, to meet a man who believed implicitly in concepts William himself could scarcely give voice to.

"But your words there, and your actions subsequently, have shown that you are a man of rare understanding. And that brings me to why Lord William sent me here."

"I'm at his service." Richard inclined his head, wondering

what the marshal could possibly want with him, a relatively humble and obscure vassal.

"Great doings are afoot. You are isolated in this small corner of the realm—forgive me if I seem to patronize. But there is much I must tell that has happened in the last months in order for you to understand what Lord William requires."

Richard gestured. "Say on."

Walter nodded. "At Epiphany this year, our king met with the barons of the northern counties, who, as you probably know, are the most vocal of all his critics. They demand certain things of him—you are familiar with some of this, I'm sure."

Richard shook his head. "Forgive me, Sir Walter. But my memory of the first part of last year was addled by the wounds I suffered in the autumn. Please, refresh me. I know the barons have quarreled with the king, but the specific issues themselves—I confess I am not familiar with them."

"In that, sir, you are not alone. There are so many demands, so many quarreling voices—you feel them little because our lord William is fair and just. But John is greedy. The wars he's fought in France have seriously bankrupted his treasury time and again, and he has sought to tax his vassals. At any rate, there was a conference with these men at Epiphany, and John sought to have the matter put off until Easter. Easter is upon us, and the barons are gathering their forces in Stamford. My lord William sent me to ask you to join him and the king at Windsor."

Richard sat back, stunned. "Me? How can I be of assistance in this matter? I am the least of Lord William's men—"

Sir Walter waved his hand. "You negotiated a peace skillfully with the Welsh. You understood Lord William better than any man he's ever seen. He needs men of your humor with him. Please, sir, will you come?"

Richard got to his feet. Such a request seemed impossible. What use could he be? He could barely speak the language. "Sir Walter, I'm flattered at the trust Lord William seems to have in me. But I'm only a soldier. I cannot even read and write, as you saw. My lady wife must read everything to me. I am not the man Lord William needs."

Walter rose as well. "My lord, one thing I have learned in all the days I have spent beneath Lord William's roof is that he is a superb judge of both men and character. If he believes you can be of use to him in this matter, you must believe it, too. The land is poised on the brink of civil war. If the king falls, the barons will be free to do as they please. Here, you may have little concern of that. But if the barons turn against the king, they will most assuredly soon turn against each other. Blood will stain the rivers red. Lord William seeks to avert that."

Richard stared at the man before him. Perhaps this was why he'd been sent to the thirteenth century. Hadn't there been a television show about a man who traveled through time, setting things right, and bouncing in and out of other bodies when his work in each was done? Richard looked down at his hands. They were strong hands, a soldier's hands. The scars crisscrossed the backs of them in all directions. And they seemed so familiar now. He could barely remember what his other hands had looked like. He straightened his shoulders and nodded. "Very well, Sir Walter. I will accompany you as Lord William requests. I have one request of my own, however. I would bring my lady wife with me."

Sir Walter shrugged. "The roads are not so bad as they

were. If that is your only request, I'm sure Lord William will not mind. You may be gone for quite some time. How soon can you be ready to leave?"

"I will have to speak to my wife about that," Richard said. The words sounded very familiar. Some things didn't change with the passage of centuries.

"As you wish, my lord. I know Lord William is looking forward to seeing you."

"Go?" Eleanor echoed. She gazed up at Richard in disbelief. "To Windsor?"

"I don't want to leave you here. Civil war is likely to break out. Sir Walter made a point of telling me that if the barons turn against the king, they will soon turn against each other. And if I leave, you will be here alone and unprotected against Giscard. What's to prevent him from attacking Barland itself in my absence?"

"There's Sir John—"

"Eleanor." Richard placed one finger against her lips. "He's a good man. But he's old. I don't want to trust your safety to a man whose best days are behind him. Hugh will come with me. You'll be alone. And we know Giscard is our enemy. We can tell the marshal about him together. But I would rather return and find that I must fight for Barland than return and find that I must bargain for your life. Do you understand?"

Eleanor looked down at the floor. There seemed to be little argument. She nodded, took a deep breath, and raised her eyes to his. "I cannot disagree with you, my lord. When must we leave?"

"As soon as possible. Tomorrow?"

She gave a little laugh. "No. Nor the day after. But in

three days—tell Sir Walter we can leave in three days time. There is an enormous amount to do between now and then— sooner is not possible."

He pressed a kiss on the back of her hand. "Is there anything I can do to help?"

At that she laughed outright. "I doubt you know much about laundry, my lord."

Richard thought about all the times he'd folded socks and underwear for his children when they were small. But the washing machines of the twentieth century were an entirely different matter. He shook his head slowly. "No, my lady. I'm afraid I know as little of laundry as I do of reading." He smiled, a little sadly, and turned to go. "I shall leave you to your preparations, my lady. In the meantime, I shall speak to Sir John. Barland must not be left vulnerable."

Spring was well along once they left the hills of the march country. The roads wound through fields and forests, and Richard was struck by the beauty of the countryside. Along the way, they passed little villages and tiny hamlets, places that in his own time would grow into towns and cities. And these rough roads, with tiny wildflowers and weeds growing in between the ruts, would someday see traffic such as his companions could never imagine. Lost in his thoughts, Richard didn't hear Sir Walter turn and speak to him.

Eleanor touched his arm. She rode beside him on a gray mare, as easily as if she had been born in the saddle. She nodded. "Sir Walter thinks it's time to stop."

"Ah." Richard looked around. "We'll make camp?"

"No," Walter shook his head. "Tonight we will sleep beneath a real roof. I'm sure you'll be happy about that, my lady." Just ahead the crenelated roof of a keep rose above the trees. "See there? That's the manor of Sir Hugh and Lady Katherine Fitzhugh. The marshal alerted them to our coming—we'll spend the night there."

Richard looked at Eleanor, who smiled. Dark smudges marred the delicate skin beneath her eyes, and he thought she looked pale and tired. Despite her protestations that she enjoyed the trip, traveling was clearly difficult for her.

Not that he blamed her. If he'd thought traveling in the autumn had been cumbersome, when he and his men had covered roughly seventy or eighty miles in a day, it was nothing compared to this. They were lucky to make half that distance. But in the interim, Sir Walter told him more about the situation in the country, and Richard was gradually able to piece together some understanding of the complex political situation he was about to become embroiled in.

The road gradually curved up a gentle slope. The trees parted, and gray stone walls rose before them, the gates partially open. Through them, Richard could see the same sort of bustle he had become accustomed to. They were spotted by a guard on the walls. He turned, crying down something unintelligible, and slowly, one of the gates opened a little more.

With a wave, Sir Walter led them through the massive wooden gates. Inside Richard reined his horse. A short, bald man whose blue silk tunic and surcoat marked him as the lord of the manor came forward smiling, his hand extended in an unmistakable greeting. "My lord de Lambert," he said. "Welcome to Bruton."

Richard slid down from his horse and took Sir Hugh's hand. "Sir Hugh? My wife and I are grateful for your hospitality."

Sir Hugh gripped his hand securely and shook it. "Ah, in

such times as these, cool heads must stick together. Right, Sir Walter?" He turned a wide smile of welcome on the younger knight.

"Indeed, my friend," said Walter. "You speak true."

Richard held up his arms to Eleanor, who slipped out of her saddle with a tired smile. For a moment, she clung to him, and he leaned down to whisper in her ear. "Are you all right?"

She nodded and smiled, but he was concerned by her obvious fatigue.

"We'll get you inside, and rest," he said, pressing her close for the briefest of moments, before turning back to their host. "Sir Hugh, may I present my wife? Lady Eleanor."

Eleanor smiled and took Sir Hugh's hand. He bowed and gestured to a woman who stood on the shallow steps that led into the keep. "I'm honored to meet you, my lady. Will you come and greet my own lady wife?"

"With pleasure, Sir Hugh." Eleanor gathered the skirts of her gown in one hand and gripped Richard's arm with the other. Sir Hugh gestured to the grooms hovering close to come and take the horses. In that moment, a dozen or so squealing piglets escaped across the courtyard. They headed straight for the horses. Richard's stallion shied, and Eleanor's mare whinnied and bucked. Richard reached for the reins, in vain, and the horse rose on her hind legs, her front hooves perilously close to Eleanor's head. "My God, look out!" he cried. "The horses—get those reins!" he grabbed Eleanor with one arm and pushed her head close to his chest, as they were surrounded by a sea of flailing hooves and squealing pigs. Richard felt a massive hoof strike his back and he collapsed to his knees, cradling

Eleanor close. "Help," he shouted. "Help!" He closed his eyes. Surely it wasn't going to end like this.

Frantically the grooms brought the horses under control and scullery maids and stable boys retrieved the piglets. Richard raised his head cautiously. Eleanor looked up at him, terror and something else, something that might be confusion in her eyes. Richard looked around and clasped her close to reassure her. "Are you all right?"

She nodded, but the expression in her eyes did not change. He looked around. The other men were standing by, staring at him with expressions that were a blend of puzzlement and concern. What was wrong? Carefully he got to his feet, helping Eleanor to hers.

"My—my lord?" Her voice was shaking. "Are—are you all right?"

"Yes," he said. What was the matter with her? She was staring at him as if he were a stranger.

"Just now . . . when you spoke—" She broke off and looked away, and Richard realized abruptly to his horror, that in the confusion, he'd spoken in English. Not the language the peasants spoke. Modern English. A language that wouldn't exist for at least another four hundred years.

Eleanor allowed Lady Katherine to lead her to a comfortable chamber above the hall, where a wide bed had been prepared for them. The woman was kind and comforting, but she, too, had heard Richard's unintelligible utterances. There had been no doubt from the tone of them what he'd been attempting to do—he was trying to save them both. But to speak in a strange tongue? A language that sounded like none she'd ever heard?

After he was wounded, when the fever had burned so

hotly through his body, she thought she'd heard unfamiliar words. But because of his throat wound, it had been impossible to understand him. He really hadn't been able to talk at all for nearly two months. Some obscure Arab tongue, she'd thought then. But why lapse into it when he was trying to save them? She thought about what Sir John had told her after Richard's return. Richard had shouted strange words. Words none of the other men had recognized. Some of those men had been with him in the Holy Land. If that were so, surely some of them would have recognized the words. But Sir John had insisted none of them did. Possession, they'd whispered. Possessed by a demon.

Eleanor turned on her side, her cheek pillowed on her hand. She closed her eyes as a wave of weariness swept over her. But Richard was anything but a demon. He was kind and considerate, even if there were something wrong with him. It was true he'd changed, but he'd changed for the better. There was no question about that. Everyone knew it. No one would prefer that Richard go back to being the way he was before the autumn attack. The fever might have left him with an addled brain—but surely he'd changed only for the better.

She rolled onto her back and stared at the ceiling. Perhaps it was the fever. Perhaps his brain had been addled. Perhaps in the heat of battle, he could not talk correctly. That didn't mean he was possessed. But would anyone believe that? Would hardened soldiers who cared only about winning a battle understand that? Or would they refuse to follow a man who perhaps wasn't . . . wasn't himself? Her mind veered away from any other characterization of it.

There was a knock on the door. She struggled to sit up, and called, "Come in."

Lady Katherine's round face peered in. "Are you quite all right, my dear? Such a terrible scare—poor lady, you look like death." The woman bustled into the room, her skirts quivering around her plump frame. She picked up Eleanor's hand and patted it. "Would you like something to eat?" She peered into the goblet of watered wine she'd left beside the bed. "I will have a tray sent up to you. My poor dear, you look quite worn out."

Eleanor nodded, feeling miserable. She wished she could tell this kind woman, but she was afraid to even give shape to her fears. How could she confide in a stranger?

"Your lord is certainly a fine figure of a man, my lady." Lady Katherine was smiling broadly. "And so brave—the way he dropped to his knees and covered you with his body—"

Eleanor listened to the woman prattle on, managing a weak smile. Lady Katherine hadn't heard Richard, obviously, and maybe in the confusion, no one else had, either. But she clearly remembered the looks of confusion on the faces of the men around them. They'd heard, she knew it. Did any of them fear the same thing she did, she wondered. Or did they think that perhaps, in all the noise—the pigs, the horses, the screams—they simply misunderstood him? She suppressed an urge to bury her head in her hands.

"My dear?" Lady Katherine had paused and was looking at her with concern. "Are you quite all right? Would you like a physic?"

Eleanor raised her eyes. Tears pricked her eyelids, and she blinked them away. "No, no, my lady. I'm fine. I'm just tired. If you would send a tray—" Suddenly she was ravenously hungry. Her mouth watered. "I'll just rest, if you don't mind."

"Of course I don't mind." The woman gave her a motherly smile. "I'll just reassure your lord that you just need rest after such a long journey. You rest, my dear. Try to sleep."

When the woman had gone, Eleanor lay back against the pillows. She gripped the woolen coverlet on both sides. Richard was fine. Richard was fine. There was nothing wrong with him, only the stress of battle—the stress that something might happen to her—had addled his brain and made his words come out mangled. He could hardly speak for the longest time, after all. It was almost as if he'd had to learn to talk all over again. She repeated these thoughts over and over in her mind, until at last she fell into a troubled sleep.

Chapter 19

RICHARD JOGGED ALONG the uneven road, his eyes focused straight ahead. A steady rain beat down, and all of them were soaked. Walter had assured them that Windsor lay just ahead, but the interminable rain made the road seem that much longer. He glanced down at Eleanor. With each passing day, she seemed to grow more and more fatigued. If he'd thought that the journey could take so much out of her, he'd never have invited her to come. He sighed inwardly, his mouth set in a grim line. Ever since that day in Sir Hugh's courtyard, things had been different between them. She jumped when he came into a room, watched him furtively beneath her lids whenever they were together. And he noticed her staring at him like a hawk at daily mass.

She'd heard him—heard the heedless English words which had jumped so readily, so easily, on his tongue. He cursed silently. He couldn't blame himself—he knew he shouldn't. But it was a serious lapse and one he knew he couldn't afford to make again.

He wondered if she'd confided in her brother. But Hugh treated him with no more or less suspicion than he'd ever had. His attitude had softened somewhat since Richard had opened negotiations with Llewellis for Angharad's hand, and if he'd heard Richard's careless words, he obviously thought little of it. But Eleanor thought of it. And thought of it often. What did she think, he wondered. That he was insane? Possessed? He sighed once more. Possessed was not exactly the wrong answer. In a sense he had possessed her husband's body. Only . . . didn't it matter that *he* was so much nicer than the original Richard?

But in this superstitious time, who could tell? Eleanor had been raised in the convent. She believed every word Father Alphonse preached. Her religion was a source of comfort and inspiration. If the priests said her husband was possessed, she would believe it.

He toyed once more with the idea of telling her the truth. He could only imagine the look of disbelief, of shock. *He* could scarcely believe it, how could he expect a woman of the thirteenth century to believe it? *You see, my dear,* he could imagine himself saying, *I'm really not your husband. I sort of landed in his body somehow. I don't have any idea how it happened, exactly, but one minute I was standing on top of the ruins of Barland Castle in 1994, and the next thing I knew, I woke up in your bedroom with an arrow in my side, and you were trying to kill me. Not that I blame you, knowing the kind of man your husband was.*

He could not even begin to imagine her reaction. She'd probably faint. Or call in the soldiers and have him taken away. Then she'd call the priest, who would call in the Inquisition. He wondered fleetingly if the Inquisition existed yet.

Rain dripped off his brow into his collar. His clothes were sodden, and the horse plodded forward with an air of resignation. Eleanor rode swathed in her cloak, her eyes fastened on the road in front of them. He wondered what she was thinking, and realized he would probably rather not know.

A pang went through him. There were so many things about this whole situation that were more complicated than he'd ever imagined. If it were true that he was here for some purpose, and he had to believe that he was, if only for his own sanity, did it mean he would leave here when that purpose was complete?

And what would happen to this body when he did? Would the original Richard come back? And if he did, what would he think? But what was even more worrisome, what would happen to Eleanor? He imagined her warm, soft, sweet body pressed beneath someone who was less than kind, who by all reports was cruel to servants and family alike. Hugh clearly despised him; Eleanor had feared him. She had begun to learn to trust him—he could only imagine how awful it would be if she had to discover her husband was once more a beast.

He glanced at her again. Her face was frozen. Perhaps she'd rather have a cruel husband, after all, than one she thought was crazy.

Sir Walter nudged his way over to Richard's side. "Less than an hour, now," he said, looking uneasily at the sky. "Would you prefer to stop, my lord? Or to press on? Your lady wife looks so tired."

Richard stole another glance at Eleanor. She looked more than tired, she looked exhausted. Dark circles seemed to have formed permanently beneath her eyes, but at night she fell asleep immediately and slept like a stone until morning. He regretted bringing her along more and more. So much for trying to give her some opportunity to see more of the world than Barland. He nodded. "I'm afraid so. Is there a likely place?"

"Just ahead. A tavern. It's frequented by the king's men and travelers coming to and from Windsor, so it's clean enough. You need have no worry for your lady there."

"Very well. Let's send a man on ahead—have them get a room and a hot meal ready."

"Good idea." Walter nodded and turned away, flapping his reins. Richard heard him order the closest guard to ride ahead, and without any urging, the man took off. He guessed the soldier was tired of the slow slog through the rain, too.

He turned to Eleanor. "Lady," he said, slowly, unwilling to break into her thoughts.

She slid her eyes over to him. They were dull and dark. "Yes, my lord?"

The words sounded so automatic. "We're not going on to Windsor today. There's an inn just up ahead. We'll stop there for the night, and then, tomorrow, you can rest there while I go on to see the king and Lord William. Do you find that"—the word "okay" nearly slipped out—"satisfactory?"

"Of course, my lord." She nodded and her hands gripped the reins tightly. Her eyes focused once more on the road ahead.

Women, Richard sighed. Couldn't she at least talk to him? Confide in him? Perhaps this evening—he would confront her that very evening. She couldn't sulk forever. He wasn't sure what he would tell her, but there had to be some way to reassure her that he wasn't crazy. At least, he thought, as he stared at the thirteenth-century landscape around him, no crazier than anyone else who had ever time-traveled.

Eleanor sank into the wooden tub, the hot water sending clouds of steam into the air. She heard the babble of voices from the tavern below—loud voices, all male, mostly drunk. She shut her eyes. The weariness spiraled through her and she shook her head. If she weren't careful, she'd end up falling asleep and drowning. Though maybe that would be preferable . . . Startled, she shook herself even harder. What was wrong with her? She was so tired. She didn't remember the journey from France making her so exhausted. And that one had been even longer.

She wondered where Richard was. He'd gone to make sure the horses were groomed and bedded down properly. He acted as though he didn't trust the landlord's grooms to see to the job. Well, maybe he was right. But it was more likely he was down in the common room, talking to the other men. Or listening. He seemed to do a great deal of listening.

She realized with a start that this was a major difference she hadn't even noticed up until this point. The old Richard—at least, that's how she thought of him before the attack—spoke loudly and definitively upon many subjects. This new Richard was far more taciturn. If anything, he'd become a man of very few words, offering an opinion or an observation only if asked. But he was likable, she had noticed that. Where others had drawn back from the old Richard, and deferred to him only out of courtesy to his rank, or out of fear—which was more likely—the new Richard's opinion was usually sought for. But only given if asked for.

She sighed once more and sank down further in the water.

Her long hair floated across the surface, and her nipples broke the surface. She glanced down at her body. They seemed swollen. Gingerly she touched them, and was surprised to feel how sensitive they were. And her breasts felt heavy and full. She sat up with a start, mentally counting back through the days. And then she realized she was with child. Richard's child. A demon's child? She felt cold all over, and she dropped her head on her knees and began to weep.

He found her like that a few minutes later, still sobbing, tears running down her face. He got a towel, and helped her out of the tub, wrapping her in a blanket he pulled from the bed. He held her until her tears stopped and then he whispered, "Can you tell me what's wrong?"

She froze. How could she tell him she was afraid he was possessed by some demon? Maybe he *was* a demon. Who knew what had happened to his soul in the dark hours he'd lain as if dead in the hall? Hugh and Sir Geoffrey had both thought he was dead—everyone had thought he was dead. Maybe he had died, and a demon had stolen into his body. She shut her eyes against such thoughts. He seemed so gentle as he caressed her hair, but didn't the priests say that the devil frequently masqueraded in order to find souls?

"Eleanor?"

She moistened her lips. "I—I'm only tired, Richard." She stumbled over his name. She couldn't even begin to tell him about the child. "Just tired."

He looked at her, forcing her chin up so she looked directly into his eyes. *My God,* she thought, *they are so blue.* "You worry me. I don't want you to get sick. I think this journey has been very hard on you, and I feel very bad about bringing you. I thought you'd like to come with us—spend more time with Hugh—" He broke off and gazed into the fire. Finally he rose, tucking her into the bed. "I'll be downstairs. Would you like something to eat?"

She nodded. She was desperately hungry.

"I'll have a maid send something up."

She nodded again and turned on her side, facing away from him. She heard him sigh deeply, and then the door clicked open. His footsteps faded down the hall, and she slept.

Richard made his way downstairs. The tavern was crowded with travelers, and he found Sir Walter and Hugh among the other men, huddled around a rough-hewn table with barely enough room for their clay mugs. Walter pushed one in his direction. "I took the liberty, my lord."

"Thank you, my friend." Richard raised his mug in Walter's direction and drank deeply.

"Is my sister all right?" Hugh asked, suspicion in his voice.

"She's fine, lad. Tired from the journey. She's not used to riding all day, every day." Richard hoped Hugh would be satisfied with that explanation. He really didn't want the boy challenging him tonight. He was tired, too.

But Hugh's attention had been diverted. He raised his head, and gazed in the direction of the door. More travelers were crowding into the little tavern. As Richard gazed into space, nursing his ale, he saw Hugh's expression change from mild curiosity to one of shocked recognition.

"What is it, Hugh?" he said, as he turned. And then he saw the reason for Hugh's surprise. Giscard Fitzwilliam stood just inside the door, stripping off his gloves, rain dripping off his face. Richard frowned.

"What's he doing here?" whispered Hugh.

Richard shrugged. "He's one of the king's loyal men. Why wouldn't he be here?"

Sir Walter looked over his shoulder, saw Giscard, and made a noise of disgust. "Loyal—ha! Men like that—" he lowered his voice—"are part of the reason His Grace is so unpopular." He shook his head. "Your holdings are not so far from Fitzwilliam's. You must know him."

Richard nodded grimly. "Yes."

"More than knows him," Hugh said. "*He* tried to kill him—"

"Hush!" Richard ordered, as heads turned in their direction. "Enough. Now is not the time."

Sir Walter frowned and spoke in low tones. "Tried to kill who?"

Richard glanced around. The tavern was noisy. "Me."

Sir Walter looked shocked. "You know this for sure?"

"As sure as we—"

"I found an arrow," Hugh said. "It was no Welsh arrow. It was of English make. And it happened twice—"

Richard held up his hands. The boy meant well but it was clear he spoke dangerously. "Not now, Hugh." He spoke in a low, firm voice.

Sir Walter looked from Hugh to Richard and back. "I understand, boy. You have evidence. You should bring this to the marshal's attention."

Richard nodded. "I intend to. But this is not a subject we should discuss here—"

"Where the walls could have ears." Walter finished for him.

"Well, well." The voice made Richard feel as though a cold hand had closed over the back of his neck. "Imagine meeting my good neighbor here."

Richard turned and met Giscard's eyes squarely. "Fitzwilliam. The king needs every loyal man."

Giscard nodded, his little piggy eyes narrowed, and his cheeks flushed red with the cold. Water still trickled from his lank hair. He looked from Richard to Sir Walter and Hugh. "You're well attended, I see, my lord. I hear you even brought your lady wife."

"I didn't want to leave her home. The times are too unsettled to leave a woman alone."

Giscard smiled. "You speak the truth. If you will forgive me, I must see to rooms for my brother and his wife. I'm sure I will see you again soon."

"Soon." Richard agreed. He lifted his tankard once again as Giscard moved off. He looked immediately at Hugh, warning him silently to say nothing. The boy scowled, but remained quiet.

Walter glanced over his shoulder. "It may well be, my lord, that you and your wife would be better served to stay here. This inn is well within riding distance of Windsor—if the castle is overcrowded, you may be offered no more than a place by the hearth. And I think your lady will be more comfortable here."

"Without question," Richard agreed.

"But as for you, my young friend," Walter said, grinning at Hugh, "you'll have a place in my lord William's household. You'll be glad for a place by a hearth, soon enough."

Hugh made a face but said nothing.

Richard smiled to himself. It would be good for the boy to get away from his sister, from the household where he felt himself to be a displaced outsider. He would speak further to the marshal about the marriage negotiations. If it were possible that the Barland demesne could be split in some way— or if some small parcel of land could be provided for Hugh—he wondered how Eleanor would react. He hoped she would be pleased, but in her present state, who knew? She didn't trust him now, that was sure. And how could he tell her the truth? He could think of no other plausible explanation.

He drained his tankard to the dregs, and tapped the table with one hand. "Excuse me. I'm going to check on my lady."

"I'm turning in," said Walter. "You should too, lad. We'll want to be at Windsor as early as possible tomorrow."

Richard nodded. Who knew what tomorrow held? The presence of Giscard Fitzwilliam certainly added a new dimension to this situation he hadn't expected.

Chapter 20

WHEN ELEANOR WOKE up, the sun was streaming across the bed, and there was hardly any evidence that he had ever been in the room. The pillow beside her bore the impression of his head, and a pack on the floor had been opened. But everything else was gone, and for the briefest of moments, Eleanor was afraid. She sat up and scolded herself. She was behaving like a foolish ninny. She should just tell Richard . . . Tell him what? she wondered. She could only imagine their conversation. *Are you possessed, my lord? Indeed, I am, my lady.* She shook her head. If only Ursula had come with her. She could have used the woman's sympathetic ear.

She made her way to the common room after she washed and dressed. The room was quiet, and empty except for one lone lady sitting by the one window. She was bent over an embroidery hoop, and she looked up and smiled when

Eleanor entered. "Good morning." She spoke with an accent that told Eleanor she had been born in southern France.

"And to you, my lady. Is the landlord about?"

"He's here and there and everywhere. Sit. He will be back soon, I'm sure."

As if summoned by the lady's words, the landlord appeared from a door that, by the sounds and smells that escaped from it, clearly led to the kitchens. "Greetings, my lady. Your lord left word that you were to have whatever you willed for breakfast. I have fresh bread and honey and new-made cheese."

Eleanor's mouth watered and her stomach rumbled alarmingly. She remembered she had not eaten dinner. Had Richard brought it up to her? She faintly remembered him gently shaking her, urging her to eat. But she'd been so tired last night, she had slept like one drugged. "That sounds fine," she said.

"Bring it here." The lady gestured to her table. "I would be so grateful for your company, lady. My lord and his brother have ridden off to Windsor, and who knows when they will return?" She pouted prettily.

"My name is Eleanor," Eleanor said, as she sat. "I was educated in Rouen—at the Abbey St. Denys."

"And my name is Marguerite—my husband is Guillaume Fitzwilliam. Ah, you know the name?" The lady saw the shock on Eleanor's face.

"My home—here—I—we have a neighbor by that name. But his first name is Giscard."

"You know my brother-in-law, then!" The lady clapped her hands together, then wrinkled her nose. "He's a pig. I don't like him at all. He's nothing like my Guillaume—nothing at all."

Eleanor smiled cautiously. Lady Marguerite seemed friendly enough, and certainly nothing at all like Giscard herself. But the idea of making friends with a woman who was related to Giscard made her wary. Further conversation was interrupted by the landlord. He placed a platter laden with bread, a jar of honey, and a round circle of cheese before her, as well as a tankard of foamy ale. "Anything else you need, my lady?"

Eleanor shook her head. "Not now. Thank you, sir."

He glanced at Marguerite. "And you, my lady?"

She shrugged. "Passage home, perhaps?"

He looked confused.

"I suppose not," she said. "No matter. Perhaps you will stay and help me while away some time—it seems we've been forever in this barbaric country. Tell me, how do you survive in such a place? Do you not miss Rouen?"

Eleanor hesitated. A week ago, she would have said no. Six months ago, her answer would have been a resounding yes. And now? She smiled and shrugged. "It's a lovely place. The convent—my aunt is the abbess—I was happy there."

"And now? How do you like—your husband's estate?"

Eleanor broke off a bit of bread and dipped it in the honey. "It's lovely there, as well. I was born there."

"Ah." Marguerite raised a delicate eyebrow.

Eleanor could see the questions in the other woman's dark eyes. She busied herself with her food, gesturing to Marguerite. "Would you care for something?"

"Oh, my goodness, no." She laughed a little. "I'm not hungry, only tired of waiting. We never expected to be here this long. The winter came so unexpectedly."

Eleanor sat back, chewing, while the other woman told

her story. There was nothing sinister about Marguerite. She
was bored and homesick, and it certainly was not her fault
that Giscard was her brother-in-law. The morning dragged
on into the afternoon and Richard did not come. The two
women walked outside, but the roads were muddy from yesterday's rain, and the villagers stared at them, and they soon
decided they'd be better off inside.

They shared a meal at noon, and by the time Eleanor had
broken up the last of her gravy-soaked trencher, they were
firm friends. It had been so long since she'd had a woman of
her own rank to talk to, she reflected, as she listened to Marguerite explain how it had happened that she and Guillaume
were married. And it had been so long since she'd had a
woman close to her age as a friend. That was something she
missed about the convent, she realized—the company of the
girls and the younger nuns, who weren't very much older
than the oldest of the girls.

They shared several glasses of wine as well, and the shadows in the courtyard were growing longer. There was still no
sign of Richard. And somehow, by the time the landlord
came in to light the fire in the great hearth, she found herself
confiding in Marguerite about her deep fears concerning
Richard. The other woman listened with a mixture of sympathy and grave concern.

"It is your own soul that is imperiled," she declared, lowering her voice lest the innkeeper overhear. "You must be
very, very careful. Who knows what wickedness he has
worked upon you?"

"But that's just it," Eleanor said unhappily. The faintest
regret about telling Marguerite was beginning to gnaw at
her. "He isn't wicked at all, just different. He's changed so
much, I scarcely think he's the same man at all. But he's not

bad—if anything, he's better than he ever was. Kinder, gentler."

"Ah, but that is just what I am speaking about. The devil doesn't woo us with hellfire. He woos us with honed words and pleasant faces. Do gluttons feast on garbage?" Marguerite waved her hand in the air. "Of course not. They want the finest of tidbits, the savoriest of meats, the sweetest of subtleties. No, no, I think you are right to be concerned. You must talk to a priest."

Eleanor stared. She knew that was the next step, and yet she hesitated to do anything that would make her fears concrete. "You don't think I should just talk to Richard?"

"What good would that do?" asked Marguerite. "He would only deny it, of course." She leaned forward and patted Eleanor's arm. "He may not even realize it. I'm sure he's a good man, at heart. If his body has been invaded by evil, he needs your help. How can he be the man you married without it?"

Well, thought Eleanor, that was part of the dilemma. She really didn't want the man she married. She liked this new Richard. But what if he really were a demon in disguise? Certainly he made her lust for his body. She twisted her hands in her skirts. "I don't know what to do."

"You must pray." Marguerite nodded. "The men are busy. There will be many hours for you to reflect and think about how you can help you husband. It is your duty as his wife to save his soul. I know if you think on it, you will see what I say is true. Perhaps you can ask your husband to send you a priest from the castle. See what he says. If he is angry, or tries to dissuade you, you might think about that. Why would any good man not want his wife to see a priest? But"—she shrugged—"he may be perfectly willing. And

that could be a sign that he is well. So you must think about
this."

Marguerite got to her feet and yawned. "I am going to
rest. We cannot be here when the men start coming in, anyway. Perhaps I shall see you tomorrow?"

"I hope so," Eleanor said. She stood up and hugged her
new friend. "I had forgotten how nice it is to have a friend."

The hour was late when Richard returned to find Eleanor
curled up in the great bed. He undressed and blew out the
one candle. He slid into bed, and touched her cheek tenderly
with one finger. It had been a long time since he'd been so
busy all day, but she had never been far from his thoughts. If
only he knew some way to talk to her. If only he could think
of some way to bridge the gap of time and understanding. It
was impossible for him to imagine that she would possibly
understand him. He sighed and turned on his side, facing
away from her.

The events of the day raced through his mind. Walter had
taken him to William the Marshal, and that spry old soldier
had welcomed him with words of praise for his skillful deal-
ings with the Welsh, as well as words of hope for his counsel in dealing with the recalcitrant barons. And then he'd
met the king.

King John. Dark, thin, but not an unpleasant-looking
man, who reminded him of a peevish client who'd tried his
best to meet the ever-increasing and unreasonable demands
of the opposition. He'd spent most of the day listening, trying to gauge how best to help in the situation. Once or twice,
he'd touched William's arm, and offered a comment or an
observation. And William had smiled, nodding in agreement. John was difficult at times, he saw that immediately.

He had to be cajoled and flattered. But then, thought Richard, in many ways he was in an impossible situation. He truly didn't understand why the barons didn't support his wars, or his causes. He truly believed he was doing his best as king, and that he had every right to impose whatever taxes he pleased, demand whatever services he required.

Richard sighed and turned on his back. Powerful men were like that. And John, a king and the son of kings, was probably the most powerful man he had ever met. Even a judge didn't have the kind of power John wielded. Checks and balances, he thought as sleep overtook him. Checks and balances.

"I want to go to Windsor." Marguerite pouted prettily, watching both her husband and his brother under her long dark lashes. "It's dull. I won't be left behind every day while you men disappear. There's nothing to do but sew."

Guillaume leaned forward and patted his wife's hand. "If you wish, my lady. But I must warn you, Windsor is not so festive either. The king has no time for feasting or other vain pursuits."

Marguerite shrugged. "But at least there are people to talk to. I had nothing to do all day here but talk to the wife of that miserable knight who lives not far from you, Giscard." She sighed, rolling her eyes. "The one you're always talking about—de Lambert."

Giscard narrowed his little eyes. "Oh?"

She shrugged again. "The poor thing thinks he's possessed—and maybe he is for all I know. It was all I heard today. Oh, please, Guillaume, say you'll take me with you tomorrow? It's bad enough we're stuck in this miserable country for another month or more. Please, take me with you."

Guillaume opened his mouth to reply, but Giscard interrupted him. "What do you mean, she thinks he's possessed?"

Marguerite waved her hands airily. "Oh, she thinks he's changed. He speaks in strange tongues sometimes, says things no one understands. She says he isn't at all the man she married." She looked at her husband. "Please, Guillaume? Please say yes."

"Ah, very well, my dear." Guillaume shrugged. "I suppose there are enough ladies there for you to keep yourself occupied. Certainly there's enough going on to keep anyone amused for quite some time. But I'll be busy, you understand. You'll be on your own there—don't look for me to amuse you."

"Humph." Marguerite made a little sound of contempt. "And since when have I ever waited for you to amuse me?" She rose to her feet and gathered her skirts. "I bid you both good night. I'm going to decide what I should wear to court tomorrow." She swept away, her skirts making a loud swish as she passed.

Giscard waited until she'd disappeared up the stairs. He took a deep breath.

"Don't even say it, brother." Guillaume signaled to the serving maid for more ale.

"What do you think I'm going to say?"

"I think you think you have a way to bring de Lambert down. Well, I'm telling you to go slowly and tread carefully. I saw him today—several times, in fact. And each time he was in the company of William the Marshal. They had their heads together on more than one occasion. If he's so close to the marshal, he has a powerful friend, indeed."

"The marshal is his liege lord. He's sworn to—"

"To give counsel? I don't think so. The marshal must trust and respect his judgment, to have him so close at a time like this. Even the king spoke to him. He's not some backwater bumpkin. He's a man who's been noticed. And I would suggest, brother, you tread very carefully where de Lambert's concerned."

Giscard scowled at his brother. "Why so cautious, brother? You had no scruples about marrying Marguerite."

"Marguerite was not the wife of another man, she was already a widow." He took a long quaff of ale. "I think you're being very foolish, Giscard. Surely there are more heiresses in England than one who's already married to a man who has the ear of not only the king but probably the most respected knight in Europe as well."

Giscard gave his brother a long look. This was the sort of thing he had always despised Guillaume for—the way he had of being supportive up to a point, and then turning back and acting as if he'd been against the idea from the beginning. He thought about arguing with Guillaume further, but decided against it. He didn't trust his brother not to go running to the marshal if he thought he could benefit in some way. His brother's opportunism was disgusting. So he shrugged instead and picked up his tankard of ale. "Well, brother," he said, studying the contents of the tankard carefully, pretending to seem lost in thought. "I suppose you have a good point."

"Better to wait until this all settles down. The king will doubtless have rewards for those who remain loyal to him. You will benefit then."

"When are you leaving?" Giscard asked abruptly.

Guillaume shrugged. "Soon. Marguerite is bored—and I am too, if the truth be told. There's no point in staying now. This situation must either resolve itself soon or the country will explode into civil war. And I don't want to be here when that happens. I'm thinking of booking passage as soon as possible."

Giscard nodded, saying nothing. Better to wait, then, until his brother was well on his way to France. A plan was rapidly forming in his mind, a plan that would ensure Richard's downfall more definitely than his murder ever could. A plan Giscard didn't want to fail.

Chapter 21

THE GRAY STONE walls of Windsor rose out of the early morning mist like a castle in a dream. Eleanor jogged along on the little mare behind Richard, silent and slightly nauseous, but determined to say nothing of her discomfort. She didn't dare disclose to him her condition, until, of course, she was sure of what she should do.

He had been solicitous and attentive when they had awoken, inviting her to accompany him to the great castle. "I would have brought you along yesterday," he said as they breakfasted on a loaf of the fresh-baked bread and honey that she'd had yesterday, "but you were sleeping so soundly, I thought it better to let you rest. But if you like, I thought you might enjoy the castle more than this place. It's dull here," he added, almost to himself.

Outwardly Eleanor was calm and quiet, but inwardly she seethed in conflict. Perhaps at Windsor she could speak to a priest, a priest more learned in these matters than Father Alphonse was ever likely to be. She regretted that she would not see Marguerite, although she doubted that Richard would approve of her friendship with a woman who was related, albeit only by marriage, to a man who was his enemy. Momentarily she wondered if perhaps she had misspoken when she'd confided in Marguerite. What if she told Giscard? But then, Eleanor decided, what man would listen to a woman's prattle, anyway? Giscard wasn't her husband, he was only her brother-in-law. And Marguerite had made it clear she cared for him not at all. Her imitations of his table manners had been devastatingly funny.

". . . so you see, it's not so much the specific items that the barons are asking for that is important, it's the very nature of the charter itself," Richard was saying.

With a start, she realized he was talking to her. "Oh, I see," she said, wondering what exactly he was explaining. "I'm afraid I'm not sure I understand."

"Well," he said, frowning a little. "For example, there are a lot of concerns about the fishing weirs along the Thames. These have all been itemized, and each grievance addressed. Who knows, though, exactly how long they can be reinforced?" She only nodded a little, to show she understood, and he continued. "Things such as that aren't really the important issue here, and that's what Lord William and the other men gathered around the king understand. The important issue is the idea that the king does not wield unlimited power, that the power of the king is limited in some way by this thing we call law. And that even the king is answerable before it. You have no idea how much of a difference this is going to make someday, Eleanor. The great charter we are working on will have an effect on the lives of every person born in Britain for hundreds of years, or more. And it's going to be the foundation for ideas that are even greater and more important—concepts such as freedom of the press and speech and—" He broke off. She was staring at him.

She gave him a little smile, wondering what on earth he was talking about. Freedom of the press? What in the world was a press? He almost sounded as if he knew far more than he was telling her. But what, exactly? It was one more item on the long list of differences between the Richard before the autumn and the Richard after it. But this was slightly different. He spoke as if he understood ideas about law and freedom that the man she had married had absolutely no interest in. But it was one thing to have no interest in something, and then to discover one. It was quite another to have acquired knowledge. And how could Richard have acquired this kind of knowledge? He'd been scarcely a week with the marshal—that wasn't long enough. A chill went down her spine. She shut her eyes and said a brief prayer as a wave of nausea washed over her. She prayed that God would keep both her and the child safe.

Richard walked slowly up the narrow stairs that led to the council chamber. He'd seen Eleanor ensconced in the solar with several of the ladies of the court, who welcomed the newcomer enthusiastically. He knew that the ladies were anxious, and for the most part, ignorant of the events that were unfolding around them. But when he tried to talk to Eleanor about what was going on, she seemed largely uncommunicative. He knew he was going to have to talk to her before long. But he'd been so busy with the recent events, so fascinated with the history that was being made every day, that he'd had no time to think of a way to talk to her.

"Richard." Walter extended his hand and Richard shook it. "I'm glad to see you again. Lord William was speaking highly of you last night. You must have made even more of an impression this time."

Since I can speak the language, Richard thought wryly. "I'm glad to be of service. Is there any word from Stanford?"

"No." Walter shook his head. "It's more important right now that we keep the king from losing his temper entirely. He's getting impatient. He wants a resolution here, and it appears to me that—"

"That the other side is deliberately holding out." Richard finished. He hadn't been impressed by the caliber of the men who had been speaking for the barons yesterday. They'd all struck him as contentious men who were more interested in quarreling for quarreling's sake than in any reforms or changes that would benefit them all.

Walter shook his head and sighed. "You're right. That's exactly what's happening. The barons want disunity. They're hoping to push the king so far that he'll be forced to take the field—and that will mean not only civil war, but chaos throughout the whole realm. And that will make all of us vulnerable."

Richard peered over Walter's shoulder. The antechamber of the council room was open, but the inner door was shut. "Who's in there now?"

"The king. Lord William. A few of the others. Stephen Langton is the most reasonable of all the men on the other side, but I doubt the archbishop will be able to keep control indefinitely. Come, let's wait inside." He gestured to the antechamber. The men took seats beside the hearth. The day was warm and Richard was abruptly reminded that spring was the season Lucy had loved best in England. And Eleanor, he wondered. What was her favorite season? And would she care to tell him if he asked.

The door of the council room opened, and William the Marshal peered out. "Ah," he said, his face breaking into a smile. "Richard. I'm glad you're here. Perhaps you can suggest some way to meet this latest demand—without shedding blood, of course."

"Of course, my lord." Richard got to his feet and bowed. It was good to think that the things he knew best could be of some use in this time and place.

"Lady Eleanor!"

The familiar voice took Eleanor by surprise. She looked up, squinted in the bright sunlight, and recognized Lady Marguerite. She smiled. It was good to see her new friend. "Marguerite," she said, as the woman reached her side, "I'm so glad to see you here."

"Well," said Marguerite with a small smile, "I couldn't leave England without seeing the court. And my husband and his brother are so important these days—all this rushing around at court. Giscard was nothing but a soldier, but now to listen to him talk you'd think he was King John's most trusted confidant. As if he would know anything at all about diplomacy."

Eleanor said nothing. She plucked at her embroidery.

"And you, my dear, how are you feeling today? Less upset, I hope? I saw your husband last night in the common room. He is a most delicious-looking man. If I were a devil and bent on possession, I'd surely possess someone who looked like him." Marguerite laughed, but broke off when she saw the stricken look on Eleanor's face. "Oh, my dear,

I'm sorry! I was joking, nothing more. Please, are you all right?"

"Oh," Eleanor said, biting her lip. "I know. I'm just so confused. He's everything you say, and more. But—"

Marguerite patted her hand. "Have you spoken to a priest, child?"

"No. I really didn't think there was anything amiss until we left Barland. And now—"

Marguerite looked around. "Wait here." She got up with a rustle of skirts and took off across the grass. In a few minutes she was back, a black-robed priest in tow. "Father Caedmun, I'd like to present Lady Eleanor de Lambert. She's sorely troubled, Father, and seeks your counsel and advice."

"Oh?" The priest smiled down at Eleanor. He was a man of middle years, his hair a gray fringe around his tonsure. He was clean-shaven, and the fabric of his black robes was of a fine quality of wool. "Can I be of help to you, my lady?"

Eleanor looked from the priest to Marguerite. "Well . . ."

"Talk to him, my dear. You'll feel much better for it." Marguerite smiled and retreated once again.

Eleanor gestured to the empty space on the long bench. "Please, sit down, Father. There is a matter that has been troubling me."

"And does it concern your soul, my lady?"

Eleanor gazed into the priest's bright blue eyes. He seemed much more human and forgiving than stern Father Alphonse ever did. "Not my soul, Father. My husband's."

"Ah." The priest nodded. "Your husband is—?"

"Richard de Lambert."

"De Lambert," the priest echoed with mild surprise. "Indeed."

"You know him, Father?" It was Eleanor's turn to be surprised.

"Ah, he's making quite a name for himself at court. The king is most impressed with his prowess at negotiating—and his ability to turn a phrase. He's had quite a hand in the document they are preparing now, from what I hear. What exactly concerns you about the state of your husband's soul?"

"Father," Eleanor lowered her eyes and blushed. "I—I hope you don't think me silly. But—"

"My dear lady, there's nothing you can tell me about your husband that will shock me or make me think you silly. Does your husband drink excessively? Have an eye for the other ladies? Spend nights gaming, or whoring with his men?"

"Oh, no, Father, nothing like that at all." Eleanor knotted her hands together on her lap. "I—I have reason to think he might be possessed."

The priest said nothing. He looked at Eleanor very carefully. "This is a serious matter, my lady."

"I am serious, Father. That is why I am talking to you."

Father Caedmun nodded. "Well, then, my lady. I suppose you better tell me why it is that you think your husband is possessed."

Haltingly at first, and then with greater confidence, Eleanor told the story of how Richard had miraculously revived after she'd thought him dead, and how he seemed to be an entirely different man since his recovery. She told how Sir John had come to her following the second ambush, adding that she had dismissed him out of hand. "But then, Father," she continued, "I heard him myself. He used words such as I've never heard anyone use. No one at all."

"And how many languages are you familiar with, my

lady?" the priest asked gently. "I am not suggesting that
your concerns are without merit. But is it possible he could
have used a language that you are unfamiliar with—Greek,
say?"

"Father," Eleanor set her shoulders. "I am convent educated. I have heard Greek, though I know it not."

The priest's brow puckered. "Lady Eleanor, I can see that
you are a godly woman. I—I cannot speak on this issue with
any certainty. But it would seem to me that this is best explained by the seriousness of those injuries he suffered in the
autumn. You say yourself that you and everyone else
thought him dead, and that he took months to fully recuper-
ate. Perhaps this evidence of his own mortality was what
Lord Richard needed to change his life. He has been a better husband to you since, has he not?" When Eleanor nodded, the priest went on. "And he is well respected here—by
the king, by the marshal, by all who have met him. I have
even heard his name bandied about the halls by men from
whom respect must be earned."

"But—but what about the strange words?"

The priest spread his hands. "Perhaps the injuries affected
his speech in some way. You said yourself his memory appeared to have been affected. There were things he seemed
to have no knowledge of when he first came to himself. This
is not uncommon. And it is not a sign of demonic possession. Is there anything else about his behavior which troubles you?"

"Well," Eleanor said slowly, "he seems to know things."

"Things? What things?"

"He talks to me about what is going on—and he uses
strange phrases—words I know, but not in the way I use
them. He talked about freedom of speech—and something

else—some phrase I didn't understand at all—'the press.' It made no sense to me. But he says this document, this charter, is tremendously important. He says it will affect the lives of people for hundreds of years to come."

The priest stared at her. His eyes were troubled. "This is not enough to convict him, lady. Does he go to mass? Take the sacraments?"

"When I do. But I have the feeling—"

"What feeling?"

"That he is merely going through the motions."

"Oh, my dear lady." The priest chuckled. "If every knight and lord in England were thought to be possessed because they were merely going through the motions of the mass, nearly all the knights and lords would be in deep trouble." He smiled. "I do not mean to laugh at your convictions, lady. I can see that this has preyed upon your mind greatly. Try to be of ease. I think it likely that he did experience some great change when he was so severely injured. Such things are not uncommon. It might even be that he is injured in some way you cannot see—he does not speak clearly, or certain words are muddled beyond recognition. It is not likely at all that your husband is possessed by the devil."

"But it is possible?"

The priest sighed. "I would be lying if I said it weren't possible. I don't think it's likely." He patted her hand. "I will see what I can learn of these cases. Perhaps there is something I can tell you definitively. In the mean time, be a good wife. Do not provoke him by accusing him unjustly. And wait to see what happens."

Eleanor sighed. Perhaps these thoughts were nothing but the imaginings of a pregnant woman. Perhaps she'd only been silly and judged Richard unjustly. She smiled at the priest, feeling as though a great burden had been lifted off her shoulders. "I thank you, Father. You've been very kind."

"Not at all, my child." His blue eyes twinkled. "Come to me at once if you have any other fears, any other suspicions."

Eleanor glanced away, slightly embarrassed. She was surprised to see Sir Walter's tall figure loping across the grass in her direction.

When he reached her, he bowed. "Lady, Lord Richard sent me to take you back to your lodgings, and to collect a few articles of clothing for him. He goes with the king and Lord William."

"Goes?" Eleanor echoed. "Where is he going?"

"To Runnymede, my lady. It's a meadow not far from here. But there both sides shall meet for the final negotiations. And pray God"—here he broke off and nodded at the priest—"that they make peace. For if they do not, I fear there will be war."

Chapter 22

THE HOUR WAS late and the tavern was dark when Richard rode his horse into the courtyard. A sleepy stable boy stumbled out of the gloom and reached for the reins with a mumble. Richard entered the common room and made his way to the room where Eleanor slept. In the moonlight, he could see her hair spilling out over the pillow. Her bare shoulders gleamed above the sheet. A little breeze blew in from the open window, and she stirred, pulling the sheet higher. He could see the curve of her hip beneath the sheet. A wave of need, and longing, and something else swept over him. She was so achingly vulnerable, and yet there was a core of resourcefulness that surprised him. She was wary of him ever since he'd reacted so indiscreetly. How would she react if—when—he told her the truth?

He undressed slowly, shivering slightly in the late spring night, and slid naked beneath the sheet. Her body gave off a warmth, and he pressed himself against her. In her sleep, she shifted her position, molding herself to the contours of his body. He slipped an arm around her waist, and drew her close, cupping one breast in the palm of his hand. Its warm, familiar weight felt good against his skin. He rubbed the nipple between his thumb and forefinger, and pressed a kiss into the nape of her neck. She stirred once more, and her round bottom pressed against his thighs. He swept the hair off her neck, and showered neck and shoulders with kisses. He heard her breathing quicken, and he raised his head. She turned her head and looked at him.

In the moonlight her eyes were clear and blue. "Richard?" she murmured.

"I'm here." He gathered her in his arms, and gently kissed her mouth.

"You—you've been gone for days."

"I'm sorry. We never thought it would take as long as it did."

She moved her whole body so that she was lying flat on her back. "I'm glad you're here." She wrapped her arms around his neck and pulled his face down to hers, surrendering wholly to him. And as they moved together, Richard was aware of a profound sense of rightness and of wholeness. *Here,* he thought, as their bodies rose and fell in the timeless rhythm of lovemaking, *here is where I am meant to be.*

In the morning, Eleanor woke to find him standing by the window, shaving. He grinned at her when he saw she was awake. "Good morning, my lady."

She smiled back. Her body felt swollen and replete, and the stickiness between her thighs confirmed that they'd made love long into the night last night. "Good morning, my lord." She bit back a giggle. "You look uncommonly happy."

He put down the razor and patted his face dry. "I am, indeed. The great charter is signed, there is peace in the land, I have a beautiful wife, and—" He paused significantly and Eleanor wondered if he might have guessed about the coming child. But his next words startled her all the more. "And I am about to be rewarded for all my time and effort, and Hugh, that young puppy, is about to reap the reward."

"Hugh?" Eleanor sat up and clasped her arms around her knees. "How so?"

"In all the negotiations, I had a chance to speak to Lord William concerning the manor of Rhuthlan. And he agreed that the demesne could be split, especially since it's about to be added to. So I will give Rhuthlan to Hugh and to Angharad as a wedding present. Hugh will not be landless, Angharad will marry Hugh, and there will be peace on the border of Wales. And," he added with a wide grin, "at least I'll know that my nearest neighbor, while he might despise me, is not likely to want to kill me."

"Oh, Richard," Eleanor said, torn between wonder and delight, "Hugh doesn't despise you. He—he's only jealous. But now he'll have nothing to be jealous about and—" She smiled at her husband. How could she have ever been so silly as to think him possessed? Truly she was a lucky woman. Whatever changes he'd gone through as a result of his accident were fortunate changes. "And I cannot quite believe it all."

He came to the bed, picked up her hand and kissed it. "Believe it. It's all true. Now. We must discuss a few other matters as well."

"Oh? Such as?"

"Well, the matter of our going home. You do want to go home, don't you?"

"Of course!"

"That's what I told the king and Lord William."

"They wanted you to stay?"

Richard shrugged. "They made it clear that my presence at court was not unwelcome, and that lodgings could be found for us—adequate lodgings, you understand—not just a blanket by the hearth. But I told them both I thought that you would want to return to Barland. And I didn't want to make any decision without speaking to you first."

"I'm pleased and proud that they want you to stay. But it's true I'd rather go home. If you don't mind."

"Mind?" He pulled her close and hugged her. "My lady, I don't mind at all. There's a great deal to be said about being at court, and there's just as much to be said about not being here. So much intrigue—so many personalities to contend with—I'm sure it would wear on me quickly. I'd rather go"—he paused just for a moment—"home to Barland too." He pressed a kiss on the top of her head. "Now, you get dressed. I'll go down and order our breakfasts, and begin to make the arrangements for our return. I see no reason to linger here any longer than is necessary."

He bounded out of the room, whistling beneath his breath. Eleanor leaned back against the pillows and froze. That tune—what was it? It didn't sound like anything she'd ever heard. Nonsense, she told herself. The priest was right when he'd suggested that she wasn't familiar with all the languages in the world, even all the ones Richard could have heard in his travels in the East. And after all, she was being ridiculous if she heard devils in a harmless tune. The man was happy, for heaven's sake. And he was trying to make her happy. Hadn't he even told the king and his liege lord that he would have to talk to her before he would consider staying at court? And hadn't he even told them he would prefer to go back to Barland, knowing that that was likely her preference?

She got out of bed. Her belly was still flat, but her breasts were definitely swollen. Her nipples looked darker too. She would have to tell Richard soon. He would notice soon enough if she didn't. It was good to think that they would be home long before the birth. Ursula would be thrilled to know that there was going to be a new generation for her to diaper and care for and love. She dressed as quickly as possible, and went down to the common room to find Richard.

He was sitting at a table near the window, a pitcher of milk and a loaf of brown bread before him. A serving maid placed a small wheel of cheese before him. "I'm sorry, my lord, there's no honey, but we have new berries just picked. Would you like some of those?"

He nodded and smiled when he saw Eleanor, rising to his feet as she approached. "You look as though the night's rest agreed with you, my lady."

"It wasn't the rest I got last night that agreed with me, my lord." She took a seat across from him.

He bowed and sat down. "May I pour you some milk?"

Her mouth watered. "Certainly."

The maid came back with bowls of strawberries, red and plump and bursting with juice. Richard cut the bread into halves with his knife, and they ate contentedly, while he told her all that had happened since he'd been gone. "And Hugh," he said. "You wouldn't know him. All dressed in William's livery, he looks five years older already. He'll be home sooner than you'll believe, Eleanor. We'll see him before we go. I think you'll be pleased."

"As will he, when you tell him the news." Eleanor popped the last of the red berries in her mouth. She reached for Richard's hand. "Thank you."

"Thank you? What for?" He grasped her hand in his and held it tightly. "Hugh's my brother, too, after all. And if he wants to be married to a Welsh hellion, he's better off sticking close to home."

She laughed. "That's not all I meant."

He met her eyes. His gaze was so piercingly serious it took her breath away. "I know, my love." He said nothing more, but their eyes held for a long moment. Then he squeezed her hand gently and released it. "I'll send word—" He broke off and looked out the window as the sound of many horses pounding into the innyard interrupted the quiet morning.

Eleanor half rose, peering outside. Soldiers, all dressed in the colors of the king, were dismounting. They strode into the tavern and paused, blinking.

Then one spoke. "Lord Richard de Lambert?"

"Yes?" Richard rose to his feet. "I am de Lambert."

"We have a warrant for your arrest, sir. You're to come with us at once."

"Arrest?" Richard demanded, even as Eleanor stared from the soldiers to her husband in dismay.

"For what?" she said.

"You're to be detained until the charges against you can be resolved, my lord."

"What are the charges?" Richard barked.

Eleanor stared at him. He sounded like the old Richard now. His shoulders were rigid and his mouth was a thin, tight line.

"Possession, my lord," answered the soldier. "You've been charged with consorting with demons."

Eleanor slumped to the floor as the world spun away into darkness.

Chapter 23

"WHAT IS THE meaning of this?" William, Marshal of England and Earl of Pembroke and Striguil, strode into the council chamber accompanied by six of his knights. He planted his feet at the end of the table and stared his king in the eye.

On the opposite side of the room, John looked up from his chess game. "My lord earl. I thought I'd see you soon."

"I haven't disappointed you then, Your Grace." William glared at the king. "May I know the meaning of this outrage against one of my most trusted vassals?"

John sat back in his chair and folded his hands over his chest. "Come and sit, William."

William did not move. "I want to know why you've had Richard de Lambert arrested and charged with this ridiculous crime. The man was nothing but a help to us all in the last weeks, and now you turn on him? Why, Your Grace? I have a right to know why."

John motioned to William. "Then come, sit. And I'll explain it to you."

Across the table, Giscard Fitzwilliam got to his feet, and picked up the board. "Shall we finish later, Your Grace?"

John nodded. "Of course. But you must stay, Giscard. The earl has questions for you, too."

With a brief shrug, Giscard placed the chess board on the table, and bowed to the earl. "My lord earl."

"Who are you?" barked William.

"Giscard Fitzwilliam, my lord."

William eyed Giscard up and down, his lip curled with scorn. His gaze slid back to the king, who lounged beside the fire. He was tempted to speak his mind to the king, but John was flushed with victory. In this mood, the king was often capricious and given to sudden changes. And the delicate peace just forged was not something William cared to risk disturbing. He walked with measured paces to the chair Giscard had just vacated and sat down. "Now." His voice was dangerously calm. "Why has one of the most trusted of my vassals been hauled off to prison like a common thief?"

John looked uncomfortable. "We can't have rumors like this one flying around, William."

"And what rumors are these, Your Grace? Exactly what are we talking about?"

John's dark eyes slid over to Giscard. He stirred from his position at the table and cleared his throat. "Possession, my lord. There's reason to believe that de Lambert is possessed."

William looked shocked, and then he began to laugh. "You're joking, right? This is an attempt to be funny."

John shrugged, saying nothing.

"Ah, no, my lord." Giscard looked distinctly uncomfortable. "Not at all."

William crossed his long legs at the knee. "Oh? And what exactly is the nature of the evidence against him?"

"He's been heard to use strange words in a language no one knows. He's been heard to hum strange songs and tunes beneath his breath when he believes no one is listening—he revived when everyone thought him dead—"

"These are not charges, Your Grace!" William leaped to his feet. "How can you listen to such nonsense? Richard de Lambert was one of the most useful men to you in these last weeks. How could you so carelessly, callously use him this way?"

"It was his own wife who made the charge," said the king. "Is that not so, Giscard?"

"His wife?" William looked shocked. "I saw her once or twice at Windsor. She's the one who said these things?"

"There are others who have heard it. His own men. There are questions, William." John stared the other man in the eye.

"I cannot believe this is true."

"But is it not true that de Lambert distinguished himself as he never had before?" John asked. "I've known of him for some time—he was never a man of words and peace. He was a man of action, who lived by the sword. And died by it, too."

"Is it not possible that de Lambert was dead, my lord?" put in Giscard. "And when he revived, it was with a demon's spirit?"

"Faugh." William spat into the fire. "You speak nonsense."

"We shall see," said the king.

William shifted his gaze to Giscard, pinning him against the table. "This makes no sense at all." He got to his feet. "I see you are set on this, Your Grace. I want to talk to de Lambert, at least. Do you agree?"

"Of course, William." John looked a little relieved that the interview was over. "Talk to him as much as you like. You might see for yourself why he's been accused."

William glanced from the king to Giscard and back again. "I shall speak to you again on this, Your Grace." With a brief bow, he stalked out of the council chamber.

John turned to Giscard. "You'd better be right about this, my friend. This de Lambert endeared himself to William rather quickly. It isn't quite as simple as you thought it would be, is it?"

Giscard shrugged. "Leave it to me, Your Grace. I wasn't the one who raised the question. It was his own wife. And there are others who can testify. I promise."

John pursed his lips. "We will see, my friend. We will see."

The tall shadow that fell across Eleanor's shoulder startled her. She turned, a wild, half-formed hope that it was Richard making her heart pound. She was even more surprised by the man who stood before her.

William the Marshal bowed with courtly grace, his face grave. "Lady Eleanor."

She got to her feet unsteadily, twisting her hands in the fabric of her gown. Her eyes were swollen with weeping, and she knew her skin was pasty from the long sleepless night. "My lord." She dropped a careful curtsey.

"Sit down, lady." His voice was sad, and he sighed. "May I sit?"

"Of—of course, my lord. You have no need of my permission."

He gave her a sad smile. "I came to you as soon as I heard the news, my lady. I've already spoken with the king."

"And what does he say?" Eleanor said eagerly. "Does he understand how ridiculous these charges are?"

William looked even more grave. "He does not. John is superstitious. His relationship with the Church has been even thornier than his own with his barons, if such a thing were possible. He dare not offend the pope. And with this recent unrest—well, let us just say John will be more than happy to lay the blame on someone else's door. And if he can work the devil into it in some way, all the better."

"So you're saying the king wants to believe that Richard is possessed by a demon? And that he is the cause of the barons' rebellion?"

William sighed once more. "I don't want to go that far, lady. But John is ever looking over his shoulder and under his bed for scapegoats. He doesn't shoulder responsibility well. He never did." William spoke with a bitter twist.

"Have you seen Richard? Will you speak to him?"

"I will, lady. But there is something I wanted to ask you about first."

Eleanor looked down.

"The king says that you were the one who raised the issue of possession—you and some of Richard's own men. Is this true? Do you believe him to be possessed?"

The marshal's steady gray gaze bore into hers. She clenched her hands in her lap to keep them from trembling. There was nothing to do but to tell him the truth. She

straightened her shoulders. "Did you know my husband before—before you met him in the autumn?"

William shrugged. "More by reputation. I met him when
he swore fealty to me, of course, after your marriage to him.
And I saw him once or twice campaigning. He was an able
and worthy knight. I have to say his reputation did not at all
match the man."

"The man you met in the autumn at Pembroke?"

"Yes. The man I met at Pembroke was not what I was expecting, that is very true."

Eleanor swallowed hard. "He's nothing like the man I
married, either." William looked at her curiously and she
hesitated.

"I knew your grandfather and your father, lady. They were
good and honest men. I hope I served them well as their
liege lord. I will do my best for you, as well. Please, try to
tell me everything. As best you can."

She saw real concern and sympathy in the piercing eyes.
"After Richard was attacked by the Welsh in September, he
was brought back to Barland in very serious condition. We
thought—I thought—he was dead." Slowly, haltingly,
Eleanor told the story of how Richard had miraculously revived under the hand of the priest, how he had slowly re-
gained strength. And how he had apparently radically
changed from a brute and a bully to someone who was kind
and considerate, loving and tender. She shook her head at
last. "I heard these words, you see. Words I couldn't understand. I realize now how foolish I was to think ill of my husband, but, my lord"—she grasped his arm—"he was nothing
like the man I married. Nothing at all. And—" She broke
off. "I was foolish. I was wrong."

"Ah, well, lady." William patted her hand. "You aren't the

first wife to swear her husband's possessed, I'm sure. But usually the behavior is a little more outrageous than that which your lord has exhibited."

"But that's it, you see," Eleanor said. "He was so—so different. And he seems to know things in ways he never knew them before. He talks about peace and law and justice—I've never heard anyone, even priests, talk about such things."

William nodded, considering. "He does have a grasp of concepts and ideas that I have never been able to express to anyone else. But an intuitive grasp of statesmanship does not a demon make." He patted her arm once more. "At least I understand now. You were frightened and confused by the changes you saw in your husband. Did you speak to your priest?"

"Not to the priest at Barland, no. But I did speak to one here. And he was reassuring. He suggested that perhaps Richard's injuries affected his speech in some way. He said such things have happened before."

William nodded. "That is very true. But now the task at hand is to get these charges dismissed so you can return to Barland with your husband."

Her hand crept to her belly. Home to Barland. The words echoed in her mind. What if they never returned to Barland together again?

"My lord, there's something else you need to know. My brother, Hugh—he believes that it wasn't the Welsh who attacked my husband in September."

William raised one eyebrow. "Oh? And who does he think is responsible?"

"A man named Giscard Fitzwilliam. I was foolish enough to confide my fears about Richard to his sister-in-law."

The marshal narrowed his eyes. "And why would this Fitzwilliam attack your husband?"

"He wanted Barland. He bid for the wardship when my father died. You were on the Continent at the time. But Richard outbid him and even though Fitzwilliam is a close friend of the king—"

"Money is far dearer to John's bosom than the best of his friends," William finished. He got to his feet. "It all makes much more sense now. Well, lady, I shall speak to your brother and to your husband. And in the meantime, try to rest. You look as though you haven't slept at all."

She shook her head. "I have not."

"Have you friends here? Women you can rely on?"

She shrugged. "No one, really."

He shook his head. "I shall see if one or two of my wife's friends are among the ladies here. You shouldn't be alone."

"Thank you, my lord."

"And I'll see you're lodged at Windsor. At least you and he can be under the same roof." He bowed once more over her hand and left her brooding again.

He found Hugh in the practice yard, drilling with the other squires. At the sight of the marshal, the young men broke out in ragged applause. He smiled and waved, and gestured to an astonished Hugh.

"I want to speak to you, Hugh."

Hugh flushed. "I—I'm honored, my lord."

William ignored the boy's nervousness. "I want you to tell me all you can about a certain Giscard Fitzwilliam."

"I hate him," Hugh burst out. "He's—"

"Hush, lad." William cut him off. "You have to learn to cool that temper. It's all well and good to hate a man, but you need to be able to think about him first. Why do you hate him? Because he bid for your sister's wardship?"

"That—and he's a lying, two-faced, hypocritical swine—"

"Enough." William held up his hand. "Why do you believe he attacked de Lambert in the autumn? Did you see him?"

"No," Hugh shook his head. "But I found an arrow just before the Welsh found me. That's why I was there, you see. I had the feeling it wasn't the Welsh. They attacked us but didn't pursue us. I wasn't hurt at all—it was clear to me, thinking about it later, that the object of the attack was Richard. And it was raining that day, we were swathed in cloaks. Unless you absolutely knew who to look for, it would have been difficult to focus that clearly on one man. Do you see?"

William nodded. "Yes, I do. Go on. Tell me about this arrow."

"It was no Welsh arrow. I know their make—everyone does on the marches. It was one of our kind. And I only found one that day—considering all the ones that had been shot, so someone was careful to go and retrieve them. Even the broken ones."

"Ah." William nodded.

"And then, when I was held by Llewellis, I got to know him. And he denied ever attacking Richard, even though he admitted he would have liked to, for reprisal against what Richard did to one of his father's men in the spring."

William frowned. "This coil grows more complicated. What did Richard do in the spring?"

Hugh shrugged. "Killed one of their chieftain's sons. He destroyed a village the day we were attacked. That's what made us all think it was the Welsh, you see."

William shook his head. "Hmm. So somewhere between the time he was wounded and the time he met with me, Richard apparently reversed his previous policies regarding the Welsh?"

Hugh shrugged again. "I wasn't there. I don't know what happened. He's damn different, that's all I know. I almost like him now."

William smiled wryly. "I see. You've heard, I suppose?"

"About his arrest? Everyone's heard." Hugh glanced at his fellow squires over his shoulder. "Everyone's asking me."

"Asking you what?"

"If it's true."

"And what do you tell them?"

"I say he's no worse a devil than any other man I ever met."

William shook his head. "As good an answer as any, young man. It seems that everyone is all agreed on one thing. Richard's recovery changed him in some way. He's not the same man he was."

"No, he's not." Hugh glanced around. "I know Eleanor likes him now—and she never used to before. But even she doesn't know some things. He fights differently now, too."

"His wounds—"

"More than that." Hugh shook his head. "Only a man who's fought him would know this. Geoffrey de Courville—Richard's second-in-command—he knew it. He kept quiet about it, though. I think he put it down to Richard's wounds. But I practiced with him after Geoffrey's death, after I was returned to Barland. Long after he was healed. And he's different. Not so sure. Certain things he used to do, he never does anymore. His stance has changed, his grip has changed—"

"All these things are possibly connected to the physical injuries, lad." William shook his head. "You can't condemn someone based on that, especially not someone who's been so badly injured. You'll see." He gave Hugh a knowing look. "All right, lad. Back to your drills. This evening, you may attend your sister. I'm arranging for her to be here at Windsor, at least until this nonsense is settled. Until then, you're excused from your duties. I think she needs you now more than I do."

Hugh bowed. "Thank you, my lord."

William watched a moment longer as Hugh rejoined his fellows. There was no doubt that de Lambert had changed in the course of his recovery. But by all accounts, he was now a far better man than he had ever been before. Perhaps he was asking questions about the wrong man. The more closely he looked, the more it was clear that Giscard Fitzwilliam was at the bottom of this coil.

Chapter 24

THE COURT WAS crowded. Men and women and even children crowded the perimeter of the great hall at Windsor Castle, and even the musician's gallery was crammed full of eager spectators. Eleanor sat on a chair to the left of the king's raised dais, gripping the arms and wondering how she would endure the coming ordeal. Several black-robed priests conferred on the opposite of the room, and every now and then one glanced in her direction. Father Caedmun sat by her side. He murmured reassurances every time that happened.

Finally she turned to him. "Father, how can this be proved?"

The priest blinked. "In truth, my lady, this is a tricky and dangerous area. This inquiry is only the beginning. There must be enough evidence for the bishop to recommend a trial. Ordinarily, that would be to the Archbishop of Canterbury. But in this case, since the archbishop himself will be here, I think matters will proceed somewhat more quickly. Though maybe not as quickly as my lady would like."

Eleanor sighed. It seemed she'd done a great deal of sighing in the last week. Hugh patted her hand. "Try not to worry, Eleanor. If there's nothing to this, the king and the bishop will see it."

She smiled weakly at her brother. She wished she could believe that. But the king was rapacious and aching to teach the barons a lesson, and as for the archbishop—she'd heard that Stephen Langton was a man of God, but who knew what they would make of all this? "What will happen, Father?"

"They'll bring your husband in, of course. He'll hear the charges, and then witnesses will be called to testify before the bishop. And if they think there's just cause to continue, the archbishop will order that he be examined more thoroughly. By the priests. Privately, of course."

Fear clutched at Eleanor's heart, and she made a little noise.

"Lady, there's nothing to fear. Your husband is a godly man. As long as he can say his Commandments and his paternoster, he'll be fine."

"My—my husband is not a learned man, Father," Eleanor said miserably. "He had no real schooling in anything but war."

Caedmun smiled at her reassuringly. "The archbishop knows that. Be easy, lady."

Eleanor closed her eyes, mentally trying to gather her strength. A blast of trumpets announced the entrance of King John and the Archbishop of Canterbury. Eleanor struggled to her feet. Hard at their heels followed the marshal, looking tired and grim. He caught Eleanor's eye as he took a seat to the right side of the dais and smiled at her. She tried to smile back, but she felt her eyes fill with tears. She clutched Hugh's hand.

"It's all right, Eleanor," he whispered, trying to console her. "Please don't worry."

"I want to believe that, Hugh," she whispered back. "I do."

She took a deep breath as the king and the archbishop conferred briefly. "Bring in the accused," the king said.

There was a rustle and murmur and then the voices of the crowd rose as a ripple ran through the assembly. There was the tramp of measured footsteps, and then the people at the front of the crowd parted. Richard, escorted on either side by six armed men, stepped before the dais. He glanced around, and saw Eleanor.

Eleanor felt her heart stop in her chest. He looked so tired, so worn. He was clean-shaven, but his hair needed a good cutting. It curled in little tendrils on his shoulders and around his ears. Those curls made him look vulnerable, she thought, noting the deep shadows beneath his eyes, and the way his skin was pale. His clothes were clean enough, though, and he didn't look as though he'd been mistreated in any way. His hands were bound in front of him. She wanted to run across the little space between them, throw herself into his arms and beg his forgiveness. But there was already forgiveness in his eyes, forgiveness and love. Her eyes filled with tears and she blinked.

"Lord Richard de Lambert, do you know the charge for which you must answer today?" The king was speaking.

Richard looked up at the king. He met the king's eyes fearlessly. "I'd like to hear it, Your Grace."

The king shrugged. "Read the charge."

An officer of the court stepped forward. "Lord Richard de Lambert, you stand accused of consorting with demons, of allowing a demon to possess your body, and of assorted crimes against our Holy Mother, the Church."

"How do you answer the charge, Lord de Lambert?" asked John.

"They're absurd." Richard looked at the priests with contempt and beside Eleanor, Father Caedmun made a little warning noise. Richard glanced in that direction. He pressed his lips together. "I deny every one."

"So you say you have not consorted with demons or allowed one to possess your body at any time?"

"Never, Your Grace."

The king glanced at Stephen Langton, who was watching Richard expressionlessly. "Well?"

The archbishop looked over at William the Marshal. "The accused has answered the charge. Let the witnesses commence."

Eleanor gasped in astonishment as the first witness pushed his way before the dais. Sir John Longshanks glanced at her with apology on his face before he turned and faced the king. "Do you swear to tell the truth as you imperil your immortal soul?"

"I do, Your Grace."

"What have you to say in this matter?"

"I've known Lord Richard in the time since he's come to Barland, Your Grace. In early December, as we were returning from Lord William's castle in Pembroke, we were attacked. And I heard Lord Richard speak in strange tongues. He fought as if another man was in his body."

"As if another man were in his body, Sir John?" Stephen Langton leaned forward. "Could you explain that?"

"Ah, he fought well enough, I am not saying he didn't. But he didn't fight the way I've seen him fight. I've had plenty of chances to see him. He was . . . not himself, that's all."

"And what did you hear him say?"

"I can't repeat the language. I don't know the words. But when someone was attacked, he would shout something at them. And I heard him call things several times—and then he'd repeat them in our tongue—almost like he was remembering he had to speak to us."

Eleanor glanced at Richard. He stood still, his hands clasped together in their bonds. His eyes were fastened on Sir John and it was impossible to read the expression on his face.

"And were there others who heard these things as well?"

"Oh, yes, Your Grace. All of the men did. I brought three of them with me—the others were needed back at Barland. But they will all swear to the truth of what I say." He looked down at his boots. "If it pleases the court, I would like to say—"

King John opened his mouth and the archbishop held up his hand. "Yes, Sir John? What else would you like to say?"

"Lord Richard did no harm to anyone. He was recovering from grievous wounds. If he fought differently, I put it down to that."

The archbishop gave the knight a long look, glancing briefly at Richard. Then he nodded. "Very well, Sir John. Thank you for that statement. Next?"

To Eleanor's horror, there were another four witnesses— a groom, a maid, and two soldiers—all of whom had heard Richard's outburst on the day the piglets had made the horses rear up. They were clearly intimidated by the court, but their testimony seemed damning enough to her. Then Marguerite stepped forward, and keeping her face averted from Eleanor, she told the story of how Eleanor had confided her fears in her. Eleanor bit her lip, desperately fighting for control. She couldn't bear to look at Richard.

And then it was Giscard who stepped forward, with the most damning testimony of all. "I saw de Lambert in the woods," he said. "He performed strange ceremonies, and lit a fire to a pagan shrine."

"That's a lie," Richard bellowed. He'd held his tongue all through the morning, and finally could stand no more. Giscard said nothing, but only met his eyes fearlessly.

Stephen Langton looked from one man to the other. "And when did this take place?"

"I saw it many times, Your Grace. Ever since Lord Richard came to Barland. He found the pagan shrine and worshiped there regularly. I saw him bring small animals and kill them there."

"That's a lie," cried Richard again, struggling in his bonds. The soldiers physically restrained him, and Eleanor wanted to rush to Fitzwilliam and attack him herself. Even Hugh scowled and cursed beneath his breath.

The hall was in a tumult, voices rising excitedly and the crowd shifted en masse as everyone tried to get a better look at the accused and his accuser.

Stephen Langton glanced at the king. "All right, my lord. You made your statement. Have you anything else to say?"

Giscard looked at Eleanor. "Nothing, Your Grace. Except that I tried to warn Lady Eleanor repeatedly. But she seemed besotted by her husband, and firmly in his thrall. She would have no time for me."

Eleanor stared at Giscard in horror.

"You lying, foulmouthed—" Hugh began.

"Hush, my son," cautioned Father Caedmun.

William the Marshal looked disgusted at Giscard's blatant perjury, and even Stephen Langton looked askance. "Very well, my lord. Thank you. You may step down."

Giscard bowed to the court, and with exaggerated courtesy to Eleanor. Her stomach twisted in revulsion and she thought she might vomit.

"Who's next?" asked the archbishop. His mouth was set in a narrow line and he looked as though he'd heard enough.

The officer looked at Eleanor. "The court calls Lady Eleanor de Lambert."

There was a gasp. Father Caedmun rose to his feet. "I beg the court's indulgence, but the lady cannot be compelled to testify against her husband."

Richard closed his eyes.

"She's not being asked to testify against him," the king replied. "This is not a trial. This is only an inquiry to determine if there should be a trial. She may speak."

Stephen Langton looked at Eleanor. "Lady," he said, and his voice was unexpectedly gentle. "Have you had concerns regarding your husband's soul?"

"I—I did." She glanced at Richard. His head was down and he looked defeated.

"And did you speak to a priest?"

"I spoke to Father Caedmun."

"And what did he tell you?"

"That my fears were unfounded. That the changes I noticed in my husband could be attributed to the seriousness of the injuries he suffered in the autumn. And that I should not worry."

The archbishop nodded. "Thank you, my lady." He

glanced around. "I would like some time to confer with my advisors before I pronounce in this matter." He rose to his feet and Giscard Fitzwilliam burst through the crowd.

"I demand a trial by combat!"

The archbishop looked down his nose at the man before him. "What?"

"If he's innocent, let him prove it to us all. If he's not, God will give me the victory and send his soul to hell."

There was a general roar from the crowd and the men on the dais glanced at each other. The marshal leaned forward, a dangerous look on his face, and the king spoke in the archbishop's ear. The two men appeared to exchange a few sentences and then the archbishop motioned to William. The three men conferred briefly. William shook his head violently once or twice. He leaned toward John and spoke rapidly. Langton stepped between the two men, a hand on both their chests. He said something to each man, and finally William shrugged and stepped back, shaking his head. He strode off the dais without a backward glance and Eleanor stared after him in dismay.

The Archbishop of Canterbury stood on the edge of the dais. He raised his hands for silence. "Good people. The judgment of the court is this. Three days hence, this inquiry will be placed in the hands of God. At the tenth hour on that morning, Richard de Lambert and Giscard Fitzwilliam will meet upon the field of honor. And there the Lord himself shall judge in this matter. May God have mercy on their souls." He crossed himself, sketched a rapid blessing over the crowd, and strode off the dais after William.

Eleanor sank onto her bench, her shoulders shaking. Trial by combat? The crowd surged forward, and the guards closed around Richard.

"Come," Father Caedmun spoke urgently. "We've got to get her out of here."

Somehow, leaning on her brother, Eleanor managed to escape the pressing crush of bodies. They brought her to the small suite of rooms William had found for her, not far from his own apartments. She stood before the hearth, staring into the empty grate, still unable to comprehend all that she'd heard.

"Eleanor?" Hugh held out a goblet of wine. "Here. Drink this."

Automatically she swallowed it. He refilled it and she swallowed that too.

"Easy, boy," said Father Caedmun. "We don't want the lady drunk."

She looked at the priest and laughed. "Drunk? That doesn't sound like such a bad idea. If I'm drunk at least I won't know. I won't know if my husband's dead. I won't know if Giscard has his way—I won't have to know—" Her laughter dissolved into tears. She sank to her knees on the worn rug. "It's my fault, all my fault, don't you see? If I hadn't said those things to Marguerite, Giscard would never have known." Tears ran down her cheeks and her whole body shook.

Father Caedmun glanced helplessly at Hugh. "My lady, my lady, please don't take on so. There's no need to blame yourself."

"Fitzwilliam was looking for a way to bring Richard down, Eleanor," said Hugh. "It's not much comfort maybe, but it's true. You meant nothing by it. I know he's changed, everyone's noticed it. And who is to say Giscard wouldn't have tried this one, anyway?"

"But all the things he said," Eleanor protested. "They're

all lies. Richard never worshiped any pagan idol—there aren't any on Barland."

"Oh," said Hugh, looking embarrassed. "But there is. There's a cairn about an hour's ride or so, near the Welsh border. I've been there myself."

"Hugh!" Eleanor looked shocked. "How can you have done such a thing?"

"I didn't say I was worshiping there, Eleanor. I said I found it. Where do you think I was all the time I was avoiding Richard and his henchmen?"

Eleanor sighed. She got to her feet. "I—I need to rest, I think."

Father Caedmun nodded. He looked relieved. "You do that, my lady. I will look in on you later." He patted her hand. "The Lord will prevail here, I promise you. Have faith." The priest was gone with a soft swish of robes.

Hugh looked at Eleanor. "Shall I leave you, too?"

"No, you stay, Hugh." Eleanor looked at her brother. She didn't trust him not to go after Giscard and attack him. And that would be a terrible mistake. She rubbed her temples. "Do you remember when you were younger, and you used to brush my hair?"

He grinned, looking embarrassed. "Of course I do. Would you like me to do that now?"

"Yes."

He got her brushes and she sat before the fire, her arms wrapped around her knees. She sighed as he drew the brush slowly through her long hair. "I'm sorry, Eleanor."

"For what?"

"De Lambert was a beast of a man. He's changed, and I'm afraid I wasn't very nice to him after I came back from Wales."

"No, you weren't," she agreed.

"Or to you." Hugh hesitated and went on. "But the real enemy is Giscard. He always was. I guess I lost sight of that. And I'm sorry."

Eleanor closed her eyes. *Please God,* she prayed, *spare Richard and keep him safe. Be with him in his hour of need.* If only she could see him, talk to him. He hadn't looked as if he were angry with her today. But she missed him. She missed him terribly. She hadn't even told him about the child. The thought of spending the rest of her life without him made her drop her head to her knees and weep slow, sad tears.

Richard sat on the narrow cot that served as his bed. He'd paced the confines of the small room endlessly in the last weeks, and now all he could feel was confusion and exhaustion. Trial by combat? He'd hoped that this morning they'd let him speak. He thought this morning that perhaps he'd have a chance to answer his accusers with accusations of his own. But William the Marshal had warned him he probably wasn't going to be given much of a chance to say anything. Except to lose his temper when the ridiculous charges were read.

But this was the thirteenth century, and there was no doubt that the charges weren't considered absurd at all. No more absurd than the idea that the matter could be resolved with swords. He rubbed his wrists where the bonds had rubbed his skin raw. Swords. Armor. Fighting. He wasn't the best fighter at all. Sir John knew it. What would Geoffrey de Courville say if he'd been alive to testify? Geoffrey was loyal, but he would be compelled to tell the truth. And the truth was—the old Richard *hadn't* just changed. He was gone.

There was a stir at the door and he got to his feet. He was surprised to see William the Marshal enter. In the last weeks, William had visited him twice. "My lord."

William looked grim. "I'm sorry, Richard."

"It isn't your fault."

"I wish I'd known the extent of Giscard's envy. I'd no idea he'd go this far."

"Neither did I," said Richard.

"That doesn't matter now. Can you be ready to fight in three days?"

"I have to be," answered Richard. "Or nothing will matter."

William met his eyes and held them. "I won't let Giscard win this, you know that. You need have no worries on that score. Barland won't fall into his hands—or your wife, either. If I have to marry her myself."

Richard gave a wry smile. "My thanks."

William eyed him up and down. "I suppose I would like to ask you one thing, though. By all accounts, you have changed. You aren't the man you used to be. Can you account for why?"

Richard hesitated. He respected William tremendously. In the last weeks, he'd also come to like him. But there was no way he was going to trust his secret to a man who saw trial by combat as a reasonable means of dispute resolution. "I was a long time recovering from my injuries, my lord." He chose his words carefully. "I could scarcely speak. And in that time, I had to listen. I did not like what I heard when people spoke to me. I realized I was feared, hated, even. My wife jumped every time I looked at her. I was not proud of the man I was. I decided to try and be better."

William nodded. "I remember your speech well—or lack of it—at Pembroke. These injuries of yours concern me, though. How badly have they affected you?"

Richard wondered how to answer. He thought he'd fought well when the party had been attacked upon their return from Pembroke. But then, maybe he hadn't. He'd come out of it alive. "I walked away from combat alive," he said aloud. "I suppose my injuries haven't affected me that badly."

William nodded. He put his hands on his hips and paced to the window. "That may be something to your advantage, actually. Every fighter has a style, and yours was well known. Giscard is not known to me at all, but if I know anything at all about bullies like him, he'll be out practicing at this very moment. I'll have some of my men give him a bout. I'll see what they can tell me about him. Have you ever faced him?"

Richard hesitated. He had no way of knowing the answer. "I don't know, my lord. My injuries affected my memory of some things. I don't recall."

William raised his eyebrows. "I see. So that is sure to account for some of these differences in you too."

Richard nodded. "I do not like to admit weakness, my lord."

William gave him a long look. "Sometimes admitting weakness is the greatest strength." He walked to the door and paused, hand on the latch. "Is there anything you would like?"

"I'd like to speak to my lady, if I could."

William nodded. "I tried to arrange that before. I'll insist

on it now. Be of good heart, son." With another nod, he was
gone.

Richard sank down onto the bed. The greatest strength. It
was time to admit his weakness to Eleanor. Or at least, to tell
her the truth.

Chapter 25

THE LATE AFTERNOON slanted across her chair. Eleanor looked up from her sewing. Hugh was lying on the hearth rug, staring at the ceiling, an abandoned chess board beside him. The past twenty-four hours had been uneventful. She felt as if time were moving like a sluggish river, hour by hour, minute by minute, all winding down inexorably to the morning of the day to come. She closed her eyes and tried not to imagine Richard dead. There was a knock on the door, and she looked up.

"Probably that priest," Hugh muttered. He got to his feet. "I'll get it."

Eleanor smiled. Father Caedmun had been kind. He'd come yesterday afternoon at this time, and then again this morning. They'd prayed together, and he'd heard her confession. With absolution, her heart seemed lighter. Hugh opened the door. A stranger in the livery of William the Marshal stood there. "My lady de Lambert," he began. "Come with me, if you will?"

"Of—of course," Eleanor said. She got to her feet, and put her sewing aside. "But where?"

The servant bowed. "My lord the marshal has arranged a visit with your husband. Will you come?"

"Hugh, stay here," she said. She eagerly followed the man. "Is he all right? Is there anything wrong?"

"Not to my knowledge, lady. But the marshal has been trying for weeks to arrange this—ever since your husband's arrest." The servant glanced at her, running his eyes over her bosom. Eleanor felt a hot flush of shame run over her. The stares and comments of the people at court were awful to deal with. She glared back but said nothing. The man gave her a lewd grin.

Finally they arrived at a narrow corridor. Two guards stood before the door. "There," the man said.

Eleanor felt their eyes on her as she advanced. She felt as if she walked naked down the hall, and she knew her cheeks were pink. The guards looked down at her, but did not question her. She placed her hand on the door. To her surprise it swung open easily.

Richard was lying on the bed, his face unshaved, his shirt wrinkled. A pitcher stood on the floor beside the bed. He leaped up as the door swung open and his eyes widened in disbelief as she stepped through it. "Eleanor!" he cried.

She pushed the door closed and stood just inside the threshold. "Richard." Her eyes filled with tears, and a lump rose in her throat. This was her fault.

He was beside her in one long stride, his arms wrapping around her to hold her close. "Oh, God, Eleanor, I've missed you so. I don't know—you don't know how much. I'm so sorry—I should have told you—"

"Richard, it's my fault, I should have trusted you—I was stupid and silly and I can't tell you how sorry I am—"

They broke off, still clinging to each other. Finally he kissed her nose. "There's nothing to forgive. You were right to doubt me."

She blinked. "I was?"

He nodded. She searched his face. "Come and sit." He led her to the narrow cot. She sat down and he backed away. She held out her hand. "No, Eleanor. What I have to tell you is very difficult for me. It's going to be difficult for you too. I'm not sure you're going to be able to believe me. I hope that you will. But—"

He broke off. He turned away, and she watched him struggle for words. Finally he faced her again. "I'm not the man you married. You—and every one else—are absolutely right. I'm not the Richard you knew."

She gazed at him, uncertain as to how to react. "Please go on," she said at last.

"My name is Richard Lambert. I was born in 1943, in a land that hasn't even been discovered yet. I was exploring some ruins of a castle called Barland one day, slipped, fell, and when I woke up, I was here. In this body. In this time and place. But I'm not the man you knew as your husband. You've been right."

She swallowed hard, trying to understand what he was telling her. "In 1943? You were born—you will be born— six hundred years from now?"

He nodded. "I don't know how to explain what happened. I don't know how it happened. I don't know why I am here. All I know is that I am here, and I don't think I can go back.

I think my body died that day I fell off the old steps. Just as Richard's body—your husband—died when he was wounded."

She sat back. "He was dead."

Richard nodded. "I think so. And somehow, in some way I can't explain, and no one else I ever met could explain either, our souls somehow crossed. And here I am." He looked at her as if he were afraid she might begin to scream. "I—I know I am not what you are accustomed to. But I thought, after I began to understand how Richard treated you, that I might be better."

She smiled, feeling a little hysterical. "You are. You are better. You aren't just better, you're quite wonderful. You treat me the way I always dreamed I'd be treated." She laughed. "And now—" She shook her head, gazing at him with disbelief. "I'm pregnant."

It was his turn to stare at her. "Is it true?"

She nodded.

He closed his eyes. "I thought so. I thought that might be it on the journey here. But you seemed so distant—you obviously didn't trust me anymore—"

"That language you spoke—those words you know—?"

"That's English. The English that will be spoken in almost seven hundred years." He grinned at her a little sadly. "I forget sometimes."

"Sweet God. You're not joking. You really do mean this."

He caught her hands in his. "Eleanor, you don't know how I've struggled to try and find a way to tell you. If you don't believe me, I understand. If you're angry at me for lying I understand. I didn't deliberately mean to lie or to deceive you. I just didn't know any way to tell you without sounding mad—or possessed."

She got to her feet, and twined her fingers around his. "Oh, Richard. I'm not angry. I'm only surprised—shocked. I suppose I knew a long time ago that something had happened—something odd and strange and in its own way, quite wonderful. I just never expected anything like this. I never heard of anything like this—ever."

"Neither have I," he said. "Do you—can you—forgive me?"

"There's nothing to forgive," she said. "I—I only feel as though I understand things so much better now. I understand now why you couldn't talk in the beginning, why you needed me so much. I suppose I can see why you wanted me to talk to you as much as you did."

He nodded.

She looked down at their hands, tightly clasped together. "I—I suppose you don't really need me anymore."

"No, Eleanor. You're wrong. I do need you, not in that way, but in others. I've realized something in these last weeks. I need you. I don't want to leave you. I don't want to go back to the world I knew. I can't bear the thought of leaving you. I'd rather stay here with you in a place where you can be accused of being possessed by the devil than live in a place where that never happens, but without you."

She raised her head. "Do you mean that? Truly?"

"I've never meant anything more." He bent his head and their lips met. She opened her mouth and his tongue danced lightly along the edges of her lips. Suddenly she felt closer to him than she ever had before. She wrapped her arms around him, holding him close, as his slid around her waist. When the kiss finally ended, they drew apart, smiling a little nervously at each other like two strangers. "If you—if that makes you feel uncomfortable, I won't do it again." He said.

"No!" she cried. He looked so lost, so alone, she wanted to take him in her arms and comfort him the way she would have with Hugh. She laughed a little shakily. "Richard, I love you. I've been so afraid to say it, so afraid to even think it. But you aren't like any other man I've ever known in my life. And I wouldn't want you any other way."

He smiled back. "I love you, too, Eleanor. I came to England because I lost my wife. She died. And I thought I would surely never love another woman the way I loved her. I still don't. But you—you're like her in some ways, and so much yourself in others. And you aren't like any other woman I've ever met either."

They looked at each other and laughed.

Then Eleanor looked around the sober little cell and sighed. "But now what?"

He drew away from her. "I suppose I do what I must."

"But—but, Richard," she said a little dubiously, "can you?"

He shrugged. "I thought I did well enough when we were attacked that night in December. But then you came riding to the rescue. I don't think I can expect that to happen again." He grinned at her again.

She could not help but grin back. There was such a cool determination about him, an unwillingness to accept defeat. He didn't want to leave her. "Are you used to fighting with weapons?"

He shook his head. "I'd laugh but it isn't funny. There's nothing like this in the twentieth century, even though I am a fighter of sorts. But I fight with words—I'm what's called a lawyer there."

"Oh!" Suddenly so much more made sense. No wonder he was willing to talk and to listen. No wonder he understood the art of negotiation. "So that is why you think the Great Charter is important."

"Yes," he said soberly. "I know it is. In more ways than anyone who signed it can possibly imagine." He looked at her and smiled. "Don't look so worried, Eleanor. Lord William has promised to come tonight and give me some ideas as to how Giscard may be defeated. He won't let me down. And tomorrow—" He shrugged. "I felt I was brought here for a purpose. If my purpose is fulfilled by the Great Charter, then . . ."

She looked up at him, her face stricken. "How can you say such a thing? You men are all alike. You talk about your own deaths so coolly, as if it were some little thing. I don't want you to die. Does that make any difference? I'm carrying your child—and it is your child—don't you want to see his face? How can you be so cruel?"

"Oh, my dear." He drew her close, stroked her hair. "Forgive me. I'm sorry. I didn't mean to sound as if I wanted to leave you—I don't. I'm as scared and worried about tomorrow as you are." He tilted her chin up to his and gently kissed her lips. The kiss deepened and his arms tightened around her. She leaned against him, savoring the hard strength in his lean muscled body. Nothing could happen, nothing. It wouldn't be fair, to leave her alone with a child, and a few months of happy memories, months that were marred by doubts. Now there would be no more secrets between them. She couldn't lose him now.

She raised her face. "God won't let me lose you. I know He wouldn't be so cruel."

He opened his mouth to answer when a hard knock sounded on the door. "Enough time, you two."

Richard kissed her head. "You should go."

"I'll see you tomorrow on the field."

"Eleanor—"

"I won't stay away." She touched his face with the tip of one finger and was gone.

He stared after her for a long time. The scent of her still lingered in the air. And then he remembered it was the same fragrance that had haunted the meadow around the ruins of Barland.

The lone candle had burned nearly to a nub when another knock came on his door. Richard sat up on his cot. "Yes?"

William the Marshal peered around the door. "Did I wake you?"

"No, my lord." Richard started to rise, but William held out his hand.

"Never mind ceremony now, Richard. There is much we need to discuss." William sat down on the one chair, which stood against the opposite wall. "Now. I sent several of my men to practice with Giscard, and each of them reported the same thing. When he attacks, he has a curious way of feinting first left, then right. The attack invariably comes from the left. But don't forget the feint. You've got to be ready for it, because if you react too quickly to the first or even the second feint, he'll have you right where he wants you. One of my men took a bad nick to his arm, but he was tired and not paying close attention." William leaned back in his chair, eyeing Richard. "Are you ready?"

"Does it matter, my lord? Tomorrow comes whether any of us is ready or not."

"That's true, I suppose. Now. The best way to attack Giscard, and I observed this myself, is from the right, even while he attacks. If you can block his blow and immediately attack, you will be able to slip in while his side is unguarded. I think an old injury forces him to turn in a rather peculiar way. It's the only explanation I can think of. He's fast with the sword, but he doesn't like to move. If you can move around him, you can force him into an attack, which will be to your advantage."

Richard wished he'd had a paper and pen. If only he could make notes. "You said you saw this attack, my lord? Could you demonstrate?"

William rose. "Of course." He stepped into a fighting stance. In a few fast motions he demonstrated what looked to Richard like an unbelievably complicated series of steps. "There. Did you catch it?"

Richard looked dubious. "Could you do it again? It's hard to see in this light."

"Ah, of course," said William. He strode to the door. "Guard, bring another candle."

There was a muttered grumble.

"Do it," said William. "Watch now." Fast as lightning, he did the same moves again. "Do you see?"

"Yes," said Richard. "I think so."

When the candle was brought, William went through the motions yet a third time, this time much more slowly. Richard felt something like a dunce. He had the sense that the marshal expected something from him, something he wasn't quite able to produce. After a few times, William had him go through the same motions, feinting and turning and striking. His muscles protested against the unfamiliar motions.

"Yes," William said, "I know it's awkward. But now you understand. I think there's a good chance you'll bring him down tomorrow, if you remember that."

"I don't want to kill him."

William shook his head. "Then don't. Just get him on the ground. The fight will be over. I wish I could say he'll offer you the same quarter."

"If I lose tomorrow, I will be judged to be possessed," Richard said. He sighed.

William did not reply. At last he said, "I'm sorry. I know this was none of your making."

"There was nothing you could do to prevent it, my lord. Giscard has had his eye on Barland for a long time. He didn't like the fact that I outbid him for the lands. I don't think he'll ever forget it."

William nodded grimly in agreement. "But if you beat him tomorrow, that will be the end of it, I think. Bullies like Giscard are mostly bluster." He offered Richard his hand. "Good luck, my boy."

"Thank you, my lord. I appreciate your help."

"And don't worry about your lady wife. You have my word she'll want for nothing if—" He broke off.

The two men exchanged a look. "I understand, my lord. And I appreciate it."

"Get some rest." With the briefest of nods, William, too, left him alone with his thoughts.

Chapter 26

THE MORNING CAME much too quickly. Eleanor, lying sleepless for the most part, watched the light change from gray to gold, and she rose, finally, when the first rays of sun slanted across her pillow. She heard Hugh stirring in the outer room where he'd slept beside the empty grate. She dressed as quickly as she could and went to join him.

"Good morning, Hugh."

He looked at her as if half afraid of what he might see. "Are you all right, Eleanor?"

She managed a thin smile. "I'll be all right. Do you think you could manage to find us some breakfast?"

"Right away." He took off, seemingly glad to have something to do. Eleanor paced the floor. The floorboards were bare and scratched, as if men in spurs had walked across them many times. She peeked out the window, but it was set high in the thick walls, and she could see nothing but a cloudless blue sky. *Please don't let him die,* she prayed. She knelt down against a chair, closed her eyes and began to pray. *Blessed Virgin, don't let him die. Be with him, holy Jesus.* She was still locked in prayer when Hugh returned. He saw her on her knees and placed the tray down.

"Eleanor?" he asked hesitantly. "I brought breakfast."

Her stomach rumbled, but the thought of food was scarcely tempting. *But you must eat,* she thought. *You have to eat for the child.* She rose to her feet with a heavy sigh. Hugh sliced bread and cheese and held out a mug of foamy milk, still warm from the cow. She drank it down, but it tasted like sawdust in her mouth. "Is it time?"

"Not yet. It's still early. I saw Father Caedmun in the hall. He asked how you slept."

She shrugged. "I didn't."

"It will be over soon, Eleanor."

"It's so ironic. Here I thought of killing Richard so many times, and now . . . now he might actually die and it's the last thing I want. The very last thing I want."

"I think he has a good chance against Giscard, who's a clumsy fighter. He plants himself in one place and hacks away. Richard's lighter on his feet. If he can move around him, I think there's every possibility he can deal a good blow of his own before Giscard even knows what happened. On the other hand, of course—"

"Stop it, Hugh." Eleanor covered her ears. "I don't want to hear all this. Go find out what time it's to begin. I want a seat in the front. Send Father Caedmun up to escort me when the time comes, all right?"

Hugh downed the last of his breakfast in two huge swallows. "I'm sorry, Eleanor. I'll go now and find a place to sit."

When he was gone, she put down the crust of bread. *Oh, God,* she prayed, *please, please, please, keep Richard safe.*

The warm summer sun beat down on the green field. Pennants flew from stakes around the marked quadrangle, giving the scene an almost festive air. Richard watched people filing in from all directions. It was a festival as far as they were concerned. He held out his arms as Hugh laced the vambraces into place on his wrists. The chain mail was a heavy weight across his shoulders, and beneath it, he was starting to perspire.

On the other side of the field, he watched Giscard making the same kinds of preparations. He hefted his broadsword and swung it in wicked arcs. He looked over at Richard and grinned.

"Don't pay him any attention, my lord," murmured Hugh, as he bent to adjust the greaves. "You'll be fine."

Richard looked down, surprised to hear such words of encouragement from Hugh. "Thank you." Hugh looked up and their eyes met and held.

"I—I misjudged you, my lord," Hugh said, his face flushing red. "You were kind to me—to arrange a marriage with Angharad. And my sister loves you."

Richard took a deep breath and scanned the field once more. He wondered if Eleanor would come today. In some ways he wished she wouldn't. Despite the marshal's reassurances and advice, and despite the practices he'd had over the winter, he wasn't a fighter and he knew it. But his body was. He had to remember that. This body—his body—was much stronger than his old one had ever been. His old body. That life was beginning to seem so very long ago and so very far away.

The king and his entourage were filing onto the royal dais beneath a brightly colored canopy. He narrowed his eyes, wondering if Eleanor had been given a seat with the king. He saw the marshal's tall figure and on his arm, a small woman clad in sober blue. Yes, there she was, a black-robed priest following close behind her. That must be the priest she'd spoken with, who'd tried to reassure her.

A procession of priests filed onto the field, carrying a portable altar. Stephen Langton raised his miter from the dais, and a priest in a white surplice began to say the Mass.

Richard crossed himself soberly. Out of the corner of his eye, he saw Giscard do the same. He knew people were watching his behavior during the ceremony, and he kept his eyes down and on Hugh for the most part, following the boy's lead. The Communion bread was not distributed. The final blessing was given, and the celebrant blessed the two combatants and the crowd. Then, altar and accoutrements in tow, the priests left the field.

A herald galloped out from the side on a black horse. "Hear ye, hear ye. We are gathered on this day to witness the mortal combat between Lord Richard de Lambert and his accuser Giscard Fitzwilliam. Victory to the innocent!" With a flash of tail and a brief whinny from the horse, the herald cantered off the field.

The king got to his feet.

Hugh put the helmet on Richard's shoulders and settled it into place. He handed Richard his sword. "God bless you," he choked. Richard was amazed to see tears in the boy's eyes.

He patted the boy awkwardly on the shoulder, and strode out onto the field with all the confidence he could muster. A shout arose from the crowd as Giscard walked out to meet him, and the king raised his arms. Instantly the crowd was still.

"Victory to the innocent!" cried the king. "Begin!"

Instantly Giscard rushed at him. Richard planted his feet and blocked the blow. He swung the heavy sword at Giscard's side and met the hard steel of his sword. Metal clashed and sparked. The two men pushed away from each other. Richard circled, watching how Giscard seemed to have picked his spot. He took one step forward, and, true to the marshal's words, feinted right then left, and attacked on the right. Richard tried to watch for the peculiar opening, but Giscard was too fast. He barely managed to evade the blow.

He backed off. The crowd was not silent anymore. There were catcalls, boos, and hisses, along with cries of "Finish him—he's a coward."

Giscard raised one hand, and in that moment Richard attacked. The two men swung and slashed. Steel thudded against steel, and sparks flew out as the blades rang together. Richard felt the force of the blows shudder down his arms to his shoulders. Perspiration streamed down his sides and down his back, and trickled down his neck. A blow to his thigh took him unaware. He was barely able to fend it off. It struck him on the leg, and bit through, inflicting a flesh wound that stung like the bite of a thousand bees. The crowd roared.

Richard tightened his grip and swung. Giscard blocked it, but the blade slipped, and landed instead on his shoulder. Richard heard the sickening thunk as the steel bit into flesh, crunching into the bone. More shouts went up as Giscard staggered back.

Richard followed, knowing that he had no choice but to bring the man down. He swung again, attacking once more on the same side. His sword thudded into Giscard's leg and the man fell, groaning, the wound in his leg fountaining blood. Instantly the crowd was on its feet, screaming for more.

Richard paused. His face was slick with sweat and his blood pounded in his ears. His arms and shoulders reverberated with the force of the blows. He put his own sword down, threw off his helmet and walked over to the king's dais. The wound in his side made him limp.

He looked the king in the eye as he placed the sword in front of him. "I have no wish to kill, Your Grace. I've proved my innocence."

The king stared from Richard to Giscard, who lay groaning and writhing on the field. "You don't want to kill him?"

"I've had enough killing," said Richard. His eyes swept over the king's entourage and found Eleanor. Her face was shining with happiness and love. "I want to go home."

"And so you shall," said the king.

The archbishop raised his miter. "Go in peace, my son."

Richard looked at Eleanor. "Are you ready to go home, my lady?"

She stood up, her whole body quivering with joy. "Oh, yes," she said, her voice trembling. "Oh, yes."

He walked to the edge of the dais and held out his arms. She rushed to the side, and he gently swept her off the platform and set her gently on her feet. Hugh came running up and picked up his sword. "Come along," said Richard. And together, the three walked off the field.

It was much, much later when Eleanor opened her eyes. The light of dozens of candles made the room seem bright as day, and a light breeze blew through the opened window. A curious sound made her look around. Richard was crouched in front of the fire, parchment and pen in hand. "What are you doing," she asked, shocked.

He turned and looked at her. In the candlelight, his bandaged leg gleamed white against his darker skin. His blue eyes crinkled at the corners in the smile she loved. "Writing, of course."

"You can write?" she whispered, astonished. "And read?"

"Of course. In the twentieth century nearly everyone can. The trouble is that I don't know how to read and write in this language. But I think, if I practice hard enough, and if you will teach me, I can learn."

Eleanor smiled and held out her hand. "And what other talents do you possess, my lord, that I know nothing about?"

He rose and swiftly enfolded her in a strong embrace, nuzzling at her throat. "Oh, I think you know what most of them are."

She giggled and pushed him away. "Not those! I know all about those talents—I meant what else can you do in the twentieth century?"

He sighed. "All sorts of things. But you can't do them here, the tools don't exist yet." For a moment he looked sad and she was suddenly afraid he would want to leave her.

"Do you miss them very much?" she asked softly.

He raised his head, and gazed into the fireplace, staring into a time and place she could never see. "Some things," he admitted. "There are some things I wish I could see again. But on balance," he said, turning back to her with a smile, "there're things here I could never see there. So it all evens out." He placed his hand on her belly. "Or it will."

She covered his hand with hers, pressing it down against the gentle swell that soon would be the mound of their child.

As he bent to kiss her, she wondered what the world he had left was like. There were so many things she was curious about. But, she thought, as he stretched out beside her, his body covering hers, there would be time enough to ask him. The future belonged to them both.